"Why have you and your sister joined this wagon train?"

Thatcher's eyes were hidden below his hat's wide brim, but Emma was sure he was scowling. She gripped the lantern with both hands. "And how is that your concern, Mr. Thatcher?"

"I am responsible for getting this wagon train to Oregon before winter, Miss Allen. *Everything* that can endanger that mission is my concern."

He called her an endangerment! Emma gave him her haughtiest look. "And how does our presence imperil your mission?"

"If you want me to name all the ways, you'd best let me light that lantern. We will be a while." He held out his hand.

"I think it would be best for you if I continue to hold the lantern, Mr. Thatcher. At this moment, you would not want my hands to be free."

Laughter burst from him, deep and full. Surprising. She had thought him quite without humor.

"Seems you might not need quite as much protecting as I figured you would." He chuckled.

Books by Dorothy Clark

Love Inspired Historical

Family of the Heart
The Law and Miss Mary
Prairie Courtship

Love Inspired

Hosea's Bride
Lessons from the Heart

Steeple Hill

Beauty for Ashes
Joy for Mourning

DOROTHY CLARK

Critically acclaimed, award-winning author Dorothy Clark lives in rural New York, in a home she designed and helped her husband build (she swings a mean hammer!) with the able assistance of their three children. When she is not writing, she and her husband enjoy traveling throughout the United States doing research and gaining inspiration for future books. Dorothy believes in God, love, family and happy endings, which explains why she feels so at home writing stories for Steeple Hill. Dorothy enjoys hearing from her readers and may be contacted at dorothyjclark@hotmail.com.

DOROTHY CLARK

Prairie Courtship

Steeple
Hill®

Published by Steeple Hill Books™

STEEPLE HILL BOOKS

Steeple
Hill®

Recycling programs
for this product may
not exist in your area.

ISBN-13: 978-0-373-82845-6

PRAIRIE COURTSHIP

"Delight thyself also in the Lord; and he shall give thee the desires of thine heart. Commit thy way unto him; trust also in him; and he shall bring it to pass."

—*Psalms* 37:4–5

This book is dedicated to my sisters Jo and Marj. My thanks to you both for being so understanding of my time constraints, and for praying me through these last two months. I wouldn't have made it without your help. I love you both.

And to my critique partner, Sam. You stand tall, cowboy. Thank you again for your encouragement and prayers. And for sticking with me through the crunch. I will return the favor when your deadline hovers! And, yes, you may have Comanche—after the next book is written. Blessings.

Chapter One

Independence, Missouri
April, 1841

"Break camp!"

That was not Josiah Blake's voice. Emma Allen turned in the direction of the barked order, stiffened at the sight of an imposing figure atop a roan with distinctive spots on its hindquarters. So the autocratic Mr. Thatcher had returned to take command. She had hoped his absence since their arrival at Independence had meant he would not be leading the wagon train after all.

Brass buttons on the front of the once dark blue tunic that stretched across the ex-soldier's shoulders gleamed dully in the early morning light. Pants of lighter blue fabric skimmed over his long legs and disappeared into the knee-high, black boots jammed into his stirrups. He rode forward, began to wend his way through the wagons scattered over the field.

Emma frowned and stepped out of sight at the back of the wagon. Mr. Thatcher did not need to wear the faded blue cavalry uniform to remind people he had been a military officer. It was in his bearing. And in the penetrating gaze of the bright blue eyes that peered out from beneath his broad-brimmed hat. Eyes that looked straight at a person, noticed everything about her—including a lace-trimmed silk gown that was inappropriate garb for an emigrant. Eyes that had unfairly impaled her on their spike of disapproval at that first meeting in St. Louis when he had simply *assumed* she was William's wife and would be accompanying him on the journey to Oregon country—and judged her accordingly. Had the man bothered to ask, she would have informed him William was her *brother* and that she was not traveling with the train.

Not then.

But that was before everything in their lives had turned upside down. Emma sighed and stroked Traveler's arched neck. How she had hated telling William that the severe nausea Caroline had developed was not normal for a woman with child. That his wife and the baby she carried were in peril, and would, of a certainty, not survive the journey to Oregon country. Her face tightened. Another prayer unanswered. Another hope shattered. William had to give up his dream of teaching at his friend Mitchel Banning's mission in Oregon country.

Emma glanced at the two wagons sitting side by side, lifted her hand and combed through Traveler's mane with her fingers. How many hours had she sat watching William plan and design the two wagons' interiors— one to hold their personal necessities and provide for Caroline's comfort, the other to carry needed provisions, the teaching materials and provide shelter for Caroline's mother? He had had such faith that things would turn out all right. *Misplaced* faith. William was, at this moment, aboard one of their uncle Justin's luxury river steamboats taking his wife home to Philadelphia. And she and Annie—who should not be traveling at all in her injured condition—were—

Traveler tossed his head, snorted. The thud of a horse's hoofs drew near. Stopped. *Mr. Thatcher.* Emma stood immobile, aware of a sudden tenseness in her breathing, a quickening of her pulse.

"Good morning, Mrs. Allen."

Emma turned, looked up at Zachary Thatcher sitting so tall and handsome in his saddle and gave him a cool nod of greeting. He was a lean man, muscular and broad of shoulder. But it was not his size, rather the intensity, the firm, purposeful expression on his weather-darkened face, the aura of strength and authority that emanated from him that produced an antipathy in her. Autocratic men like Zachary Thatcher were the bane of her life, had caused the demise of her dream. She refused to feed this one's vanity by exhibiting the slightest interest in him or what he had to say.

A frown tightened his face, drew his brows together into a V-shaped line. "I see your lead team is not hitched yet. Tell your husband from now on every wagon is to be ready to roll out by first light."

Emma stared up into those judgmental, sky-blue eyes. Clearly Mr. Thatcher expected an acknowledgment. "I will relay your order." Her conscience pricked. She quelled the unease. It was the truth as far as it went. As for the rest, let the pompous Mr. Thatcher who formed his own conclusions believe what he chose.

He glanced toward the second wagon. "I understand your husband hired the oldest Lundquist sons to help him out—drive his wagons, herd the stock and such. Is that right?"

"They have been hired, yes." There was that prick of conscience again. She clenched her hands and yielded to its prompting. "But I must explain that William is not—"

"I have no time for explanations or excuses, Mrs. Allen. Only make sure your husband passes my message on to his drivers. Tomorrow we start traveling at the break of dawn. Any slackers will be left behind to turn back or catch up as best they can." He touched his fingers to his hat's brim and rode off.

Tyrant! It was a wonder he did not make the members of the train salute and call him "sir"! Emma glared at Zachary Thatcher's strong, straight back and shoved her conscience firmly aside. She had tried to tell him the truth about William. It was not her fault if he would not take the time to listen.

"Whoa, now, whoa!" Oxen hoofs thumped against the ground—stopped. Chains rattled at the front of the wagon.

Emma hurried forward. "Mr. Lundquist, Mr. Thatcher has returned. He ordered that from now on all wagons are to be hitched up and ready to leave by first light, else they will be left behind. Please inform your brother."

Her hired driver's head dipped. "I'll see to it." He

leaned a beefy shoulder against an ox and shoved. "Give over, now!"

Emma left him to his work, glanced around the field. Everywhere she looked men were making last-minute checks of equipment, climbing to wagon seats or taking up their places beside oxen teams. Women and girls were dousing cooking fires, stowing away breakfast paraphernalia and gathering small children into the wagons. All was as she had watched their company practice over the past few days under Josiah Blake's guidance—and yet completely different.

"Form up!"

The words cracked through the cool morning air, sharp as a gunshot. Zachary Thatcher's order was picked up and echoed around the camp. Emma caught her breath and tugged her riding gloves snug. This was it. There was no more time. A tremble rippled through her, shook her hands as she loosed the reins tethering Traveler and led him to the side of the wagon to use the spoke of a wheel as a mounting aid. The light wool fabric of the long, divided skirt of her riding outfit whispered softly as she stepped into the stirrup and settled herself into the strange saddle with the horn on the front. William's saddle. William's horse.

Tears flooded her eyes. Her brother, her staunch protector, the only one of her family who shared her blood, would soon be out of her life—forced by his wife's illness to remain at home, while she, who wanted only to return to Philadelphia, traveled with this wagon train bound for Oregon country. Oh, if only William had sold the wagons! But he had kept hoping. And then Annie had declared she would go to Mitchel Banning's mission and teach in William's place!

Emma's shoulder's slumped. When Annie would not be dissuaded, *her* fate had been decided. What choice had she but to come along to care for her injured sister? The sick, hollow feeling she had been fighting for days swelled in her stomach. Would she ever see William again? Or Mother and Papa Doc, who had taken them into their hearts and adopted them so many years ago she could remember no other parents?

Emma blinked to clear her vision, brushed the moisture from her cheeks and focused her attention on the last-minute rush of activity to block out the dear, loved faces that floated on her memory. Her heart pounded. Men's mouths opened wide in shouts she could not hear over the throbbing of her pulse in her ears. Whips snaked through the air over the backs of the teams. Here and there a wagon lurched, began to move. She tensed, counted. William's wagon—no, *her* wagon—was to be fourth in line...to what? A primitive, unknown land inhabited by heathen. It was insanity!

"Haw, Baldy! Haw, Bright!"

The command penetrated her anxiety, the roaring in her ears. Emma drew her gaze from the camp, watched the oxen her brother had purchased lean into their yokes and move forward at Garth Lundquist's bidding. The wagon shuddered and creaked, rolled over the trampled grass. She swallowed hard against a sudden surge of nausea, made certain only the toes of her riding boots showed from beneath the fullness of her long skirts and rode forward beside the wagon. All through the eight-day steamboat journey from St. Louis up the muddy Missouri River to Independence she had managed to hold her apprehension at bay. Even when the steamer had run aground on one of the many sandbars, or when it had been raked by hidden snags, she had maintained her calm. But now…

Now there was no more time.

Emma closed her eyes, took a deep breath to steady her nerves. Still, who could blame her for her fearfulness? She opened her eyes and stared at the western horizon. This was not merely another drill to ensure everyone could drive their wagons and herd their stock on the trail. This was *it*. She was leaving behind family, friends and all of civilization and heading into untold danger. And for what? Someone else's dream. If Mitchel Banning had not started that mission in Oregon country none of this—

"Haw, Big Boy. Steady on, Scar."

Emma glanced over her shoulder, watched Garth Lundquist's brother, Ernst, bring William's second wagon into line behind hers. Anne's wagon now. She and her adopted sister were on their own. A tremor snaked through her. Traveler snorted, tossed his head and danced sideways. She leaned forward, patted the arched neck. "It's all right, boy. Everything is all right." The horse calmed.

Emma gave him another pat and straightened in the saddle. How lovely it would be if there were someone to reassure her, to ease her fear. Disgust pulled her brows down, stiffened her spine. She had to stop this self-pity that eroded her courage and undermined her purpose. Still…

She halted Traveler and glanced over her shoulder. Perhaps she should try once more—now that the time of departure was upon them—to dissuade Anne from going to Oregon country. Perhaps the reality of the leave-taking had softened Anne's determination. Perhaps. Hope she could not quite stifle fluttered in her chest.

Emma reined Traveler around, halted and stared as Anne, riding Lady, the bay mare William had bought for Caroline, emerged from behind her wagon. So Anne had, again, ignored her advice. She was supposed to be in the wagon. Abed.

Worry spiraled upward, crowded out every emotion but concern. Anne's face was thin and pale beneath the russet curls that had escaped from beneath the stiff brim of her black bonnet, her body frail and tense in her widow's garb. That she was in discomfort was obvious in her taut face and posture. If only she would give up this madness!

Emma tapped Traveler with her heels and rode to her sister's side. "Annie…" She frowned, changed her tone. She had tried pleading. "Anne, this is your last chance. It will soon be too late to change your mind. As your doctor, I am advising you to reconsider your decision to make this journey. You are not yet recovered from—"

"Do not say it, Emma!"

Anguish flashed across Anne's pale face. Emma's heart squeezed, her professional doctor's facade crumbled. "Oh, Annie, forgive me. I did not mean to—" She stopped, stared at the silencing hand Anne raised between them, the uncontrollable twitching fingers that were the outward sign of Anne's inward suffering. She reached out to touch her sister's arm. It was jerked away.

Emma pulled back. She stared at her younger sister, once so happy and loving, now so grim and distant, and closed her hand in a white-knuckled grip on the reins. All Anne had ever wanted was to marry and have children. But that dream was now as lifeless and cold as the stone that marked her loved ones' graves.

"I know you mean well, Emma. And I do not mean to be sharp with you. It is only—I cannot bear—" Anne's hesitant words stopped on a small gasp. She clutched her side.

Emma took note of Anne's closed eyes, the increased pallor of her skin, and clenched her jaw. She could not bring back Phillip and little baby Grace, but she could treat the physical injuries Anne had sustained in the carriage accident that had killed her husband and child. Only not here. Not on a wagon train.

Almighty God, if You can change the heart of a king, You can make Anne change her mind and return home to Philadelphia where Papa Doc and I can properly care for her—where the love of her family can help her over her grief.

Emma shifted in the saddle, closed her heart against the useless words. The prayer would only be heaped atop all the countless others she'd offered that had gone unanswered. She cleared the lump from her throat. "Annie—"

"No!" The black bonnet swept side to side. "I am

going on, Emma. I cannot face the…the memories at home." Anne opened her eyes and looked straight into hers. "But I want you to go home, Emma. It is foolish for you to come along, to place yourself in harm's way so that you may doctor me when I no longer care if I live or die." Anne's voice broke. She took a ragged, shallow breath. "Turn around and go home, Emma. You still have your dream. And all you desire awaits you there."

Emma's vision blurred, her throat closed. She looked away from her sister's pain, stared at the wagons that had become the symbols of William's lost hope and Anne's despair—of her own thwarted ambition. *Why God? Why could not at least one of us have our dream?*

Emma huffed out a breath and squared her shoulders. Pity would help nothing. But the truth might help Anne. At least it would keep her from feeling guilty. "How I wish that were true, Anne. But though Papa Doc has taught me all he knows of medicine, his patients do not accept me as a doctor. And they never will." The frustration and anger she held buried in her heart boiled up and burned like acid on her tongue. "It is time for me to set aside my foolish dream. I will never be a doctor in Philadelphia or anywhere else. *Men* will not allow it. They will not permit me to treat them or their families. And who can be a doctor without patients?"

She lifted her chin, tugged her lips into the facsimile of a smile. "So, you and I will journey on together. And we had best start, or we will fall out of place behind our wagons and be chastised by the arrogant Mr. Thatcher." She urged Traveler into motion, gave an inward sigh of relief as Anne nudged her mount into step beside her.

"What slow and lumbering beasts these oxen are. It will take us forever to reach Oregon country at this pace."

Anne stared at her a moment, then turned to face forward. "Forever is a long time to live without a dream."

The words were flat, quiet...resigned. Emma shot a look at Anne but could see nothing but the stiff brim of her black bonnet, the symbol of all she had lost. *Oh, Annie, you cannot give up on life. I will not let you!*

Emma set her jaw and fixed her gaze west, her sister's words weighing like stones in her heart.

Zach stopped Comanche at the edge of the woods, rested his hands on the pommel and studied the wagons rolling across the undulating plains. The line was ragged, the paces varied, but it was not bad for the first day. Too bad he'd had to scout out the trail conditions. Things would be better had he been around to run the practice drills himself. Still, Blake had done a fair job, but he was too soft on the greenhorns. They had to learn to survive, and there was more to that than simply learning a few new skills. They had to develop discipline, and a sense of responsibility to the group as a whole or they would never make it to Oregon country.

Zach frowned and settled back in the saddle. There had been a lot of grumbling when he pushed them to an early start this morning. The problem was the emigrants' independent spirit. They balked like ornery mules being broke to harness when given orders. It was certainly easier in the military where men obeyed and performed duties as instructed. But it was not as lucrative. And, truth be told, he had his own independent streak. No more fetters of military life for him.

"We are going to be free to roam where we will, when we will. Right, boy?" Comanche flicked an ear his direction, blew softly. Zach chuckled, scratched beneath the dark mane. Of course he had his ambitions, too. A trading post. One that would supply both Indians and army. And the fee for guiding this wagon train to Oregon country, combined with what he had saved from his army pay, would enable him to build one next spring. The large bonus promised—if he got the emigrants to Oregon before the winter snows closed the mountain passes—would buy the goods to stock the place. He intended to earn that bonus. But in order to do that he would have to drive these people hard and fast. It snowed early in those high elevations.

Zach gave Comanche a final scratch and settled back, his lips drawn into their normal, firm line. Too bad they were not all reasonable men like Mr. Allen. It was obvious, even at his first meeting with the emigrants back in St. Louis, that the man understood the need for rules and limitations. Of course that wife of his was a different matter. She had no place on a wagon train with her fancy, ruffled silk dress. He had learned in his days of command to spot troublemakers, and Mrs. Allen spelled trouble with her challenging brown eyes and her small, defiant chin stuck in the air. She looked as stubborn as they came. Beautiful, too. More so today, standing there by the wagon in the soft, morning light.

Zach again crossed his hands on the saddle horn, drew his gaze along the line of wagons. There she was, riding astride, and looking at ease in the saddle. He never would have thought it of her with her fancy gowns and her city ways, but astride she was. Must have had that outfit made special. He'd never seen anything like it. She looked—

He frowned, jerked his gaze away. The woman's beauty was but a shallow thing. He had overheard her complaining to Allen of their wagon being too small to live in. He shook his head, glanced back at the slender figure in the dark green riding outfit. Coddled and spoiled, that was Mrs. Allen. But she was her husband's problem to handle, not his. And a good thing it was. He was accustomed to commanding men, not obstreperous women.

The lowing of oxen and braying of mules pulled him from his thoughts. Zach straightened in the saddle, stared at the mixed herd of animals coming over the rise behind the wagons. Those fool boys were letting the stock wander all over the place! And that bull in front looked wild and mean. If he caught a whiff of the river ahead and took it into his head to run—

He reined Comanche around. "Let's bunch up that herd, boy." The horse needed no further urging. Zach tugged his hat down firm against the wind, settled deep in the saddle and let him run.

Emma climbed to the top of the knoll, lifted the gossamer tails of the fabric adorning her riding hat and let the gentle breeze cool her neck as she looked back over the low, rolling hills that stretched as far as the eye could see. White pillows of cloud drifted across the blue sky, cast moving shadows on the light green of the new grass. It was a glorious day…except for the occasion.

She frowned, let the frothy tails drop back into place and turned toward the river. Her chest tightened, her breath shortened—the familiar reaction to her fear of water. She'd been plagued by the fear since the day William had pulled her, choking and gasping for air, from the pond on the grounds at their uncle Justin's home. She'd been reaching for a baby duck and—

"Randolph Court." Speaking the name drove the terror-filled memory away. Emma closed her eyes, pictured her uncle Justin's beautiful brick home, with its large stables where she and William had learned to ride along with their cousins Sarah and Mary and James. It was there her mother had taught her to ride astride instead of sidesaddle. A smile curved her lips. She could almost hear her uncle Justin objecting to the practice, and her mother answering, "Now, dearheart, if riding astride is good enough for Marie Antoinette and Catherine the Great, it is good enough for—"

"Lundquist, get that wagon aboard! Time is wasting! We have ten more wagons to ferry across before dark."

Emma popped her eyes open at Zachary Thatcher's shout. Was her wagon—"Haw, Scar! Haw, Big Boy!"— No, it was Ernst moving Anne's wagon forward. She held her breath as her sister's wagon rolled down the slight embankment toward the river. A figure, garbed in black, appeared briefly at the rear opening in the canvas cover, then disappeared as the flaps were closed.

Annie! What was she doing? She knew Mr. Thatcher had ordered that no one cross the river inside the wagons for fear they would be trapped if— *I want you to go home, Emma. It is foolish for you to come along, to place yourself in harm's way so that you may doctor me when I no longer care if I live or die.* A chill slithered down her spine. Surely Annie did not mean to— Her mind balked, refused to finish the horrifying thought.

The wagon halted at the edge of the riverbank. Men rushed forward to help Ernst unhitch the oxen. Others took up places at the tongue, wheels and tailgate. "No! Wait!" Her shout was useless, lost in the clamor below. Emma yanked the front hems of her long skirts clear of her feet and raced down the knoll.

"The teams're free! Get 'er rollin'!"

The men strained forward, pushed the wagon onto the short, thick planks leading to the deck. Emma dodged around the wagon next in line and ran toward the raft.

"Sutton! Thomas! Chock those wheels fore and aft!" Zachary Thatcher grabbed chunks of wood from a small pile and tossed them onto the deck. "And see you set the chocks firm so that wagon can't shift or roll. There'll be no stopping her if she starts slipping toward the water." He turned toward Ernst. "Lundquist, you get those oxen ready to swim across."

Emma halted her headlong rush as the men, finished with their work, jumped to the bank. She stood back out of their way and stared at the raft sunk low under the heavy load. Only a few inches of the sides showed above the rushing water of the Kansas River. Every bit of courage she possessed drained from her. But Anne was in that wagon. Anne—who did not care if she lived or died. She drew a deep breath, lifted the hems of her skirts out of the mud with her trembling hands and ran down a plank onto the bobbing ferry.

"Mrs. Allen!"

The authoritative shout froze her in her tracks. Emma grabbed hold of the top of the rear wagon wheel, turned and looked full into Zachary Thatcher's scowling face.

"Come off the ferry and wait for your husband, Mrs. Allen. Everyone is to cross with their own wagon."

The ferry dipped, shuddered, slipped away from the bank. Muddy water sloshed onto the deck and swirled around her feet. Emma tightened her hold to a death grip on the wheel and shook her head. "My sister, Anne, is lying ill in this wagon, Mr. Thatcher." She instilled a firmness she was far from feeling into her voice. "I am crossing the river with her."

"Your *sister!*" Zachary Thatcher's face darkened like a storm cloud. "*What* sister? When did—"

"And I have no husband. William Allen is my *brother.*"

The ropes attached to the ferry stretched taut with a creaking groan. Emma gasped, turned and fixed her gaze on the men on the opposite bank hauling on the rope. Frightened as she was, the view across the water was preferable to the one of Mr. Thatcher's furious face. The raft lurched out into the river then turned its nose, caught the current and floated diagonally toward the other side. She closed her eyes and hoped she wouldn't get sick.

Chapter Two

"The last wagon is safely across, Anne. They are hitching up the teams to pull it up the bank." Emma hooked back the flap of canvas at the rear of the wagon to let in the evening light. "Perhaps now the camp will settle into a semblance of order."

"Perhaps. Please close the flap, Emma."

How she hated that listless attitude! Emma let the flap fall into place and fixed a smile firmly on her face as she stepped to the side of her sister's bed. "Would you care to take a short walk with me before the sun sets? I want to make certain Traveler and Lady swim across safely."

"No. You go, Emma." Anne lifted her hand and pushed a wayward curl off her forehead. "I am weary."

"And in pain." Emma dropped the phony smile and frowned. "You cannot move without wincing, Anne. I warned you riding would not be good for your injured ribs. It has irritated them. Your breathing is shallow. I will go get my bag and give you some laudanum to ease the discomfort." She stepped to the tailgate.

"Please do not bother, Emma. I want no medication—only rest."

"Annie—"

"I'll not take it, Emma."

"Very well." Her patience had run its course. Emma pushed the canvas flap aside, climbed through the opening then stuck her head back inside. "But I shall return when Mrs. Lundquist has prepared our supper. And you *will* eat, Anne. You are my patient and I shall not allow you to die—even if you want to!" She jerked the flaps back into place for emphasis, whirled about and headed for a spot beneath a tree to watch the men swimming the stock across the river.

A low hum of voices, broken by the shouts and laughter of children, vibrated the air. From the adjoining field came the lowing of cows and oxen, the neighing of horses and braying of mules. Chickens and roosters, imprisoned in cages lashed to the sides of wagons, cackled and crowed. Dogs barked and snarled at enemies real or imagined.

Such a din! Emma nodded and smiled at the woman and daughter working over a cooking fire and made her way to the outer rim of the men grouped around the lead wagon. Heads turned her direction. Faces scowled. Her steps faltered. She braced herself and continued on.

"Did you want something, Mrs…"

Emma met a thin, bearded man's gaze. The look of forebearance in his eyes caused a prickle of irritation that fueled her determination. "Only to be obedient to Mr. Thatcher's order to assemble."

"This meeting is only for the *owners* of the wagons. The heads of the families."

Emma glanced toward the condescending voice coming from her left, stared straight at the rotund, prosperous-looking man who had spoken. "Yes. That was my understanding."

A frown pulled the man's bushy, gray eyebrows low over his deep-set eyes. "Now, see here, young woman, we men have business to discuss. This is no time for female foolishness! Go back to your wagon and send your husband, or father, or—"

"My name is Miss Allen, sir." She kept her tone respectful, but put enough ice in her voice to freeze the Kansas River flowing beside their evening camp. "I have no husband. And my father is in Philadelphia. I am the owner of—"

"Impossible! I personally signed up every—did you say Allen?" The man's eyes narrowed, accused her. "The only Allen to join our train was William Allen and his *wife*."

The man had all but called her a liar! Emma forced a smile. "William Allen is my brother."

"Then your brother will speak for you, young lady. It is not necessary for you to attend this meeting."

Emma took a breath, held her voice level. "My brother's wife took ill and he was unable to make the journey. My sister and I have taken their place on the train."

"Two lone *women!*" The exclamation started an uproar.

"Gentlemen!"

The word snapped like a lash. Every head swiveled

toward the center of the group. Silence fell as those gathered stared at Zachary Thatcher.

"The trail to Oregon country is two thousand miles of rough, rutted prairies, bogs and marshes, quicksand, swift, turbulent rivers, steep, rocky mountains, perpendicular descents and sandy desert—most of the terrain seldom, if ever, traversed by wagon. Factor in thunderstorms, hailstorms, windstorms, prairie fires and—if we are too often delayed—snowstorms, and everything gets worse. You will never make it to Oregon country if you waste time arguing over every problem that arises. There will be legions of them. And this particular situation is covered by the rules and regulations settled upon by Mr. Hargrove and the other leaders of this enterprise before our departure. Now, to the business at hand. Miss Allen…"

A *problem* was she? Emma lifted her head, met Zachary Thatcher's cold gaze and traded him look for look.

"This meeting is about tending stock and standing guard duty. Each wagon owner must shoulder their share of the work. I understand your hu—*brother* hired drivers. As it states in the rules, hired drivers will be permitted to stand for wagon owners—in this instance, you and your sister. Therefore, Mr. Hargrove is correct—your presence is not required at this meeting." He turned to the thin man beside him. "Lundquist, your sons—"

The man nodded. "I'll fetch 'em in." He faced toward the river and gave a long, ear-piercing whistle.

She was dismissed. Rudely and summarily dismissed. Emma clenched her jaw, stared at the backs of the men who had all faced away from her then turned and strode toward her wagon. A *problem!* You would think she *wanted—*

Emma stopped, gathered her long, full skirt close, stepped around a small pile of manure and hurried on. Why was she so discomposed? Her demeaning treatment by the men was nothing new. She had become accustomed to such supercilious attitudes in her quest to be a doctor. Thank goodness Papa Doc did not share such narrow vision! Not that it mattered now. Her dream was not to be. Instead she was on this wagon train of unwelcoming men, headed toward an unknown future in an unknown, unwelcoming country.

Bogs, marshes and quicksand…swift, turbulent rivers…high, steep, rocky mountains… Emma shuddered, looked at her wagon. Her *home*. It was all she had. The reality of her situation struck her as never before. She sank down on the wagon tongue and buried her face in her hands to compose herself. Not for anything would she let Mr. Zachary Thatcher and those other men see her dismay.

Zach looked at the grazing stock spread out over the fields and shook his head. The men on first watch were taking their duties lightly, in spite of his instructions. But one stampede, one horse or ox or cow stolen by Indians, one morning spent tracking down stock that had wandered off during the night would take care of that. They would learn to listen. Experience was a harsh but effective teacher. So were empty stomachs. A few missed breakfasts would focus their attention on their duties. As for the camp guards—they, too, would learn to take advice and stay alert. Most likely when one of them was found dead from a knife wielded by a silent enemy. His gut tightened. He'd seen enough of that in the army.

He frowned, rode Comanche to the rise he had chosen for his camp and dismounted. He stripped off saddle and bridle, stroked the strong, arched neck and scratched beneath the throat latch. "Good work today, boy. If it weren't for you, those emigrants would have lost stock while swimming them across the river for sure. But they'll learn. And your work will get easier."

The horse snorted, tossed his head. Zach laughed, rubbed the saddle blanket over Comanche's back. "I know, they're green as grass, but there's hope." He slapped the spots decorating Comanche's rump and stepped back. "All right, boy—dismissed!" He braced himself. Comanche whickered softly, stretched out his neck, nudged him in the chest with his head then trotted off.

"Stay close, boy!" He called the words, though the command was unnecessary. Comanche never ranged far, and he always returned before dawn. And there wasn't an Indian born who could get his hands on him.

Zach smiled, then sobered. They were safe from hostiles for now, but once they moved beyond the army's area of protection it could be a very different story. Sooner, if one of these greenhorn emigrants pulled a stupid stunt that riled the friendlies. "Lord, these people are as unsuspecting of the dangers they're heading into as a newborn lamb walking into a pack of wolves. I sure would appreciate it if You would help me whip them into shape and grant them Your protection meanwhile."

He looked toward the red-and-gold sunset in the west, took off his hat, ran his fingers through his hair, settled his hat back in place and headed for the wagons. There was one more piece of business to attend to before he turned in.

The small dose of laudanum she had finally convinced Anne to swallow had eased the pain. She would sleep through the night now. Emma pulled the quilt close under Anne's chin, climbed from the wagon and secured the flaps. It would be a comfort if Anne would consent to share a wagon, but she insisted on being alone. Not that it was surprising. She had resisted all physical contact, all gestures of comfort since Phillip and little Grace had died.

Emma sighed and looked around the center ground of the circled wagons, now dotted with tents. It was so quiet she could hear the murmurings of the few men and women who still sat working around cooking fires that had died to piles of coals. Traveler, Lady and a few other personal mounts were grazing in the center of the makeshift corral, their silhouettes dark against the caliginous light.

She walked to her wagon, lifted a lantern off its hook on the side but could find no means to light it. She heaved another sigh and looked up at the darkening sky. She should probably retire as others were doing, even if sleep eluded her. But to be alone in the wagon without light—

"Good evening."

Emma gasped and whirled about, the lantern dangling from her hands. "You startled me, Mr. Thatcher!" She pressed one hand over her racing heart and frowned at him. "Is there something you wanted?"

"I need to know why you and your sister have joined this wagon train. What purpose takes you to Oregon country?"

His eyes were hidden by the darkness below his hat's wide brim, but she was sure he was scowling. She brushed back a wisp of hair that had fallen onto her forehead at her quick turn, then, again, gripped the lantern with both hands. "And how is that your concern, Mr. Thatcher?"

He tilted his hat up, stared down at her. "I am responsible for getting this wagon train to Oregon before winter, Miss Allen. *Everything* that can endanger that mission is my concern."

First he called her a "problem" and now he named her an endangerment! Emma lifted her chin, gave him her haughtiest look. "And how does our presence imperil your mission?"

"If you want me to name all the ways, you'd best let me light that lantern. We will be a while." He held out his hand.

Emma tightened her grip. "I think it would be best for you if I continue to hold the lantern, Mr. Thatcher. At this moment, you would not want my hands to be free."

Laughter burst from him, deep and full. Surprising.

She had thought him quite without humor. Of course he was laughing at her.

"Now that erased one of the reasons on my list, Miss Allen. Seems you might not need quite as much protecting as I figured you would. All the same, I'll take my chances on freeing up your hands." He reached for the lantern.

This time she let him take it. She needed that lantern lit. Even more, she needed to know how he would light it. She watched as he walked to a nearby fire, squatted down and held a twig to one of the dying embers then blew on it. The twig burst into flame. Of course! She should have thought of that. He lit the lantern, tossed the twig on the embers and returned to her.

"Easy enough when you know how, Miss Allen. And that is my first reason." All trace of amusement was gone from his voice. His expression was dead serious. "If you do not know how to light a lantern out here in the wilderness, how will you manage all the other things you do not know how to do? You are a pampered woman, Miss Allen. Because of that pampering—and without a husband *or* brother to care for you—you are a burden and an endangerment to all the others traveling with you. And I assume it is the same with your sister. Only worse, because she is ill."

"My sister is not a *burden,* Mr. Thatcher! And she is my responsibility to care for, not yours or any other man's!" Emma snatched the lantern from his hand, held her breath and counted to ten as she adjusted the wick to stop the smoking. When her anger was under control she looked up at him. "What you say about me was true, Mr.

Thatcher—until a moment ago. But I now *know* how to light a lantern here in the wilderness. And I will learn how to do all the other things I must know the same way. I will observe, or I will ask. I may be a pampered woman, but I am not unintelligent, only untaught in these matters. And I will rectify that very quickly. As for my needing protection—do not concern yourself with my safety. I am an excellent shot with rifle or pistol. As is my sister. We will look to our own safety."

"And your wagons and stock?"

"We have drivers to care for them—as the rules permit."

His face darkened. "Accidents happen, Miss Allen! Your drivers can be injured or killed. And then—"

"And then I would be no worse off than a wife who has lost her husband." Emma lifted her chin and looked him straight in the eyes. "We have paid our money, and you yourself said we have met the rules and regulations set in place by Mr. Hargrove and the other leaders. My sister and I are going to Oregon country with this wagon train, Mr. Thatcher. Now I bid you good evening, sir."

He stared at her a moment, then tugged his hat back in place. "As you will, Miss Allen." He gave an abrupt nod and strode off into the darkness.

Emma turned to her wagon, packed and prepared by William for him and Caroline to live in on the journey. Everything had been so rushed after Anne's surprising announcement, only her own clothes had been added at the last minute. She should have spent some time at Independence exploring it, locating things. But she had stayed at the hotel caring for Anne.

A burden and endangerment indeed! She would show Mr. Zachary Thatcher how competent a woman she was! She set the lantern on the ground, untied the canvas flaps, then reached inside to undo the latches that held the tailboard secure. Try as she might, she couldn't release them. Fighting back tears of fatigue and frustration, she grabbed up the lantern, walked to the front of the wagon, stepped onto the tongue and climbed inside.

Zach untied his bedroll, rolled it out and flopped down on his back, lacing his hands behind his head and staring up at the stars strewn across the black night sky. He was right. That woman was trouble. And stubborn! Whew. No mule could hold a patch on her. Spunky, too. She hadn't given an inch. Answered every one of his concerns. Even turned his own chivalrous deed of lighting her lantern back on him.

A chuckle started deep in his chest, traveled up his throat. Mad as she was at him, she'd have stood there holding that lantern all night rather than admit she didn't know how to light it. And that tailboard! She never did figure out how to open it. Must have spent ten minutes or so trying before she gave up and climbed in the wagon from the front. It had been hard, standing there in the dark watching her struggle. But she probably would have parted his hair with that lantern had he gone back to help her.

I think it would be best for you if I continue to hold the lantern, Mr. Thatcher. At this moment, you would not want my hands to be free. His lips twitched. She'd been dead serious with that threat to slap him. The spoiled Miss Allen had a temper, and did not take kindly to his authority over her as wagon master. He'd send Blake around with some excuse to examine her wagon tomorrow. He could show her how the tailboard latches worked.

He stirred, shifted position, uncomfortable with the thought of Josiah Blake spending time around Miss Allen. That could be trouble. She was a beautiful woman. No disputing that. 'Course, he'd never been partial to women with brown eyes and honey-colored hair. He preferred dark-haired women. And he liked a little more to them. Miss Allen was tall enough—came up to his shoulder. But she was slender—a mite on the bony side. Though she had curves sure enough.

Zach scowled, broke off the thoughts. It was time to sleep. Tomorrow was going to be a rough day. Those greenhorns weren't going to like the pace he set. But he intended to break them in right. Which meant he would have them awake and ready to roll at the break of dawn. He chuckled and closed his eyes. Fell asleep picturing the pampered Miss Allen trying to build a fire and cook breakfast.

Emma used the chamber pot, dipped water into a bowl from the small keg securely lashed to the inside of the wagon and washed her face and hands with soap she found in a large pocket sewn on the canvas cover. There was a hairbrush in the same pocket. And a small hand mirror. She took them into her hands, traced the vine that twined around to form the edge of the silver backings. It was a beautiful vanity set. Caroline had excellent taste. Her fingers stilled.

Emma placed the mirror and brush on top of the keg, unfastened her bodice and stepped out of her riding outfit. Was Caroline's severe nausea improving? Was the baby she carried still alive? She untied her split petticoat, spread it overtop of the riding outfit she had laid on a chest. *Please, Almighty God, let William's wife and child live. Grant them—* Bitterness, hopelessness stopped her prayer. God had not spared Phillip and little Grace. Why would He spare Caroline and the unborn babe in her womb?

Emma pulled an embroidered cotton nightgown from a drawer in the dresser sandwiched between two large, deep trunks along the left wall of the wagon, slipped it on, then shrugged into the matching dressing gown. She took the pins from her hair, brushed it free of tangles and wove it into a loose, thick braid to hang down her back. From her doctor's bag she pulled her small crock of hand balm and rubbed a bit of the soothing beeswax, oatmeal and nut-butter mixture onto her hands, then smoothed them over her cheeks. A hint of lavender tantalized her nose. Papa Doc's formula. One he'd made especially for her.

Loneliness for her parents struck with a force that left her breathless. She stood in the cramped wagon, stared at the lantern light flickering on the India-rubber lined canvas that formed the roof over her head. What would she do without her family? Would she ever see or hear from them again?

A soft sound beneath the wagon set her nerves a tingle.

She tensed, listened. There it was again—a snuffling. A dog? Or some wild animal that was drawn to the light of the lamp? She turned, reached up and snatched down the lantern hanging from a hook screwed into the center support rib but fear stayed her hand. If she doused the light she would not be able to see.

Something howled in the distance, then was answered by a frenzied barking beneath her feet. Only a dog, then. Still… Heart pounding, Emma put the lantern on the floor and tested the ties to make sure the ends of the canvas cover were securely fastened. Her hand grazed the top of the long, red box. She went down on her knees and lifted the wood lid. A fragrance of dried herbs, flowers and leaves flowed out. She caught her breath and peered inside—stared agape at the stoppered bottles, sealed crocks and rolls of bandages. Medical supplies! And a letter! In William's hand.

Tears welled into her eyes. She propped open the lid and lifted out the missive, held it pressed to her heart until she got the tears under control, then blinked to clear her vision, lowered the letter close to the lamp and read the precious words.

> My dearest Em,
> I know you think your dream is dead. But I believe it is God's will for you to be a doctor. I believe God placed the desire to help others in your heart. And I believe He will fulfill His will and purpose for you. Yes, even in Oregon country. The Bible says: "Delight thyself in the Lord; and he shall give thee the desires of thine heart. Commit thy way unto

him; trust also in him; and he shall bring it to pass." I am praying for you. And for Anne. I know you will care well for her injuries, but only God can heal the hurts of her grieving heart. Remember that, Em, lest you take upon yourself a task no one can perform.

After Anne's startling announcement and your determination to accompany for her, I asked the local apothecary what you would need to ply your doctoring skills. I have done my best to procure the items he recommended in the limited time available before your departure. I will bring more when Caroline, our child and I join you in Oregon country. Until then, have faith, my dear Doctor Emma. And always remember that I am very proud of you.

With deepest love and fondest regards,
Your brother, William

Her tears overflowed, slipped down her cheeks and dropped onto the letter. She blotted them with the hem of her nightgown lest the ink run and smear, then placed the letter back in the box where it would be safe so she could read it over and over again on the long journey. A smile trembled on her lips. Even here in this cramped wagon with wild animals howling and the whisper of a river flowing by, William could make her feel better.

Weariness washed over her. She turned down the wick of the lamp and stepped to the bed. It was exactly as William had designed it. A lacing of taut ropes held two mattresses—one of horsehair, the other of feathers—covered in rubber cloth secure inside a wood frame that was fastened to the wagon's side by leather hinges at the bottom and rope loops at the top. She unhooked the loops and lowered the bed to the floor. A quilt was spread over the top mattress. A quick check found a sheet and two feather pillows in embroidered cases beneath it.

A horse snorted. A dog barked. In another wagon, a baby cried. Emma shivered in the encroaching cold and slid beneath the quilt, relishing the welcoming softness of the feather mattress, wishing for secure walls and a solid roof. Silence pressed, broken only by the whispering rush of the nearby river.

Commit thy way unto him.... If only it were that simple a thing. She stretched, yawned and pulled the quilt snug under her chin. Her eyelids drifted closed. William had such faith. But William was not a woman who longed with her whole heart to be a doctor. And he did not have to contend with despotic men like Zachary Thatcher. Nonetheless, for William...

She opened her eyes and looked up at the canvas arching overhead. "Almighty God, all of my life I have dreamed of being a doctor. That dream is dead." Accusation rose from her heart. She left the words unspoken, but the bitterness soured her tongue, lent acidity to her tone. "I have no other to replace it. Therefore, do with me what seems right in Your eyes. I commit my way unto Thee. Amen." It was an ungracious yielding at best. A halfhearted acknowledgment that God could have a purpose for her, should He care to bother with it. But it was the best she could offer.

She frowned and closed her eyes. It was not worth a moment's concern. Why did any of it matter? God did not deign to listen to her prayers.

Chapter Three

Emma lifted her face to the sunshine and breathed deep of the fresh, sweet fragrance the grass released as it was crushed under the wagon wheels.

Traveler snorted, tossed his head and pranced. She leaned forward and stroked his neck. "I know, boy. I am weary of this slow pace, too." She pursed her lips, glanced over her shoulder. Anne had yielded to her discomfort and exhaustion and taken to her bed in her wagon after their midday rest stop. She did not need her. And it was such a fine day. Surely it would not hurt to explore a bit. Perhaps ride out to see what was over that rise ahead on their right.

She shifted in the saddle, took a firmer grip on the reins. For over a week they had been plodding along, and she was tired of seeing nothing but wagons. She was longing for a real ride. And Traveler needed a run. Surely that was reason enough to disobey Mr. Thatcher's edict to stay by the wagons. *His* mount was being exercised. She smiled and touched her heels to the horse's sides.

Traveler lunged forward, raced over the beckoning

green expanse toward the gentle swell of land. Emma let him have his head, thrilled by his quick response, the bunch and thrust of his powerful muscles, the musical drum of his hoofbeats against the ground.

Hoofbeats. Too many. And out of cadence.

She glanced over her shoulder, spotted a rider astride a large roan bearing down on her from an angle that would easily overtake her. A rider in faded blue cavalry garb and a wide-brimmed, once-yellow hat. She frowned, slowed Traveler to a lope. The roan's hoofbeats thundered close. Zachary Thatcher and his mount raced by her, wheeled at the top of the rise and stopped full in her path.

Emma gasped and drew rein. Traveler dug in his hoofs, went down on his haunches and stopped in front of the immobile roan with inches to spare. Fury ripped through her. She leaned forward as Traveler surged upright, then straightened in the saddle and glared at Zachary Thatcher. "Are you mad! I could have been thrown! Or—"

"Killed!" He jerked his arm to the side. One long finger jutted out from his hand and aimed toward the ground behind him. Or where ground should have been.

Emma stared, shivered with a chill that raced down her spine at sight of the deep fissure on the other side of the rise.

"This is not a well-groomed riding trail in Philadelphia, Miss Allen!" Zachary Thatcher's cold, furious voice lashed at her. "It is foolhardy and *thoughtless* for you to race over ground you do not know. There are hidden dangers all over these prairies. That is why I scout out the trail. Now go back to the wagons. And do not ride out by yourself again! I do not have time to waste saving you from your own foolishness."

Emma fought to stem her shivering. "Mr. Thatcher, I—" She lost the battle. Her voice trembled, broke.

"I am not interested in your excuses, Miss Allen." He gave her a look of pure disgust, reined the roan around and thundered off toward his place out in front of the wagon column.

Emma stared after him, looked back at that deep, dark gape in the ground and slipped from the saddle. "I'm sorry, boy. I'm so sorry. You could have—" Her voice caught on a sob. She threw her arms around Traveler's neck, buried her face against the warm flesh and let the tears come.

The sameness was wearying. Day after day, nothing but blue sky, green, rolling plains and wagons. And slow, plodding oxen. Emma arched her back and wiggled her shoulders. She was an excellent rider, but though she was becoming inured to sitting on a horse all day, it still resulted in an uncomfortable stiffness.

"Whoa, Traveler." She braced to slide from the saddle and walk for a short while, heard hoofbeats pounding and looked up to see Zachary Thatcher racing back toward the train.

"Get to the low ground ahead on the left and circle the wagons! Lash them together! Move!" He raced on down the line of wagons shouting the order.

What—

"Haw, Baldy! Haw, Bright!"

Garth Lundquist's whip cracked over the backs of the lead team. Cracked again. The oxen lunged forward. He jumped onto the tongue and grabbed the front board. Emma caught her breath, watched him climb into the wagon box even as the vehicle lurched after the wagons in front that were already bouncing their way over the rough ground. She sagged with relief when he gained his seat.

"Hurry on, Scar. Move, Big Boy! Haw! Haw!"

Ernst's whip and voice joined the din. Emma looked back. Anne's oxen teams were settling into an awkward run, the wagon jolting along behind.

Annie! That jarring was not good for Annie!

Emma halted Traveler, waited for the oxen teams to pass so she could tell Ernst to slow down. Wind rose, whipped the gauzy tails of her riding hat into her face. She brushed them back and turned to lower her head against the force of the blow, gasped. The western half of the sky had turned dark as night. Black clouds foamed at the edge of the darkness, tumbled and rolled east at a great speed. Lightning flashed sulfurous streaks across the roiling mass. Thunder rumbled. And rain poured from the clouds to earth in a solid, gray curtain.

The old terror gripped her, lessened in intensity from the span of eighteen years, but still there. She braced herself against the memory of lightning striking the old, dilapidated shed where she and Billy had lived with other street orphans—closed her mind to the remembered crackle of the devouring flames, the screams of Bobby and Joe who had been trapped inside. She heeled Traveler into motion, urged him close to her sister's wagon, then clapped her hand over her hat's crown and leaned toward the canvas cover as the horse trotted alongside. "Anne, there is a terrible storm coming. Brace yourself for a rough ride." The wind fluttered the canvas, bent the brim of her hat backward. She raised her voice. "Hold on tight, Anne! Protect your ribs! Do you hear me? Protect your ribs!"

"I hear—"

The iron rim of the front wagon wheel clanged and jerked over a stone. The wagon tilted, slammed back to earth. There was a sharp cry from inside.

"Anne?"

A sudden drumming sound drowned out any answer. Hail the size of a cherry hit her with stinging force, bounced off the canvas cover. Emma raced Traveler ahead, fell in behind her own wagon to gain some protection from the driving wind and pelting ice. The rain came, soaked her clothes. She lowered her head, hunched over and rode on, the hail pummeling her back.

Garth Lundquist guided the oxen toward the inside of the forming circle, stopped the wagon in place with the outside front wheel in line with the inside back wheel of his father's wagon that had stopped ahead of them. Emma sighed with relief, thought of the dry clothes awaiting her inside and would have smiled if her lips hadn't been pulled taut with cold and fear.

She glanced across the distance, watched as Ernst pulled Anne's wagon into place on the other side. Other wagons followed on both sides until the circle was complete. The enclosed oxen bawled, bugled their fear. Men jumped from their wagon seats and ran forward to calm their teams and lash the wagons together as ordered. Wagons rocked. Canvas covers fluttered and flapped.

Emma slid from the saddle, tethered Traveler to the back of the wagon then slipped through the narrow gap between the two side-by-side wheels. She skirted around her nervous, bawling oxen being calmed by her driver, and headed for Anne's wagon. Wind buffeted her, whipped her sodden skirts into a frenzy. She reached to hold them down and her hat flew away. Hail struck with bruising force against the side of her face. The rain stung like needles. She turned her face away from the wind and struggled on across the inner oval to the side of the wagon. "Are you all right, Anne?" The wind stole her words. She raised her voice to a shout. "Are you all right, Anne? I thought I heard you cry out." She cupped her ear against the fluttering onsaburg.

"I'm all right, Emma. Come in out of the rain!"

"I have to get out of these wet clothes. I will come back when the storm is over!" Water dripped off her flailing hair, dribbled down her wet back. Emma shivered and turned. A hand grasped her arm. She lifted her bowed head, looked into the fear-filled eyes of a sodden woman holding a folded blanket to her chest. The woman's lips moved. She leaned forward to hear her.

"Please, Miss. You were ridin'. Did you see my little girl, Jenny? I've checked with everyone and she's not here. She must of fell out of the wagon, and—" Lightning flickered through the darkened sky, streaked to earth with a crack that drowned out the woman's voice. Thunder clapped, rumbled. "—did you see her?"

"No. I am sorry, but I did not."

The woman swayed, sagged against the side of the wagon. Her lips trembled. "You were my last hope. Oh, God…my baby…my baby…" She lifted her hands, buried her face in the blanket.

Emma's throat constricted. She put her arm about the woman's shoulders, though she wanted desperately to go to her wagon. "Please don't—there is still hope. My head was bowed, I was not looking—" She stopped. Closed her eyes. If the child had fallen out of the wagon she was probably injured, or worse. But if she did survive the fall, this storm… *The storm!* She took a shuddering breath and held out her hand. "Give me the blanket. I will go back and look for your daughter."

The woman lifted her head. Hope and doubt mingled in her eyes. *"Now?"*

Emma nodded, took the blanket from the woman's hands. "She will need this when I find her." *If I am not too late.*

She battled her way back to her wagon, climbed over the chains Garth had used to lash the wheels together and reached up to untie the back opening in the canvas. There was no time now to change out of her wet clothes, but she needed her doctor's bag. And Caroline's rain cape. She bit down on her trembling lips, tried to stop shivering and concentrate on her task. It was no use. The flapping had drawn the knots too tight—her chilled fingers could not undo them.

Lightning sizzled to earth with an ear-deafening

crack. Emma cringed against the wagon, shivering and shaking so hard she feared her joints would detach. Hot tears stung her eyes. She tugged again at the knots, yanking at the bottom edge of the canvas when they did not yield. A spatter of water from the canvas was her only reward. A chill shook her to her toes. She sagged back against the wagon, ceding defeat.

The patient's welfare must always come first, Emma. A good doctor does not hesitate to sacrifice time or comfort, or to do whatever he must to save a life.

How many times had Papa Doc said that to her when they were called to a patient's side in the middle of the night? Strength of purpose flowed into her. "Thank you, Papa Doc." She shoved away from the wagon, unhitched Traveler and mounted. Coat or no coat, doctor's bag or not, she would go. The child did not have a chance of surviving the storm without her.

Please, God, let me find her soon. She cannot live in this storm. Emma lifted her lips in a grim smile. Why did she pray when she did not expect God to answer? Why did it make her feel better? It was foolishness.

Her teeth clattered together. She clenched her jaw, but could not sustain the pressure. She had never been so cold. But at least the hail had stopped and the wind was at her back. She tried to use her misery to block out her fear. It was impossible. Every time the lightning flashed across the sky and streaked to the ground with a thunderous clap that made the very air vibrate, she had to hold herself from screaming. She dare not let Traveler sense her terror. Thank goodness he was not a horse to panic at the flashes and rumbles.

"Good b-boy, Traveler." She patted the horse's neck, studied the ground in front of her. The rain and hail had beaten the grasses down so that it was difficult to make out the wagon tracks. If only the land were not all the same! Had she come far enough? Was this where they had started the wild run with the wagons? Was she even looking in the right place?

Almighty God, for that little girl's sake, guide me to her, I pray. She lifted her head and peered through the deluge, trying to spot something familiar. Something she had noticed earlier that afternoon. There had been a rise with a dip in the middle of the top. She had wondered if there was a pond….

Lightning glinted, turned the sky into a watery, yellow nightmare with a coruscating tail dropping to the earth. Thunder crashed. She rode on, topped the next swell and spotted the rise she was looking for off to the right. She had been going the wrong way. She slumped in the saddle, discouraged, frightened. What if she got lost out here? What if—

"Stop that this i-instant, Emma Allen! That little g-girl needs y-you!" She could barely hear her own voice above the pounding rain. But the scolding worked. She squared her shoulders, wiped the rain from her eyes and reined Traveler around. The wind slapped a long tress of freed hair across her eyes. She brushed it back, wiped the sheeting water from her forehead. She would surely find the wagon tracks now. Then she could line them up with that rise and backtrack. She rode down the other side of the swell into a broad swale, urged Traveler into a lope and came up the knoll on the other side. And there, lying on the sodden grass, was the child.

"Whoa!" Traveler danced to a stop. "Please G-God. Please l-let her be a-l-live." Emma slid from the saddle, led Traveler close and dropped the reins to the ground. *Please let him stand.* She grabbed the blanket she had been sitting on to keep it dry, knelt beside the child and touched a cold, tiny wrist. A faint throbbing pulsed against her fingers. Tears sprang to her eyes, mingled with the rain on her cheeks. She blinked her vision clear, leaned over the child to protect her from the bone-chilling downpour and began to examine the small body.

The storm had let up, except for the relentless rain. The occasional glimmer of lightning and grumble of thunder in the distance held no menace. Zach circled the herd of stock one last time. They were bunched and settled, the threat of a stampede past. The others would be able to handle them now. He slapped the water from his hat, peered through the rain at the wagons. Some had not moved, despite his relayed order. Must be there were problems Blake couldn't handle. He rode down into the shallow basin and headed toward the Lewis wagon.

"Be reasonable, Lorna."

"I'm not moving from this place without her."

"Blake said it's only a short ways. If she—"

"Don't say *if,* Joseph Lewis. Don't you dare say *if!*" The Lewis woman buried her face in her apron and burst into tears.

Zach scowled. This was no time for a domestic argument. "I ordered all the wagons moved to higher, dryer ground, Lewis. They'll bog here when the water soaks in. Unless you have a broken wheel or axle, get rolling."

"It's not the wagon, sir. It's—it's—" The man looked at his wife, cleared his throat. "Our little Jenny has come up missing. The missus asked all around for her and no one has seen her. We—we figure she fell out of the wagon during our run here. But I'll find someone to move the wagon while I go look—"

The wife jerked the apron from her face. "I ain't leaving this place 'till she comes back, Joseph Lewis! If this wagon moves, it goes without me. She'll come here, and I've got to know one way or...or the other."

"Hush, Lorna! I told you if Miss Allen—"

"Miss *Allen?*" Zach's scowl deepened. "What does Miss Allen have to do with your daughter?"

"She went to look for her."

Anger shot him bolt upright in the saddle. Fool woman! He'd told her not to go riding off by herself. Now he'd have two lost people to search for! At least she couldn't have much of a head start on him. His face tightened. "How long ago did Miss Allen leave?"

"Why, right away. When I was askin' round about Jenny. She said she would find her, and she got on her horse and rode off."

"During the *storm?*"

The woman nodded. Her lips quivered. "She took the blanket with her. To warm Jenny when she found her."

The fury of the storm was nothing compared to the anger that flashed through him. Zach stood in the stirrups, looked behind him. "Blake! Get these wagons moving! Every one of them!" He looked down at the man beside him. "Lewis, you move your wagon out with the others. I know this land, and if it's humanly possible, I'll bring your daughter back to you."

He glanced up at the misty light filtering through the rain. It would soon be night—and Miss Allen was out there searching unknown land with no trail experience to fall back on. *Fool women. May he be spared from them all!* He urged Comanche into a lope and started back along the wagon trail.

Chapter Four

Zach swiped off the water sluicing from his hat brim and squinted through the rain at the dark shape ahead. It was a horse, all right. One with an empty saddle. Where was the Allen woman? He scanned the area as far as he could see through the downpour. There was no sign of her. Had the horse been frightened by lightning and thrown her? Had he ridden past her unconscious, injured body in the storm?

He muttered a couple choice words he'd picked up in the cavalry and urged Comanche into a walk. If he spooked her horse, he might have to chase it for miles and he needed it to carry Miss Allen and the child back when he found them—no matter what their condition. His stomach knotted. He was used to handling injured or wounded or even dead soldiers—but a woman and child…

Zach shoved the disquieting thought away and focused on the job at hand. The first thing was to catch the horse. He reined Comanche to circle wide to the right, so the horse would not perceive them as a threat and bolt.

He watched the horse, saw it lower its head and kneed Comanche left to move in a little closer. If he— *There she was!*

Zach halted Comanche, stared at the figure kneeling on the ground in front of the horse, head down, shoulders hunched forward, her back to the driving rain. It was, indeed, Miss Allen. And she was likely injured, else she'd be riding. He told the wind what he thought of foolish women, slid from the saddle and dropped the reins.

Water squirted from beneath his boots as he strode to Miss Allen's huddled body. Why was she holding that blanket instead of— *She'd found the child!*

"Miss Allen?" Zach touched her shoulder, felt the icy-cold flesh beneath the soaked gown, the shivers coursing through her. She lifted her head, stared up at him. Blinked. Her trembling lips moved.

"I f-found her."

He nodded, swept his gaze over her. "Where are you injured, Miss Allen?"

"Not inj-jured."

"Not—" Irritation broke though his control. "If you can ride, why are you *sitting* here?"

An expression close to disgust swept across her face. "Sh-she's injured. I c-can't mount."

Zach stared. Scowled. What was she planning to do? *Sit* here all night in the storm, shielding the child with her body? She could have— He squelched the thought. What did he expect of a greenhorn woman? "You can now." He leaned over and held out his arms. "Let me have the child."

She shook her head.

"Miss Allen! You and the child both need to get back to warmth and shelter. And I—"

"Have to...b-be careful. Her arm is broken... h-head injured. I will c-carry her. And we m-must walk horses."

"Walk them! But you need to get out of—" He stopped, stared at her lifted chin, the sudden set look of her face. "All right, Miss Allen, you will carry the child, and we will walk the horses. Now, give her to me, and let's get you mounted." He took the blanket-swaddled child, cradled her in one arm and held out his free hand.

Holding the child was a handicap. And Miss Allen was so stiff and sluggish with cold, so weighted down by her long, sodden skirts, it took him three tries, but at last he had her in the saddle. He handed her the reins, placed the child in her shivering arms and whistled for Comanche. The big roan came dutifully to his side.

"I'll have you warmer in a minute." Zach unlashed the bedroll from behind his saddle and yanked the ties. He shook out his blanket, tossed it over Miss Allen's shoulders and covered it with his India-rubber ground-sheet. He grabbed the flapping ends, crossed them over each other in front to cover the child and secured them to the saddle horn with one of the ties. It was the best he could do to warm and protect them.

"Th-thank you."

Zach looked up. Rain washed down Miss Allen's face, dropped off her chin onto the rubber sheet and sluiced away. She was shivering so hard he had doubts of her ability to stay in the saddle. He took off his hat and clapped it on her wet hair. It slid down to her eyebrows. "Keep your head down, we'll be facing into the storm on the way back. And hold on to that horn, I'll lead your horse." He took the reins from her and leaped into the saddle, started Comanche toward the wagons at a slow walk.

Rain drenched his hair, funneled down his neck to soak his coat collar and dampen his shirt. Zach frowned and hunched his shoulders as a drop found an opening and slithered down his back. It was going to be a long ride.

A pinpoint of light glowed in the darkness ahead. Only one reason for that. Someone had got a fire started. Zach stared at the welcome sight, a frisson of expectation spreading through him. That should cheer the Allen woman. It made him feel better. There was nothing like a fire when you were cold and wet and feeling miserable. Especially if there was a pot of coffee simmering on the coals.

Zach scanned the area as best he could through the rain, trying to spot the night guards. It wouldn't do to startle them. The greenhorns were liable to shoot before they were sure of their target. He looked back at the fire, close enough now that he could see the light flickering and make out the crude, canvas canopy someone had rigged. He hadn't expected any of the emigrants to figure a way to start a fire in a rainstorm, let alone know how to protect it. Likely it was the Lewises, guiding their way back.

The fire disappeared, blocked from his view by the wagons as they approached. He spotted it again through a gap between the bulky vehicles. Looked like Lewis had switched places with the Lundquists. Joseph Lewis and his wife were tending the fire. He could make out the two of them silhouetted against the rosy glow as he rode to the Allen wagon. They appeared to be the only ones about. Not surprising, given the late hour, the weather conditions and the hard day. But where were the guards? They should have challenged him on their way in.

He frowned, halted Comanche at the back of the Allen wagon, slid from the saddle and tethered the woman's horse. "We're here, Miss Allen."

"Yes."

She sounded about done in. Zach turned his head, raised his voice loud enough to be heard over the beating of the rain on that canvas canopy rigged to protect the fire. "Lewis, give me a hand. I've got your daughter and Miss Allen." He turned back, began to untie the rawhide thong holding the blankets to the saddle horn. "I'll have you free in—"

"My baby! Where's my baby?" Mrs. Lewis squeezed through the narrow space between the wagons' wheels, her husband right behind her.

"She's right here." Zach undid the last turn of the thong and threw back the edge of the blankets.

"Oh, give her to me!" The woman reached up for her child.

"Don't h-hug her." Miss Allen's teeth chattered, broke off her words. She threw him a look of appeal.

Zach stuffed the thong in his coat pocket, and gently

lifted the child from her arms. "Your daughter has a broken arm and a head injury, Mrs. Lewis. She has to be handled careful."

The woman gave a little cry, sucked in a breath and nodded. "I understand."

Zach placed the swaddled toddler in her arms, turned back to remove his blankets and help Miss Allen from the saddle.

"T-take her into my wagon, Mrs. Lewis. I'll s-set her arm."

"You!" Joseph Lewis shook his head. "I'm right grateful to you for going to look for our Jenny, Miss Allen. But we need someone knows what they're doing to care for her. I reckon—"

"I know how to care f-for your daughter, Mr. Lewis. I'm a d-doctor."

A doctor! Zach froze, stared at Miss Allen—there was a look of grim forbearance on her face. He frowned and tossed his bedding over his saddle. A woman doctor. Judging from the argument going on between Lewis and his wife, it would cause a furor among the emigrants if she plied her trade. That was all he needed. Another problem to get in the way of his getting this train to Oregon country before winter hit the mountains.

He scowled, grasped the Allen woman around her waist and lifted her out of the saddle to the ground. Her knees buckled. She fell against him.

"S-sorry." She placed her trembling hands against his chest and tried to push herself erect.

Zach's face tightened as he steadied her. *Me, too, Miss Allen. Sorry you ever joined this train.* He leaned down, lifted her into his arms and stomped toward her wagon, heedless of the water in her sodden gown soaking through the wet sleeves of his coat.

The dry nightclothes and fire-warmed blanket felt wonderful. But it made her want to sleep. Emma swallowed the last sip of hot coffee and set her cup on the floor. She was losing her battle against the fatigue that dragged at her. Her eyes had closed again.

She forced her reluctant eyelids open, glanced at the child lying on the pallet made out of her feather pillows. Unlike her own still-damp hair, the toddler's had dried, and soft, blond curls circled the small face now pink with warmth. Jenny looked like any other sleeping toddler. Except for her splinted arm and unnatural stillness.

Emma lifted her gaze to Jenny's mother, sitting on the floor with her back against the long red box and holding her baby's hand.

"Jenny's got blue eyes. Like her papa's. I wishst she'd open 'em." The woman's chest swelled as she took a deep breath, sunk as she let it out again. "Will I ever…see her blue eyes again, Miss—Dr. Allen?"

Emma stiffened. That's what Anne had asked. Just before— She shoved the thought away, looked into the fear-filled eyes begging for hope and summoned a smile in spite of the bitterness squeezing her heart. "I cannot say for sure—such things are in God's hands—but I believe you will, Mrs. Lewis. Jenny's pulse is steady and strong, and that's a good sign." *Little Grace's pulse had been uneven and weak…*

The woman nodded, pulled the blanket draped over

her shoulders closer together across her chest. "I've been prayin'." She looked up, and the lamplight glimmered on the tears swimming in her brown eyes. "I wasn't meanin' to make you uncomfortable, askin' you things only God Hisself can answer."

Yes. Only God, who had chosen to let little Grace die. "I understand, Mrs. Lewis." *If only she could.*

Silence fell. Rain pattered against the canvas cover. The faint sound of snoring came from the Lewis family's wagon. A child's yelp. And then— "Move over, Gabe! Yer pokin' me with yer elbow!"

The woman glanced that way, looked back and shook her head. "You were right to have Jenny stay here in your wagon. With four youngsters, things are a mite crowded in ours. Special with the Mister havin' to sleep inside 'cause of the rain. 'Tis mortal kind of you to let me stay here with her."

"Not at all. Jenny will want you when she wakes." *If she wakes.* Emma blinked and gave her head a quick shake, rubbed her hands up and down her arms beneath the blanket to ward off sleep.

"You've had a hard time of it tonight, what with going out in the storm after Jenny and all. Why don't you get some sleep, Dr. Allen? I'll keep watch over Jenny."

Emma stifled a yawn, shook her head. "Her condition could change and…"

"I'll wake you if it does." The woman's eyes pleaded with her. "Please, Dr. Allen. It would make me feel better for you to rest."

She was so sincere. Emma swallowed back her fear. Her being awake had not saved little Grace. She sighed and gave in to her exhaustion. "All right. But you must wake me the moment there is the slightest change, Mrs. Lewis. Any change at all. A whimper…or a twitch… anything…" She stretched out on the feather mattress she was sitting on, pulled the quilt over top of the blanket wrapped around her and closed her eyes.

"Not meanin' to put myself forward, Dr. Allen. But I'd be pleased if you would call me by my given name, Lorna."

"Lorna…a lovely name." Emma tucked her hand beneath her cheek. Jenny had her pillows. "And you must call me Emma…"

"I'd be honored to, Dr. Emma."

Dr. Emma. The name echoed pleasantly around in her head. William had called her that in his letter. She snuggled deeper into the warmth of the quilt and smiled. If only she could…write William and…tell him she had a…patient…

"I gave the order to break camp, Lewis. Get this canopy down and your oxen hitched. We've wasted enough daylight. We move out in ten minutes."

Emma lifted her head at the sound of Zachary Thatcher's muffled voice coming through the canvas. She had been hoping for an opportunity to properly thank him for rescuing them last night. She pulled the blanket back over Jenny's splinted arm and turned toward the front of the wagon, paused to run her hands over her hair and down the front of her gown. The feel of the sumptuous fabric brought the memory of their first meeting leaping to the fore. She looked down at the three tiers of lustrous, rose-colored silk trimmed with looped roping that formed the long skirt and frowned. She could well imagine Mr. Thatcher's opinion of her inappropriate frock. But there had been no time to have gowns made after Anne announced her intention to take William's place teaching at the mission. With only two days of preparation time, the best she could manage was to purchase dress lengths of cotton and other sensible materials to bring—

"I ain't travelin' today."

Oh dear! Emma jerked her attention back to the conversation outside the wagon. Mr. Lewis sounded… truculent.

"What do you mean, you're not traveling today? You don't have a choice. Lest you want to go on by yourself."

And Mr. Thatcher sounded…adamant, to be charitable. Perhaps this was a poor time to—

"Tell that to that Allen woman what calls herself a *doctor!* She's got the missus all in an uproar over Jenny. Says Jenny can't travel, and the missus won't go without her. With three other young'uns that need carin' for, I—"

"You speak respectful of Dr. Emma, Joseph Lewis. She rode out in that storm and found your baby. Likely saved her life."

Lorna! Emma peeked outside. Joseph Lewis was glaring at his wife, who was glaring back at him from their wagon.

"*If* she lives, Lorna. We don't have a real doctor to—"

A *real* doctor! *Ohhh!* Emma hiked up her voluminous skirts, climbed onto the red box and reached to shove the front flaps of the cover aside. The back of her skirt snagged on the latch. *Bother!* She reached back.

"Don't you say *if,* Joseph Lewis! The Good Book says, 'According to your faith be it unto you.' And don't think I'm goin' to move one foot from this spot 'till Dr. Emma says it's safe for Jenny to travel, neither."

Emma freed her skirt and turned back. Lorna had climbed from their wagon and stood facing her husband. The sight of their angry faces turned her own anger to regret. She had not meant to set husband and wife at odds. But all was not lost. If Zachary Thatcher would agree not to travel out of consideration of the child's poor condition… She scooted out onto the driver's seat, cast a longing glance at her sodden, mud-stained riding outfit crumpled in the corner of the driver's box and stood. "Good morning."

All three people turned to look at her. Zachary Thatcher swept his gaze over her fancy gown and his expression did not disappoint her expectations. She abandoned the idea of relying on his understanding and sympathy. In the cold light of day, it appeared Mr. Thatcher did not have any. She looked down into his steady, disapproving gaze and stiffened her spine. "I regret the wagon train cannot travel today, Mr. Thatcher. But it would be dangerous for Jenny to be jolted and bounced around in her condition."

She watched his face tighten and stood her ground as

he rode his horse close to the wagon and peered up at her. "I understand the child is ill, Miss Allen. But you must underst—"

"*Dr.* Allen, Mr. Thatcher."

His eyes darkened and narrowed. His lips firmed.

She was familiar with the disparaging expression. She had seen it far too often on the faces of her Papa Doc's male patients. Very well. If that was how it was to be. Emma trotted out her armor for the battle ahead. "I am a fully trained, fully qualified doctor with credentials from a celebrated surgeon with the Pennsylvania Hospital—" she registered the growing disdain in his eyes and rushed on "—which I will produce if you doubt my word." Her challenge hit the mark. Anger flashed in those blue depths.

"This is not about your qualifications, *Miss* Allen. It is about getting this wagon train to Oregon country before winter snows close the mountain passes. To that end, these wagons will move forward *every day*—including today." He touched his hat brim and reined his horse around to leave.

Emma clenched her hands into fists. "Whether you acknowledge me as a doctor or not, Mr. Thatcher, Jenny Lewis is my patient. And I cannot—*will* not—allow her to be jostled around in a moving wagon. It could very well take her life."

Zachary Thatcher turned his horse back around, stared straight into her eyes. "And if this train gets caught by a blizzard in a mountain pass it could well cost us *all* our lives, Miss Allen."

"That is conjecture, Mr. Thatcher. Jenny's condition is fact. This wagon does not move until it is safe for her to travel."

Stubborn. He knew it the moment he set eyes on her. Stubborn and spoiled. But he never expected this. A doctor! And if this morning was any indication, one that would give him a good deal of trouble. Zach held the horseshoe nail against the hickory rib in front of him and lifted the hammer. "Ready, Lewis?"

"Hammer away!"

Zach hit the nail with such force the rib thudded against the sledgehammer Joseph Lewis was holding against it outside and twanged back. The nail was buried deep enough in the wood he didn't need to hit it again. "That will do it!" He tied a long, thick leather thong to the nail, tugged to make sure the knots would hold then picked up the oblong piece of canvas with the big knots on the corners and tied the other end of the thong around one corner and tugged. There was no way the thong could slip off past that big knot. He repeated the process with the other three thongs hanging from the nails he'd driven in other ribs, then gave the canvas a push. It swung gently through the air. There! That would take care of any jolting.

He gave a grunt of satisfaction, picked up the hammer and extra nails and leaped lightly from the wagon. "The bed is ready, *Dr.* Allen. Now tell Garth Lundquist to get your oxen hitched. Time is wasting!" He took the sledge from Lewis and strode off toward the Fenton wagon to return the tools to the blacksmith.

Emma stared after him, reading disgust and anger in the rigid line of his broad shoulders, the length and power of his strides. Her own shoulders stiffened with resentment. He made the word *doctor* sound like an *expletive*.

Joseph Lewis cleared his throat. "I'll go fetch Lundquist for you. Have him bring up your teams, Miss… er…"

Emma turned her gaze on him. He flushed, pivoted on his heel and hurried off.

"It ain't *Miss,* Joseph Lewis! It's *Dr.* Allen."

Emma glanced at Lorna Lewis. The woman was staring after her husband, her face as flushed as his. She tamped down her own anger. "Please, Lorna, do not trouble yourself on my behalf. I do not want to be the cause of discord in your household."

"Well, it ain't right, Joseph not givin' you your rightful due—an' Mr. Thatcher gettin' riled at you for holdin' up the train so's to keep my baby safe an'…" The woman's words choked off.

"And nothing, Lorna." Emma whirled around, her long, ruffled skirts billowing out then rustling softly as she climbed into her wagon. "I care not a *fig* for Mr. Zachary Thatcher's opinions or anger. And even less for his orders. As for Mr. Lewis's reluctance to name me a doctor…I am accustomed to that. Keeping Jenny safe is all that is important. And this wagon will not move until I am satisfied it will do her no harm. Now, give Jenny to me and climb in so we can see what sort of bed Mr. Thatcher has contrived."

She turned and carried the toddler to the canvas sling

hanging lengthwise over the long red box just behind the driver's seat.

"Well, I never…" Lorna Lewis set the sling swinging.

"Nor I." Emma handed Jenny to her mother and examined the clever contraption from all angles. "I find no fault in this. It will make Jenny a wonderful bed." She lined the sling with her pillows, covered them with a blanket then gently placed Jenny on them and folded the sides of the blanket over her.

Chains rattled. An ox snorted, bumped against the wagon in passing, causing the bed to sway gently. "You want I should hitch up now, Miss Allen?"

Emma smiled and stuck her head out of the opening behind the driver's box. "Yes, hitch up the teams, Mr. Lundquist. We will travel today after all. But drive the oxen carefully, mind you. No hurrying."

She ducked back inside, pulled a long scarf from a dresser drawer and held it out. "Wrap this twice around both Jenny and the sling, Lorna. Then tie it so Jenny cannot fall out. I will be right back." She climbed down, lifted the hems of her skirts above the still-wet ground and ran across the oval to check on Anne before the wagons began to roll.

Chapter Five

Emma sighed and clutched the edge of the driver's seat to steady herself as the wagon lurched over the rough terrain. And she thought she was uncomfortable riding Traveler all day. She could only imagine how sore she would be tonight from this day's continual bone-shaking travel. But at least her patient was being spared. The sling bed Mr. Thatcher had created worked perfectly. No matter how badly the wagon bucked, Jenny simply swung back and forth, the length of the leather thongs keeping the bed from too violent a motion.

Emma tightened her grasp against another lurch and grimaced. Too bad the driver's seat was not a sling. It would certainly make her ride more comfortable. She considered the idea a moment, then discarded it and resigned herself to endure the punishing jolts. A sling seat was not possible. The box beneath her held Traveler's feed.

The front wheels dropped into a rut and Emma glanced over her shoulder at Jenny. Her stomach—her personal measure of concern—tightened. The toddler looked perfectly normal. But if she did not wake soon…

Emma's face drew as taut as her stomach. She lifted her hands to adjust her scoop bonnet that had been jarred awry. The wagon ricocheted off some unforgiving obstacle, and she bounced into the air, then slammed back down onto the hard wood seat. "Ugh!"

A shrill whistle sounded ahead. Emma looked forward, saw Josiah Blake standing in his stirrups and circling his arm over his head, and heaved a sigh of relief. It must be time to rest and graze the stock. Which meant the buffeting would stop—at least for a while. And the break would give her time to check on Anne and ease her feelings of guilt for being unable to watch over her today. She would insist Anne come and ride beside her wagon when their journey resumed.

"Circle up!" The call passed from wagon to wagon, faded away down the line.

Emma frowned and worried her bottom lip with her teeth. Anne's pain had been worse last night and she was sure the wild ride in the wagon yesterday had reinjured her sister's mending ribs. Not that Anne had complained. As usual, she said nothing, simply endured whatever pain assailed her mending body. It was only an increased pallor, an involuntary wince and tightening of her sister's face that had alerted her to Anne's worsened condition.

Emma gripped the seat harder. Sometimes Anne's quiescence made her want to shake her. She and William, cousin Mary, even Mary's pastor had tried to reason with Anne, but none of them could sway her from her notion that her pain was deserved punishment for surviving the accident that had claimed the lives of her husband and baby. It made treating her more difficult. Anne did not want to get better.

Emma heaved a long sigh and released her grasp on the edge of the seat as the wagon followed the Lewis vehicle into the familiar circle and stopped. Across the oval, the source of her concern and frustration rode into view behind her halted wagon and dismounted, her movements slow and careful. Clearly riding was irritating Anne's injuries, but being tossed around in the wagon was little better. Oh, if only Anne had listened to reason, at this moment they would both be aboard one of their uncle Justin's steamboats on their way home to Philadelphia with William and Caroline! Home to the bosom of their family where Anne would receive the love and attention she needed.

A sick feeling washed over her. Emma swallowed hard, faced the thought that had been pushing at her all day. Perhaps she did not possess the skills needed to be a good doctor. She did not know what more to do for Anne. Or for little Jenny. Her learning was but a poor substitute for Papa Doc's medical experience, or her feisty temperament for their mother's patient, loving care.

"Mama? Maaaamaaaa!"

Jenny! Emma whipped around and scurried over the red box into the wagon, all speculation about her possible inadequacy forgotten at the toddler's frightened wail.

"Shhh, Jenny, shhh. Everything is all right." She smiled and patted the little blanket-covered shoulder.

Round blue eyes, bright with tears, stared up at her. She studied their clear, focused gaze, held back the shout of relief and joy swelling her chest. The toddler's tiny lower lip protruded, trembled. She touched it with her fingertip and shook her head. "No, no. I will get your mama for you. But you must not cry, Jenny. It is not good for you to cry."

She turned and leaned out over the wagon seat. *"Lorna!"*

Lorna Lewis glanced her way, paled then sent a stern look toward her children standing by the wagon. "Don't you young'uns move from this spot 'till I say! Lily, you hand out the biscuits." She shoved a crock into her daughter's hands and turned, her movements stiff as she moved toward the wagon. "Is it—is Jenny—"

Emma smiled. "Jenny is *awake,* Lorna! And she wants her mama." She laughed her delight at the joy that spread across the woman's face and ducked back inside the wagon to untie the knot in the scarf that held Jenny secure.

"You must feed Jenny only broth, perhaps some thin gruel until we see how she tolerates food, Lorna." Emma smiled at the toddler resting happily on her mother's lap. "And keep her calm. Do not let the others overly excite her."

"C'n I ride in the swing bed, Pa?"

Oh dear! Emma turned around on her camp stool and looked up at the other Lewis children crowded together on the driver's seat watching Zachary Thatcher and their father hang the sling bed inside their wagon. Had she made a mistake suggesting the transfer of the bed? What if—

"You'll ride on that seat or walk same as you been doing, Gabe. And that goes fer the rest of you, too. Jenny's bad hurt and this bed is special to help her get better. The rest of you young'uns ain't to be crowdin' round or hangin' on it. You hear me?"

"Yes, Pa!"

Emma smiled and let her worry drain away. Joseph Lewis's gruff orders and the children's chorused answer left no doubt as to Jenny's safety.

"Dr. Emma! Jenny's—her eyes closed sudden like."

The fear in Lorna Lewis's voice caught at her throat. *No! Not again! Please, not again!* Emma turned back. Jenny's color was good. She lifted the edge of the blanket covering her small patient and placed her fingertips on a tiny wrist. The pulse was strong and steady. "She's only fallen asleep, Lorna."

"Oh. Praise be to God. It was so sudden like, I thought…"

Emma nodded, closed her eyes against a surge of relief so strong she was lightheaded.

"Doctor?"

"Yes?"

"I been thinkin' on how we can pay you for savin' our Jenny. We ain't got much cash money. We put about all we had into outfittin' the wagon an'—"

"There is no charge, Lorna." Emma opened her eyes and smiled at the grateful mother. "I am pleased to have helped."

"All the same…" Lorna gave her a hopeful look. "Mayhap I can cook your meals?"

Emma shook her head. "That is a very generous offer. But I have engaged Mrs. Lundquist to prepare meals for my sister and me. And truly, you need not—"

Lorna's pointed chin lifted. "We pay our way. I'll think of somethin'."

"Miss Allen."

The deep voice brought a tautness to her stomach that had nothing to do with worry. Emma turned. Zachary Thatcher was striding toward her. She rose. "Is the bed ready for Jenny, Mr. Thatcher?"

"Yes." He stopped in front of her. "But what I wanted was to warn you *again* not to go off by yourself like you did last night. These foolhardy—"

"Foolhardy!" Emma glanced over her shoulder at the sleeping toddler, snagged her bottom lip with her teeth and flounced over to her wagon. She stepped into the shade on the other side and whirled to face the wagon master following in her wake. "I find your comment both inaccurate and insulting, Mr. Thatcher. I did not go for a *pleasure* ride in that storm. I went after a lost and, I assumed, injured child. And I found her!"

"Yes. By luck. It is certain it was not any measure of trailing skills on your part that led you to the child. All you did was endanger yourself."

Ungracious words. But true. Pride kept her back stiff. "I concede the danger, made greater due to my lack of frontier skills, Mr. Thatcher. I was aware of it last night. But I am a doctor. I could not leave that child to the mercies of that storm knowing she would likely die. I had to try and find her."

He shook his head. "No, you did not. That was my responsibility, Miss Allen. Or her father's." His gaze bored down into hers. "Given the gravity of the situation, Mrs. Lewis—or you—should have come to one of us. Had you gotten lost it would only have made the situation worse. I would have had two people to search for instead of one."

Emma clenched her hands, stared up into those unflinching, unforgiving blue eyes. The man had no understanding. No *compassion*. "Mrs. Lewis was trying to find her *child* while you men were busy securing wagons or herding stock. She needed help. Her *child* needed help. I provided it."

"Because of luck!" The words were all but snorted. Zachary Thatcher snatched his hat off, ran the fingers of his left hand through his hair, then slapped the hat back on his head. "Had I been informed of the situation, I would have found the child because of skill. With no danger to any other."

Emma raised her chin. "And would you have recognized and known how to treat her injuries, Mr. Thatcher? Are your *skills* equal to that? Jenny needed a *doctor*. I went to her then, and I will go to anyone who needs my help in the future—in spite of personal risk." His blue eyes darkened. She took a step back as he moved closer. He took another step, trapped her against the wagon.

"Have you no *sense?* That is feckless, thoughtless reasoning. You were fortunate this time, Miss Allen. The next time that may not be the case."

The words were chilling. More so because of the slow, quiet way he spoke them. They brought to mind that deep hidden chasm, the many dangers he had warned the emigrants about. She tore her gaze from his eyes, stared at a brass button on his shirt. "Then should I come to danger, it will be on my head. You, sir, are exonerated of all blame."

A strange sort of sound, not unlike a low growl, emanated from him. Emma jerked her gaze to his face. He opened his mouth, clamped it shut again, pivoted on his heel and strode away. She took a long breath, sagged against the wagon and watched him go.

Comanche's hoofs thundered against the ground, crushing the new grass, flinging small clods of prairie soil into the air. Zach leaned forward as they climbed a rise, urged Comanche to greater speed as they pounded down the other side. Stubborn! Stubborn! Stubborn! Downright mulish! That's what she was. The woman had no common sense! Standing there looking up at him with those big brown eyes and declaring he was exonerated of all blame if she came to harm. As if that was what worried him—being blamed. How did you reason with someone like that? "God, give me patience to deal with foolish women!"

Zach glanced up at the sun, frowned. Two hours' travel time left today, at best. Snows would catch them for sure if they moved at this pace. His frown slid downward into a scowl. It was early—little more than two weeks out—but the Allen woman was going to endanger them all if she continued to delay the train. Not to mention she would cost him his bonus, as well. He had to make her see reason. But how?

Zach lifted his head and sniffed the air, caught the scent of water. He slowed Comanche to a trot, headed for the slight rise on his left to look over the lay of the land and choose their camping spot for the evening. He had wanted to cross this stream today and camp on the other side, but the morning's delay had squelched that plan.

So what could he do? If she were a man, he would have no problem. He had dealt with insubordinate troopers. But he had no jail to throw her in. And he sure couldn't beat sense into her with his fists, though he was tempted to tie her up, toss her in her wagon and keep her there until they reached Oregon country! The woman was going to get herself hurt, or killed…or worse.

Memories of the mutilated bodies of settlers unfortunate enough to be caught in the path of angry hostiles flooded his head. His stomach knotted. By all that was holy, if it were not for her ill sister, he would throw Dr. Emma Allen over his saddle, heel Comanche into a gallop and not stop until they reached Independence where he would put her on a steamboat for parts e ast!

Emma walked beside the wagon, grateful to be spared the punishment of riding. Still, her legs were beginning to tremble in protest of the exercise. She sighed and swatted at the insects buzzing around her head. If only she could ride Traveler. But that was not possible without her riding outfit. She had no sidesaddle, and she certainly could not ride astride in this dress.

Her lips twisted in disgust. She was beginning to realize how very inappropriate her gowns were for her situation. The opulent skirts dragged against the grass, making walking difficult and tiring. And the shimmer and color of the silk seemed to attract insects. She waved her hand through the air in front of her face, putting a stop to the annoying buzzing and humming for a moment. When she stopped, the insects returned. She sighed and trudged on. If only she had not lost her riding hat in the storm, she could have rearranged the gossamer fabric that formed the long tails into a protective veil.

"Oh!"

Emma stopped, glanced in the direction of the startled cry. A woman was struggling to rise from the ground, a small boy beside her. The woman gained her feet, took a step, cried out and fell forward. Emma grasped her voluminous skirts, lifted the hems free of her feet and forced her tired legs to run across the grassy distance. She pushed her skirts aside and knelt beside the woman seated on the ground holding her foot. "What happened?"

"I stepped in a hole and my ankle turned. My foot hurts... It's swelling."

"Yes, I see. I shall have to remove your shoe." Emma smiled reassurance, undid the laces and eased the shoe off to an accompanying hiss of sucked-in breath. "This will hurt a bit, but I must examine your—" The foot was drawn aside. She looked up. A flush crept over the woman's pale face.

"You're that doctor woman I've heard talk of, aren't you?"

Doctor *woman*. Emma's heart sank. She held her face impassive. "Yes. I am a doctor."

The woman nodded. "Thank you for the kindness, but I'll manage now."

"And how shall you do that, Mrs…?"

"Swinton." The flush deepened. The woman looked down and picked up her shoe. "Edward will help me. My husband said I was to have naught to do with you."

Would there ever come a time when those words did not hurt or make her furious? Emma nodded and looked at the boy. He was too young to send to the wagons for help. "I understand, Mrs Swinton. And I have no desire to force my ministrations on you. But I am afraid you are going to have to accept my assistance. Without examining you, I cannot tell if the injury is a break or a bad sprain, but the swelling tells me it is severe. You should not walk on it lest you do it further damage. And your son is not big enough to help you back to the train." She forced a smile and drove bitter words out of her mouth. "I am sure, under the circumstances, your husband will forgive you. You are not disobeying his edict. You have refused my doctoring skills. I will only help you back to your wagon, as would anyone. I am certain he would not want you left here helpless and in pain."

The woman looked toward the wagons filing by in the distance, pressed her lips into a firm line and nodded.

Emma rose and looked at the boy. "I shall need you to stand just here and help balance your mother for she must not put her foot down. Are you strong enough to do that?"

The boy gave an eager nod and moved into place.

Emma moved to the woman's side and bent to put her arm around her waist. "Now, Mrs. Swinton, place your arm about my neck and we shall rise together on the count of three. But do *not* put your foot down." She reached up to her shoulder, grasped the woman's wrist and braced herself to lift her. "Ready? One…two… *three*."

"These wagons give a very punishing ride. And they are so confining it makes me restless." Emma gave her sister a hopeful look. "Do you feel well enough to come outside and sit with me until nightfall, Anne? It is a lovely evening."

"Perhaps tomorrow, Emma. It has been a long, wearying day and I want only to retire." Anne reached to pull the pins from her hair, winced, gave her a wan imitation of her once-vibrant smile and picked up her brush.

"I shall leave a dose of laudanum should you need it to sleep." Emma pulled a tiny, cork-stoppered vial from her pocket, placed it on a trunk holding teaching supplies and climbed from the wagon. She closed and latched the tailgate, straightened the end flaps of the cover that fell into place. A canvas curtain that effectively shut her out of Anne's life. She sighed and turned away from the wagon toward the openness of the prairie. William was right. She could not heal Anne's grief. It was an impossible task. Yet she could not simply give up and let Anne perish of a broken heart. There had to be *something* that would make her want to live again. And she would not rest until she found that something.

She strolled on without direction or purpose, musing

over possibilities, found herself near a thin band of trees, plucked a leaf from a low-hanging limb and absently shredded it as she worried over the problem. If only she could find some spark of interest in Anne for *something*. But she kept to herself day and night. Spoke to no one—

"Miss Allen."

Emma jumped, turned and stared at the stocky young man striding toward her. "Good evening, Mr. Blake." She glanced toward the distant wagons. "Is there a problem?"

"Not if you turn back." A smile curved a line through Josiah Blake's dark, stubbly beard. "Night's about to fall and you're getting a mite far out for safety."

She glanced at the setting sun, the darkness under the trees beyond the reach of its gold-edged rose and purple-colored rays. A shiver slid down her spine. "Are you speaking of Indians?"

"Always a possibility. More so the farther west we travel. But there's other dangers—wolves and such."

Her skin prickled. Her imagination placed the beasts among the trees, skulking through the deep grass all around her. "Thank you for coming to warn me, Mr. Blake. I did not realize how late it is getting, or how far I had wandered." She started back toward the wagons, grateful for his presence as he fell into step beside her, but still frightened enough her feet itched to run. The band of trees along the stream now seemed a menace instead of a cool comfort from the sun.

"I was sorry to hear your sister's ill, Miss Allen. She's

fortunate to have you to care for her. I mean, you bein'
a doctor and all."

His words soothed the ache in her heart over her
inability to help Anne out of her grief—eased her hurt
from the Swinton rebuff earlier. She turned her head and
gave him a grateful smile. "Thank you, Mr. Blake. You
are most kind."

Zach watched Josiah Blake approach Emma Allen,
saw them exchange words, then walk together toward
the wagons. She would be safe now. Good man, Blake.
Though his second-in-command had been a little too
eager to accept the task he'd set him.

Zach scowled, edged through the trees and stalked
back to the wagons to set the night guards. Emma Allen
was a beautiful woman and that could become a major
problem. There were quite a few single men on this train.
What was she doing wandering off by herself this time
of night anyway? Strolling around as if she was in some
park back in Philadelphia without a care in the world.

He glanced back, saw Blake had escorted her safe
to her wagon, caught the smile she gave him before he
walked away. The second one. She'd never smiled at
him.

Zach let out a disgusted snort. That could only be
counted as a blessing. Emma Allen was nothing but
trouble, and he'd wasted enough time watching out for
her safety. He aimed for the herd and lengthened his
stride. It would not happen again. He had enough work
to do.

Chapter Six

Emma bunched her dressing gown to make a pad under her knees, pushed her long, thick braid back over her shoulder and delved into the trunk to sort through the material she had purchased for gowns before she boarded the steamboat and began this journey. She was *not* going to suffer another day of torment from those voracious insects. The veiling she bought to trim her hats would— What was that?

She slipped her fingers between the hard, smooth object and the pile of household linens it rested on, took a firm grasp and tugged it out from under the stack of fabric.

"Oh, my!"

Emma rested back on her heels, staring at the unearthed treasure in her hands. Light from the lantern flame danced in reflected golden luster across the waxed wood of the small lap desk. She placed it on her knees, ran her fingertips over the smooth, polished surface, felt the minor scar a sharp object had made in the wood.

A coyote howled, the sound mournful in the night stillness. Somewhere in the distance an owl hooted.

She rose, carried the desk to her bed, propped up her pillows and positioned herself with her back braced against the sidewall of the wagon. The circle of light from the lantern sitting atop the water keg fell across her knees. She raised the slanted top of the desk, touched the stationery inside, lifted a pen and swallowed hard as tears welled. How precious the most ordinary things had become. These were her connection with her loved ones at home.

A smile tugged at her trembling lips. She closed the desk and uncorked the inkwell that had been sealed with wax, then closed her eyes and thought about what she would write. Should she tell them of her aching loneliness for them? Yes. But nothing that would cause them worry or fear for her safety.

The coyote howled again. Another answered. She lifted her head, listened to the plaintive calls tremble on the air before the sad notes faded away, then dipped the pen and began to write.

My dearest William, Mother and Papa Doc,
How I miss you all. The coyotes are howling tonight, their sad, lonely song echoing what is in my heart as I take up my pen. *Your* pen, William. For I have found your lap desk in the chest of linens. A wonderful, precious treasure for it allows me to write you all, and thus, feel a bit closer to you.

Every day, every step carries me farther from

you and my heart is burdened with sadness at day's end. It would be less so if Anne were improved, but she is much the same. She keeps always to herself. And the effort of riding Lady, or the constant jolting of the wagon delays her healing. I confess, Papa Doc, I do not know what more to do for her. She disobeys my instruction and refuses my medicines. I wish I had your forbearance, Mother. But alas, I do not. And at times I find myself quite out of patience with her. But I persevere. For I am determined to find that which will bring our Annie back to life. Back to us.

I am well. But though I ravenously partake of the meals Mrs. Lundquist prepares for us, the miles I travel each day have made me quite thin, though stronger. My gowns hang loosely upon my frame.

William, my dear brother, I know you are longing for news of our journey. I am told we shall reach the Big Blue River tomorrow or the day following. The river must be forded, for, as the dictatorial Mr. Thatcher says, there are no ferries here in the wilderness. As you will know, I am dreading that.

How I wish I could receive a letter from you. I have read your note over and over, William. It is a comfort to me. Thank you from my heart for the medical supplies, though I fear I will have little use for them. Still, your faith in my doctoring skills warms my heart.

My dearest love to you all, always,

Your Emma

She blotted the ink, blew on it to hasten its drying, then folded it to the inside, inscribed William's name and directed the letter to the Twiggs Manor Orphanage in Philadelphia. He would be back there teaching by now. Tears flowed. She swiped them from her cheeks, lifted the desk lid and took out the small candle of sealing wax and the little metal stamp. William's stamp, with its capital *A* for Allen.

The tears came again, faster. She placed the lap desk on the floor, lifted the chimney of the lantern, lit the candle and tilted it downward over the letter. The melting red wax dropped in a tiny puddle securing the loose edge to the letter body. She blew out the candle and pressed the stamp against the cooling wax, stared down at the *A* it imprinted. Would there be a way to send the letter home? Would they ever receive it and know how much she loved and missed them?

A sob broke free from her constricted throat. Another. And another. She grabbed a pillow, hugged it to her chest and threw herself on the bed to cry out her loneliness and fear.

"Follow us! Stay on our path!"

Emma turned her face from the river. Zachary Thatcher and Josiah Blake were leading the first wagon into the water and she could not bear to watch. She looked at the low hills in the distance, drew her gaze back to Garth Lundquist, thought of how odd it was to have him sitting beside her, and concentrated on the rumble of the wheels bumping down the sloping bank and the sound of the swiftly flowing water of the Big Blue.

"Gee! Gee!" Garth Lundquist cracked his whip in the air over the broad backs of the oxen. The teams plunged into the water, turned right, following the wagons ahead. The front wheels rolled into water, turned brown with mud churned up by hoofs, that splashed against the rims and rose quickly to cover the hubs.

Emma gripped the edge of the seat and stared down at the toes of her boots poking out from under the long, ruffled skirt of her watered-silk gown. An incongruous sight. But one to be preferred over watching the water rushing by beneath the floorboards. She stole a quick glance at the opposite bank. They were halfway there. *Please let us cross safely.*

The wagon dropped sharply to the right, jolted to a stop. Her grip broke. She slid along the canted seat.

"Haw! Haw!" The whip cracked. The oxen lunged. The wagon slipped farther right, sank deeper.

Emma threw herself toward the center of the seat, groped for a handhold to stop her slide, found only the smooth surface of the seat top, the protruding lip too small for her searching fingers to grasp. Fear squeezed her throat, froze her thoughts on the silky whisper of her gown against the smooth boards as she slipped toward the water waiting to embrace her.

"Hold those oxen, Lundquist!" An arm slid beneath her abdomen, plucked her from the seat, dragged her onto a saddle. The horn dug into her leg, water swirled around her feet, wet her skirts and boots. She twisted her torso, clutched hold of fabric and buried her face against a wool shirt that smelled faintly of horse, leather and man. The horse beneath her lunged. Water sloshed higher. She shuddered.

"Blake, get a rope around that front axle and hold her fast so she can't slip to the right! I'll get the back." Zachary Thatcher's deep voice fell on her ears, vibrated in his chest beneath her hands. "Let go of my shirt, Miss Allen. I have to tie my rope to the back axle." He loosed his arm from around her, withdrew the circle of safety.

Panic pounced. She pressed closer, held tighter. His muscles rippled. His strong hands gripped hers, tugged them from his shirt front, lowered them. "Hold to my holster belt." She seized the leather strap her fingers touched, felt him lean sideways and reach down. The saddle creaked. Cool air replaced the warmth of his body—emptiness stole her security. Panic gnawed at her nerves. She kept her eyes closed tight, fought the scream filling her throat, surging into her mouth.

Zachary Thatcher straightened, snagged her around the waist with his left arm, lifted her and held her tight against his chest. "Sorry, I have to snub the rope." He shoved aside her skirt, wrapped the rope around the horn and settled her back in place. "Lundquist, move those teams forward! And don't stop!"

Garth Lundquist's whip cracked. The wagon lurched.

"Back, Comanche!" The horse backed up, the wagon slid left, leveled out and rolled forward. "That's got it!" Zachary Thatcher urged his horse forward, leaned down and unhooked his rope, rode behind the moving wagon and up the other side. He spanned her waist with his hands, lifted her onto the wagon seat and rode away.

She sat gripping the sideboard and looking after him, fighting back tears and an unreasonable, overwhelming feeling of being abandoned.

"Now hold very still." Emma put fresh padding on Jenny's arm, added the splints and bound them in place, grateful for the need to think of something other than the terror of the fording—and the comforting strength of Zachary Thatcher's arms. "All done. You were a very good girl." She smiled at the toddler who promptly turned and buried her face against her mother's chest. Emma patted the child's back and looked up at Lorna. "Jenny's arm is healing fine."

The woman nodded. "Thank you, Dr. Emma. I watch her careful. An'…well, I been thinkin' whilst you was checkin' her arm. Like I told you afore, Mr. Lewis and I haven't got the cash money, but I can wash your clothes—an' your sister's—to pay for you takin' care of Jenny an' all. I got my water heatin' by the river. So if you'll fetch the clothes for me, I'll get Jenny settled and get to the washin'."

There was unyielding pride in Lorna Lewis's voice. Emma looked at her set face and nodded. "That is a very generous and welcome offer, Lorna. I will bring our clothes to you." She rose and started away, turned back. "Would you care to continue to take on that task while we journey? My sister and I will be happy to pay you." She gave a helpless little shrug. "I am afraid neither of us are trained in such skills."

Lorna studied her face for a moment then nodded.

"Wonderful! I shall tell Anne our laundry problem has been solved." Emma smiled and hurried to her wagon. She climbed onto the step attached to the tailgate and tossed back the flaps. If Lorna cleaned her riding outfit she would be able to—

"Pardon me, Miss."

Emma turned. A worried-appearing young woman holding a crying baby was looking up at her.

"Are you the doctor lady?"

The woman was close to tears. Emma nodded, gave her a reassuring smile. "Yes, I am a doctor."

Relief spread across the woman's face. "I need help, Doctor. It's Isaac. He won't eat nothing. And he won't stop crying. And he's such a good baby… It's been two days." Tears spilled down the woman's cheeks. "I've tried all I know, and what others have said…" She caught her breath. "My husband didn't want me to come, but I think Issac's fevered. And if he's sick…"

"Perhaps I should look at him." Emma stepped down and took the baby into her arms. "How old is Isaac?"

"A bit over a year." The woman wiped away the tears, stared at her child with fear-filled eyes.

Emma sat on the step, laid the baby on her lap, held his tiny, too-hot hands and swung her knees side to side, humming softly to calm him. There was a red flush on his chubby little cheeks, his eyes were squeezed shut. She let go of his hands, felt his forehead…*fevered*—gently probed the glands in his neck…*swollen*. She slipped her hands up and checked behind his ears…*nothing*.

"Is he…sick?"

Emma lifted the baby off her lap, held him in front of her and peered into his mouth when he opened it to squall his protest. The telltale spots were there on the inside of his cheeks. She snuggled the baby against her shoulder, rubbed his tense back, wishing with all her heart she had been wrong. She fixed a calm expression on her face and looked up at his mother. "Isaac is coming down with the measles."

The young woman's face blanched. "Measles?"

Every tale of every death caused by the disease was in the whispered word. "Yes. But Isaac looks to be a healthy, robust baby. And we will do everything we can to keep him that way." *Please, God, grant that it may be so.* She rose and gave the baby back to his mother.

The woman cuddled her son close, pressed her cheek against his soft curls, then looked up and squared her shoulders. "Tell me what I must do."

Emma looked into the determined face. The fear was there in the young woman's eyes, but the firm line of her mouth said she would not let it defeat her. And she had already defied her husband for her child's sake when she brought him to her. Isaac would be well cared for. "You must keep Isaac as calm and comfortable as possible. And keep him warm at all times—a chill will be very bad for him. And keep him inside the wagon. The bright sunlight will hurt his eyes." She had a momentary flash of Papa Doc closing the curtains on the window above her bed in the orphanage. "Encourage him to nurse as often as he will, and feed him only a thin gruel that is easy to swallow, for his throat is sore."

She looked up and met the mother's gaze. "What is your name?"

"Mrs. James Applegate…Ruth Applegate."

Emma dipped her head in acknowledgment. "And have you other children, Mrs. Applegate?"

"No…only Isaac."

Relief spread through her. Perhaps it was not too late to contain the spread of the disease. "If your husband will permit it, Mrs. Applegate, I will come to your wagon and check on Isaac every day. If he will not—" she reached out and touched the soft hair curling behind the baby's ear "—check here often. In the next day or two the rash will begin and it usually starts here, or on the forehead, then spreads. An oatmeal paste will help soothe the itching." She gave her another encouraging smile. "The disease will run its course in a week or so. But you must keep Isaac warm and quiet for several weeks after. Meanwhile, if he shows signs of distress, or develops a deep cough, send for me immediately."

The woman nodded, bit down on her lip. "Doctor, I…" A flush crept across the woman's cheeks. She lifted her head a notch. "My husband will give me no money to pay you. Have you any sewing or—"

"Sewing?" The pile of fabric tucked away in the trunk in the wagon flashed into her head.

"Yes. I was a dressmaker back home, before my marriage."

Zach stood beside Comanche and watched the emigrants herding the stock, settling them down for the night. Only a few animals had wandered into deep water and been forced to swim to the other side during the fording. He and Comanche had only had to save one milk cow. Everything considered, the greenhorns had done a good job today. Hopefully, they would do as well when they faced the whirlpools, swift water and quicksand in the rough river fords ahead.

He lifted his hat, ran his fingers through his hair then settled his hat back in place and tugged the brim low over his forehead. "Well, boy, there's no reason for us to be standing here. Let's get to camp so you can start grazing." Comanche twitched his ears, tossed his head. Zach gathered the reins, glanced in the direction of the wagons and frowned. Who was he fooling? He wasn't ready to turn in. There was a restlessness in him that wouldn't let sleep come easily tonight. And the reason was in that fourth wagon.

He turned away, yanked his hat down lower. What he needed was a hard run with Comanche's hoofs thundering against the ground. Or some combat with an Indian brave determined to have his scalp as a trophy. That would take his mind off the way Emma Allen had felt in his arms this afternoon. The way his heart had pounded when she grabbed his shirt and hid her face against his chest. He sure hadn't wanted to let her go when he put her back in her wagon. He'd wanted to pull her tight and kiss her. And now there was this sense of something unfinished inside him. He scowled, whipped around toward his saddle. "Let's make a final scout of the area before we go to camp, boy."

There was a whisper of sound behind him. He clasped the haft of his knife and pivoted, stared as Emma Allen stepped out of the shade of a tree into the soft, rosy glow of the setting sun. She glanced around and headed his way, a picture of beauty and grace. His heart kicked. He frowned at the involuntary reaction, grabbed Comanche's reins and strode to meet her. He had no idea why the woman would be seeking him out. But whatever the reason, he had already learned, if Dr. Emma Allen was involved, it spelled trouble for him. Whether it was as a doctor or as a woman, she was trouble for him.

Chapter Seven

"Measles." Zachary Thatcher removed his hat, ran his fingers through his hair, settled his hat back in place and frowned down at her. "You're certain?"

Emma stiffened at the implied doubt of her competency. "Yes, Mr. Thatcher, I am certain."

"But you say there's no rash…"

"The preceding signs are all there. The rash will appear sometime in the next two days."

He nodded, rubbed the back of his neck, stared off into the distance for a moment then blew out a long breath and again fastened his gaze on her. He looked as if he would like to shoot the messenger. "How likely is it to spread?"

Emma squared her shoulders. "Beyond doubt. All those who have been in contact with the Applegates are in danger of coming down with the disease. How far it spreads depends on you. Mr. Applegate has little faith in my doctoring skill—" she let her tone tell him she was aware that he shared Mr. Applegate's opinion "—and, as he will not listen to me, you must tell him he and his family will be quarantined until—"

"Quarantined!" The frown on Zachary Thatcher's face deepened to a scowl. "This is a wagon train, Miss Allen."

"Yes." She fought down her impatience, held her voice calm and reasonable. "And unless you want this disease to run rampant through its members, you must quarantine the Applegates."

"And how do you suggest I do that?"

Emma clenched her hands, took a breath and forced herself to stand her ground instead of whirling about and walking away as she wanted to do. She was sick of fighting these battles with men who dismissed her doctoring ability simply because she was a woman. "You must have Mr. Applegate move his wagon a safe distance from the others and then *stay* with his wagon. And you must inform everyone they are not to go near the Applegates, nor their wagon, until they are able to rejoin the train and we travel on. Those who come down with the disease meantime, will be treated in the same fashion."

"Until we 'travel on.'" He fixed a withering gaze on her. "And when will that be?"

His voice had gone hard as stone. Emma put steel into hers. "When I pronounce the wagon train free of the disease."

His eyes darkened. "Now look here, Miss—"

"Doctor."

He stared at her.

She stared back.

He sucked in air, let it out. "These wagons roll west at dawn tomorrow, *Doctor*. *All* of them."

The words were final. The tone implacable. Emma opened her mouth, then pressed her lips together to hold back her retort. The bright blue eyes staring down at her had gone as flinty as the voice. Obviously, Mr. Thatcher would not be moved by her challenging him. She would have to take another path. "*Mister* Thatcher, I understand that, as captain and guide, it is your duty to get these wagons to Oregon country in a timely manner. But to travel when the Applegate baby is ill may well cause his death. If he is to have a chance to live, he needs to be kept calm and comfortable. He needs to sleep as much as possible and with the jolting of the wagon continually disturbing him—" She caught her breath, taken by the glimmer of an idea that could prove the resolution to their stalemate. "Have you had the measles, Mr. Thatcher?"

"I have." He eyed her as if she were a beaver trap ready to spring. "Why?"

"Because that means it is safe for you to go to the Applegate's wagon." She lifted her hand, tapped her lips with one fingertip and looked into the distance, feeling her way through the idea. "If you will make a sling bed for baby Isaac—as you did for Jenny—he will be warm and comfortable and able to sleep in the moving wagon." She brought her gaze back to meet his. "And if you will break your rule and allow some of the wagons to exchange places in the train, that will solve the problem. We can have a moving quarantine."

"A *moving* quarantine?"

Emma stared at him. It wasn't exactly a sneer, but it might as well have been. She stiffened.

"And how do 'we' accomplish that Miss Allen? It seems to me the idea defies the very meaning of the word."

"In ordinary circumstance, yes. But we have an extraordinary circumstance here." She plunged ahead, too desperate to find a solution to be deterred by his touch of sarcasm. "If you place the Applegate wagon in the rear with my wagon in front of it and Anne's wagon in front of mine, it will keep the Applegates separated from the others as we travel. Anne has had the measles so there will be no danger to her. When the train halts, we shall camp some distance behind it, thus maintaining the quarantine. That way I can care for both baby Isaac and Anne. And—"

"And what of you, Miss Allen? Have you had the measles?"

Surely that hint of concern was not for her? No, of course not. He was thinking of his wagon train. She gave a brisk nod. "Yes, I have. Anne gave them to me." A smile tugged at her lips. "*And* to William. *And* Mother, though she was only Laina Brighton to us then. *And* to a dozen or so of the other children in her orphanage. We were quarantined for *weeks* while Papa Doc treated us." She shook off the memories, sobered. "As I was saying, if any others come down with the measles they shall place their wagon in the rear behind the Applegates where I will be able to tend them also."

He shook his head. "I see you have experience with this quarantine business, Miss Allen, but, as you say, this is an uncommon situation. What you propose will not work. To place the wagons in the rear as we travel makes good sense. But to have separate camps at night is foolhardy. It weakens the train and puts us all at peril. Every day we travel takes us closer to the hostile tribes. I am hoping we will not have problems with them because of a show of force, and having a few wagons camped off by themselves, thus minimizing that force, is asking for trouble."

"As is a wagon train of ill or dying people, Mr. Thatcher." She clenched her hands, watched his frown return, brought back, no doubt, by the asperity in her voice. Well, she could not help it! Why could the man not see reason?

"True enough. But I cannot permit your plan. It's too risky. I haven't men enough to guard two camps."

Emma lifted her chin and looked him full in the eyes. "And how will you get this train to Oregon country if there are no men well enough to drive the wagons or herd the stock or stand guard?"

Zachary Thatcher didn't so much as twitch. He simply looked at her. But some change in his eyes made her suddenly feel crowded…threatened in the same way she had that day by her wagon. It was an odd sort of feeling that shortened her breath and brought heat to her cheeks. It made her want to turn and flee.

"And if the Lundquists have not had the measles and you and your sister are left with no drivers? Have you solved that problem also, Doctor Allen?"

His voice had softened, but the tone was still resolute. She stared up at him irritated by her sudden unease and nettled that he had found a weak spot in her argument for which she had no answer.

He turned away, took hold of Comanche's reins. "I'll give the matter some thought. For now, I will have a talk with Applegate and make that sling bed. Meanwhile, I suggest you return to your wagon." He touched the brim of his hat and walked away, the big roan with the dappling of spots decorating his rump plodding beside him.

The man was *insufferable!* Emma took a deep breath, unclenched her hands and turned back toward her wagon. Zachary Thatcher had said he would make the sling bed for the baby and talk to Mr. Applegate. At least that was something.

Emma lifted the lap desk from the trunk, set the lamp on the closed top and shifted her position to lean her back against the firm support. Her hands trembled as she took out the writing supplies and opened the inkwell. It was small wonder. If William was right, and it was God who put this desire to be a doctor and help others in her, why hadn't He made her a *man?* God was supposed to know everything. And if so, He had to realize there was no other solution to keeping her dream from being unfulfilled because of the small-mindedness of stubborn, arrogant men like Zachary Thatcher!

She scowled down at the blank paper in front of her, sorely tempted to write out her frustration. Instead, she took a deep breath and yanked her thoughts from her confrontation with Mr. Thatcher. She needed to write William, to feel close to him and his belief in her abilities, not spew her agitation into her letter and upset him. She relaxed her tense shoulders, adjusted the position of the desk on her lap and dipped the pen into the well.

My Dearest William,

How I wish you were here. I think of you often, knowing of your curiosity about the country and the animals so different from what we have known. The terrain is endless and bears a perfect resemblance to the waves of the sea. Antelope with their budlike horns, white throats and round black eyes peer at you from above the tall grasses. Wolves and coyotes howl at night. We do not see them by day. There are snakes in abundance. They slither from beneath the oxen's hoofs and the drivers kill them with their whips. Do not fear, for I stay close by the wagons, as ordered. Most annoying are the swarms of insects. I have attached veiling all around my wide-brimmed straw flat to keep them from my face and neck.

The weather is hot now. The sun blazes down upon us all day. And we suffer thunderstorms, unlike any I have before seen in severity. There is hail the size of the cherries that grow on the tree in the backyard of the orphanage. Do you remember, William, when I became so ill from eating the unripe ones?

I must tell you of my patient. A toddler who injured herself falling out of the family's wagon. I set her arm and continue to watch over her. Others reject me as a doctor. I fear there is a measles outbreak in the offing, but Mr. Thatcher ignores my warning and refuses a quarantine. In this, things are much like there at home.

I hope this finds you all well. It is distressing not knowing if Caroline's health has improved. I comfort myself that Papa Doc is caring for her and the babe she carries. And that I shall have a niece or neph—

A fist thumped the side of the wagon. "There's a meeting called. Come to the head wagon!"

Gracious! Emma righted the desk that had tilted when she jumped, swallowed to force her heart down out of her throat back into her chest where it belonged and frowned at the ink blotch on the paper. She considered staying in her wagon to finish her letter, then sighed and rose to her feet. Most likely Mr. Thatcher was going to tell them of some obstacle ahead tomorrow. She had better go and listen to what he had to say.

Along the circle of wagons the dying embers of cook fires winked red into the dark night, appearing and disappearing as the men and women of the train crossed in front of them on their way toward the lead wagon. Zach watched them come, found himself searching for the slender, graceful figure of Emma Allen, frowned and squatted to add a broken branch to the fire.

It was only right he should look for her—she was the cause of this meeting. But the tense knot of anticipation in his gut told him that wasn't the only reason. He huffed out a breath, watched the dry bark smolder then burst into flames. The branch would soon be reduced to a pile of ashes and embers. He figured the same thing happened between a man and woman. Things burned hot for a while, then there was nothing left except the residue trapped within the circle of rocks that had walled in the flames. He wasn't looking for any walls.

Zach brushed the clinging bits of bark from his hands and rose. He wanted no relationship with any woman, let alone one as troublesome as Emma Allen. He intended to be free of all fetters, to roam where he chose, when he chose. That was the life he wanted. And it was the life he would have once the trading post he intended to build was up and running under a hired manager. But he needed the bonus for getting this wagon train to Oregon country to make that happen. And that meant they had to push forward every day in order to get through before the snow closed the mountain passes. There simply was not time for delays.

The murmur of voices, punctuated by the lowing of oxen or the neighing of a horse, disturbed the night's quiet. A wolf howled. A coyote yipped nearby. Zach tensed, listened, decided they were real and relaxed. He scanned the faces of the people gathering around the fire so unaware of the myriad dangers surrounding them. Moonlight silvered their features, revealed worry and concern, curiosity and puzzlement. Everyone was wondering what this hastily called meeting was about. He spotted John Hargrove hurrying toward him and stepped to meet him.

"What's going on, Thatcher?" The older man's

bushy gray eyebrows fairly bristled with indignation. "What is the purpose of this meeting? And why was I not informed? As the one who formed this train I expect—"

"Calm down, Hargrove." It was the voice he'd used to deal with insubordinate soldiers and it had the same effect. John Hargrove looked angry, but he held his tongue. Zach threw balm at the resentment. "There's no need to get riled. I would have told you about the meeting had there been time. I appreciate your coming forward to stand with me. It's always good to show a united front."

"Indeed. Indeed." The eyebrows drew close over John Hargrove's deep-set eyes. "That, of course, is my purpose."

Zach nodded, swept his gaze over the assembled people, spotted the fire reflected in a shimmer of silk. She was standing off to one side, next to a wagon, her frilly dress incongruous among all the other plain, sensible gowns of wool or cotton. Another reason not to allow his attraction to Emma Allen free rein. The woman was totally unsuited to life on the frontier. He shifted his gaze toward the wagons, noted that there was no one else coming and stepped forward into the light of the fire. The murmuring stopped. An expectant hush hung on the air.

"I called this meeting because we have a problem that needs to be dealt with quickly."

"A problem... Must be Injuns... What kind of problem... Must be somethin' he discovered when he was scoutin' the trail... Is it Injuns..." The questions and speculations shouted out in dozens of voices collided in the air, made an undecipherable din. Zach gave a shrill whistle, held up his hands. The clamor stopped.

"The Applegate baby has the measles." The words hung in a sudden, dead silence. "You all know what that can mean. But with your cooperation we are going to do our best to head off an epidemic." He swept his gaze over the crowd. "First off, I want those of you who have had the measles to come to the left side of the fire, and those of you who have *not* had the measles to come to the right side. Mothers, some of your children may be too young to remember, so you help them get to the right place. And don't be concerned, you will not be separated from your family. This is only so we can know how to go on with our plan."

There was a general muttering. People exchanged glances. A few started to move. He looked at Emma Allen. She was frowning, looking perplexed.

"Hold on, Thatcher!" The words rang out. People froze in place and looked toward Tom Swinton. "My wife says she was holding the Applegate baby earlier, and he hasn't got any spots on him. How do you know he has the measles?"

"Dr. Allen examined him."

"That woman charlatan!" Tom Swinton snorted. "I'm not having any part of this, lest a *real* doctor says that baby has the measles. We're going back to our wagon. Come along—"

"That is your right, Mr. Swinton." Zach raised his voice to carry over the muttering that had started with Tom Swinton's declaration. "But if you take your family back to your wagon, you hitch up and move on. You will no longer be allowed to travel with this train." He looked out over the people. "And that goes for any of the rest of you, as well. Make your choice now." His tone left no doubt he meant what he said.

Emma Allen stared at him, her mouth agape. No one moved.

"Come with Mother, Edward." Pamelia Swinton's soft words carried clearly on the frozen silence. Zach fixed his gaze on the woman. She took her young son by the hand, grasped the limb she was using for a cane and hobbled toward the right side of the fire.

"Pamelia, I forbid—"

The woman stopped, drew herself up straight and faced her husband. "Not this time, Thomas. I obeyed your order to have nothing to do with Dr. Allen when I injured my foot and I still cannot walk on it. I will not take the same risk with our son's life, nor with the life of the babe I carry."

Her words galvanized the women in the group to action. In a flurry of movement they herded their children where they should be and took up their own places. The men exchanged looks with one another, shrugged and followed. Tom Swinton strode off to his wagon. Pamelia looked up at him. "Thomas stands on this side also, Mr. Thatcher."

Zach nodded, slewed his gaze to his left and took a head count of those that had already had measles. Twenty-five people—fifteen of them men or boys old enough to drive wagons, herd stock or stand guard. Garth Lundquist was not among them. He searched faces, settled his gaze on Josh Fletcher. The boy was young, only fifteen or so, but he was strong, sensible, and good with oxen and rifle. Better, perhaps, than Garth Lundquist with the rifle. He looked back to his right. Twenty vulnerable people, the majority of them children. Several of the families were split between the two sides, which complicated matters. He did some rapid calculating in his head, cleared his throat. *Make this plan work for their sakes, Lord.*

"As I said earlier, we have a plan. Dr. Allen proposed a way to quarantine the sick to protect the rest of you as best we are able while still continuing to travel. I concur. Therefore, there will be a change in the formation of the train tomorrow. Listen carefully for your new place. The two Applegate wagons will be in the rear. The two Allen wagons will be next in line so Dr. Allen can tend the sick. In front of them will be those families who have all had the measles and are in no danger. That would be the Hargroves and the Suttons. In front of them will be the Fentons, the Swintons, the Lundquists, the Fletchers and the Lewises. The lead wagon maintains its place. *No one* is to leave their assigned position."

He fixed his gaze on the burly young man standing at the back of those on his right. "Garth, you will stay with your family, help out with herding the stock of those who are in quarantine." He slid his gaze left. "Josh, you are to take over as driver for Dr. Allen."

The boy looked at his father, received a nod and squared his shoulders. "Yes, sir."

"What happens if one of us gets sick?"

Zach slid his gaze over the crowd, sought out the

questioner. "If anyone in your family gets sick, your wagon goes to the rear of the train and the quarantine continues."

Axel Lundquist nodded. "Sounds like this thing might work."

There was a murmur of agreement.

"It will as long as you all stay in your own wagons with your own families until the disease has run its course and the danger passes. Of course, those driving for the owners of the wagons in quarantine will have to stay at the rear of the train. They will not be allowed to go to their family's wagon during the quarantine period. I will provide a tent for them." He allowed himself another glance at Emma Allen. She looked astounded. But there was a warm glow deep in her lovely brown eyes that made his heart beat faster in his chest.

Emma made a last pass with the strip of fabric under the arch of Pamelia Swinton's foot, brought it back over the top, wound it around the ankle again and tied it off. "That should help relieve your pain, Mrs. Swinton. But you must not put your weight on your foot until it is healed. When you use it, it sprains it all over again."

"Thank you, Dr. Emma. This time I shall heed your warning." Pamelia Swinton glanced up. "I'm sorry, I did not mean to sound disrespectful, Dr. Allen. I have heard Lorna Lewis call you Dr. Emma and it slipped out."

Emma laughed. "I like the sound of Dr. Emma. It is… friendlier than Dr. Allen."

Her patient smiled and reached for her stocking. "Then you must call me Pamelia."

Emma nodded and reached to help stretch Pamelia's stocking over the thick winding around her foot and ankle. "Pamelia, did your husband say at the meeting that you held little Isaac Applegate tonight?"

"Yes. He has been so fussy and fretful he is wearing Ruth out. She wearies quickly since she's been with child. And I was sitting resting my ankle anyway so—" She stopped tugging at her stocking and looked up. Her face paled. "*Edward*. Mr. Thatcher said there is to be a quarantine to keep us safe..." Tears glistened in her eyes. "Have I endangered Edward?"

Emma looked at the fear in Pamelia's eyes and wished there were some way she could erase it. "There is no way to tell, Pamelia. But Edward is a fine, strong boy. I believe he will be fine if he does come down with the measles. He will be uncomfortable, but fine." She made her voice calm, reassuring. "Of course, you must let me know if he becomes fevered. Or if he has the sniffles, or a cough." She smiled and picked up Pamelia's shoe. "I am afraid this will not fit over the bandage. Have you some boots you can wear until your sprain is better?"

"Yes. And if they do not fit, I shall borrow one of Thomas's." She placed her hand on the edge of the tailgate and pushed herself upright, took a firm grip on her branch cane and reached for her shoe. "Thank you again, Dr. Emma. My ankle feels better already. I am sorry I cannot pay you now, but the money is in the wagon. I...I suppose now you shall have to wait for your fee until after the...the quarantine."

Emma nodded, placed her hand on Pamelia's arm. "Do not fret, Pamelia. Edward is a strong little boy, and he may not get the measles. The disease is a chanceful thing. Now, let me help you to your wagon."

"Thank you, Dr. Emma. You are very kind, but you had best not. Thomas is—you'd best not."

Emma stood and watched Pamelia hobble off into the darkness. The poor woman was so worried about her little boy she had not thought of the possible danger to herself and her husband.

Emma sighed. Sometimes it was difficult being a doctor. Still… *Dr. Emma.* It had a lovely sound. She smiled, picked up her lantern and headed for Anne's wagon to check on her and tell her all that had happened at the meeting. She was halfway across the inner circle when it hit her. Tonight these people, well…*some* of these people had accepted her as a doctor. Even Mr. Thatcher. Was it possible her dream was not dead? That it could still come true?

Commit thy way unto him; trust also in him; and he shall bring it to pass.

Could it be… She looked up at the star-strewn night sky, holding her breath, waiting for she knew not what— some sign? A sense of reassurance? There was nothing. Only the dark, and the sounds of the night. She raised the lantern and continued on her way. The truth was, she had a few patients because she was the only doctor on this wilderness journey, not because God had suddenly decided to answer her prayers. And Mr. Thatcher had acquiesced to her quarantine recommendation in order to keep the men healthy and able to work—not because he believed in her doctoring skills. Would she never learn to stop hoping for something that could not be?

Chapter Eight

Emma ladled water from the barrel lashed to the side of the wagon into the wash bowl she now placed on the shelf beside it whenever the wagon train stopped. She lathered and scrubbed her hands with lye soap as Papa Doc had taught her to do whenever she treated the ill. Wonderful Papa Doc, who for many years had been scorned by his fellow physicians at Pennsylvania Hospital for what they called his "foolishness," his insistence on cleanliness during and after seeing patients or performing surgery. And for using alcohol to cleanse wounds and hands and instruments. That is, they had scorned him until they realized how many of his patients survived. Now most of them had adopted those same practices. But Papa Doc had been the first.

Thoughts of her adopted father brought tears to her eyes. She blinked them away, dumped the water on the ground then dipped her fingers into the small crock sitting beside the wash bowl and rubbed the balm he had formulated especially for her into her hands. She closed her eyes, wiped her hands over her cheeks then cupped her hands over her nose and inhaled. The fragrance of lavender tinged with a hint of soap transported her back to Papa Doc's office—to their discussions over his experiments, and those of the other doctors he exchanged letters with across the country, even across the ocean.

She sighed, tugged the long sleeves on her new, sensible dress of dark blue cotton back over her wrists and replaced the top on the crock. Would he write her of his findings about the medical use of sulfuric ether? She stared down at the crock, remembering his excitement when he had discovered the substance some of his pupils and their friends used to exhilarate themselves at parties rendered them insensitive to pain. He had pondered and mulled over possibilities for weeks. And then, two days before she left for St. Louis to visit Mary while William prepared for his journey to Oregon country, he had removed a tumor from Mr. Jefferson's back while the man smelled the sulfuric ether she had mixed and placed on a towel. Excitement tingled through her at the memory. Mr. Jefferson had felt *nothing*. He had not even made objection to her presence during the surgery. In truth, he had been most amenable while smelling the ether. A smile tugged at her lips, turned into a grin. Perhaps she should administer some ether to Mr. Thatcher.

Her amusement drowned in a wash of reality. She looked around the inner circle, then stared out at the wilderness surrounding the circled wagons. If Papa Doc wrote her, would she ever receive his letter? Would she ever again know of the new and exciting things he and his fellow doctors discovered?

Boots rasped against the sandy soil. "Dr. Emma, Ma says supper is ready."

She turned and smiled. "Thank you, Matthew. I'll be right there."

The tall, lanky young man nodded, stuffed the half a biscuit he held into his mouth and ambled off toward his wagon.

Emma brushed the wayward wisps of hair off her temples and forehead, tugged the button-front bodice with its high collar into place and smoothed down the long skirt of her new dress. It was the first of the two gowns she had commissioned Ruth to make for her. The woman had sewn it while sitting in the wagon watching over baby Isaac.

She looked down, ran her fingers over the rolled-ribbon trim at her narrow waist that was the dress's one vanity. The dress fit well. Ruth truly was a gifted seamstress. She was eager now for the other dress Ruth was making her to be finished. The dark red wool fabric would be welcome for the cooler weather of the mountains. She wiggled the toes of her shoes peeking out from under the hem of the long, full skirt and smiled. These gowns would not drag along the ground and snag on every little thing as she walked beside the wagon. And Mr. Thatcher would no longer look askance at those opulent silk gowns better suited for drawing rooms than rough trails and wilderness prairies. Not that she had seen much of Mr. Thatcher since the quarantine started. She seldom caught even a glimpse of him from here at the back of the train. He was always out front, scouting the trail for the best camping places, then leading the wagons to them. But he had kept his word and provided a tent for their drivers to sleep in.

Emma shrugged off the thoughts and turned her mind toward supper. It would mean another battle to get Anne to eat. Well, so be it. She respected her sister's grief, but she refused to allow it to kill her. She placed her foot on the step, leaned into the wagon and took tin plates and flatware from the trunk beside the tailgate, hopped down and walked forward to the Hargrove's wagon.

"Good evening, Mr. Hargrove." The older man nodded and went on eating. He made no secret of his poor opinion of a woman doctor. Nor did he hide his displeasure with her for initiating the quarantine that kept everyone confined to their own wagons. But she did not expect he would change his mind about that. Mr. Hargrove liked to strut his importance as the organizer of the wagon train among its members and the quarantine made that impossible.

Emma turned from his frowning face and smiled at his wife. "Hello, Lydia. What have you for us tonight?"

The plump woman straightened from stirring the contents of one of the cast-iron pots sitting on the glowing coals of the cook fire, lifted the long skirt of her apron and wiped the perspiration from her face. "There's side meat and gravy, beans and stewed apples. And biscuits." She shot a pleased look at the pots. "Matthew found wood to make fire enough to cook us a satisfying meal. Those buffalo chips we've been using don't make coals for baking, so I made biscuits enough for tomorrow, too." Her lips lifted in a wry smile. "I never thought I would cook over such things! But when there's no wood..." She shrugged and held out her hand.

"You always make a good meal, Lydia." Emma smiled, handed her one of the plates then bent and spooned food onto the other. "I may be a doctor, but Anne and I would have perished of starvation over these last few weeks had you not offered to cook for us."

Lydia Hargrove laughed. "I figured as much when I saw you coughing and choking on the smoke rising from those potatoes you were trying to cook that first night of the quarantine. I never saw anything as burnt as those potatoes. They weren't good for anything but dumping into the fire for fuel."

Emma joined in her laughter. "I remember. I also remember how relieved and grateful I was when you came to my rescue."

Lydia Hargrove spooned food onto the plate she held and added a biscuit. "Truth be told, I enjoy cooking for you and your sister. It remembers me of before Sally and Ester married and left home." A frown wrinkled her forehead. "But I do wish I could manage something that would make your sister eat more. She looks mighty frail and peaked. But I suspect she will eat hearty again, once her grieving is done." She shook her head, stared down at the plate she held. "It takes the heart out of a woman to lose her husband and her babe. Takes time to get over a thing like that." The older woman lifted her head and Emma saw remembered sorrow in her eyes before Lydia smiled and held out the filled plate. "Listen to me, talking on and on, and keeping you here while the food gets cold. You'd best be on your way."

Emma nodded and hurried to Anne's wagon. The end flaps of the canvas cover were down as always. She sighed and stepped close. "Anne, I have your supper. And it will do you no good to tell me you have no appetite for you know I will simply come inside and pester you until—"

"Oh, Emma, why will you not let me be?" The flaps parted. Anne appeared against the dusky interior of the wagon, her black dressing gown hanging on her too-thin frame, her russet curls tumbling askew around her pale face. "Truly, I am weary and want only to sleep."

"After you have eaten, Annie." Emma kept her voice firm and pleasant. "I promise I will go away when you have eaten half of what is on your plate. But if you do not, I will stay and recite—"

"No, Emma. Truly I cannot eat any—"

She squared her shoulders and cleared her throat. "The sun had clos'd the winter day—"

Anne sighed. "Robert Burns, Emma? You know—"

"—The curlers quat their roarin play—"

"Enough, Emma! You *know* I cannot bear your atrocious Scottish accent." For a tiny moment Anne's voice seemed to lose its tone of grim bitterness, seemed to hold the merest ghost of her old humor. And then it was gone. She stepped back into the wagon. "Come inside. If it is the only way to silence you, I will try to eat."

Emma placed the cleaned dishes back in the trunk, turned on the tailgate step and looked out over the land. When they had reached the Platte River the prairies had given way to a wide valley. One with only occasional clumps of trees that rose like shadowed islands along the many ribbonlike streams that wound their way through it. They had crossed so many streams she had quite gotten over her fear of fording them. Now—

"Come down from there, Miss Allen!"

"Oh!" Emma whirled, lost her balance and fell forward.

Zachary Thatcher caught her in midair, lowered her to the ground. His arms were as strong, felt as safe as she remembered. She looked up, straight into those bright blue eyes. They held her gaze, then darkened. His arms tightened around her. Or did she imagine that? Warmth crept into her cheeks, spread to every part of her. She bowed her head to hide her flushed cheeks from him, stepped back and pressed her hand over the wild thumping at the base of her throat. "Forgive my clumsiness, but I did not hear you approach, Mr. Thatcher."

He cleared his throat, gestured toward his feet. "Moccasins. They are quieter than boots—better for tracking." A frown creased his forehead. "Come here, beside the wagon."

His voice held his normal, autocratic tone. For some reason it made her feel safer. She moved back to stand beside the water barrel, then glanced down at the leather moccasins that rose from his feet to cover his muscular calves. Leather thongs held them in place. "What are you tracking?"

"Whatever is needed. How are your patients faring?"

It was an evasive answer. She studied his face, could detect nothing from his expression. She formed a cautious answer. "Very well. Emily and Susan Fenton's measles are gone. And they are the last ones to fall ill. Two more days and the quarantine will be over. There is only—"

"The quarantine is over now." He turned away.

An owl hooted. Another answered.

"Mr. Thatch—"

His raised hand silenced her. Quick and quiet as a shadow, he slipped into the narrow space between the aligned wheels of hers and the Hargrove's wagons and stood looking out into the distance. The soft light of dusk outlined his straight nose, his square jaw and strong chin. Something in the way he held his head sent a chill skittering along her spine—prickled her flesh. "What is it?" The sudden tautness of her throat turned the words into a whisper. She stepped close to him.

He pivoted, grasped her elbow and in two steps had her back behind the wagon. "Stay out of sight. There are Cheyenne out there."

"Cheyenne? You mean *Indians?*" Her jaw dropped, her eyes widened with shock.

He nodded, turned and strode to the Hargrove wagon. "John… Matthew… Get your rifles and assemble at the driver's tent!"

Before she could take a breath, he turned and headed for the Applegate wagons. What was he *doing?* These men were not yet recovered enough for…for *battle?* Emma made a valiant attempt to regain her composure, stepped away from the security of her wagon and ran after him, feeling the malevolent gazes of hundreds of savages fastened on her.

"James… Seth… Get your weapons and assemble at the driver's tent!"

The Applegate men scrambled for their wagons at his order.

"Mr. Thatcher! I must—"

He wheeled, scowled. "I told you to stay out of sight." He gripped her upper arms, stared down at her. "For once, will you do as you're told? Go back to your wagon and—"

"Not until I know—"

The muscle along his jaw twitched. "As you will. I haven't time to argue the matter." He released her and pivoted.

Hosea and Jasper Fenton were striding toward them, rifles in their hands. "We heard." Hosea jerked his head backward. "Nathan's gettin' his rifle, he'll be along." They swerved toward the tent. Carrie Fenton stood by their wagon, her body tense, her face pale. Nathan hopped down and loped off after his father and brother.

"Carrie, keep your girls calm and inside the wagon!"

It was all she had time to say. Zachary Thatcher was headed for the Swinton wagons. Emma ran and stood in his path. Ezra Beason, Thomas Swinton's hired driver, rushed by her, headed for the tent, rifle in hand. She took a breath to calm her racing heart. "Mr. Thatcher, I do not know what you want with these men. But whatever it is, you cannot involve Thomas Swinton. He was very ill and is not yet recovered. He could well die if he gets chilled or overtired."

Zachary Thatcher stared into her eyes, took a step toward her. She backed up.

"*Doctor* Allen, I have yielded to you as the medical expert on this wagon train to the point of allowing almost half of the able-bodied fighting men to be quarantined. But I *will not* cede you one iota of power beyond that."

He closed the gap between them. She tipped her head back, stared up into eyes that had darkened to the color of blue slate.

"The leadership and safety of the people on this train are my responsibility. One for which I am well qualified. Now do me the service of respecting *my* ability and get out of my way."

The last words were all but hissed. Emma caught her breath and shook her head. "I cannot. Not if it will mean Mr. Swinton's death."

Those blue eyes flashed. Zachary Thatcher made that sound low in his throat—the sound he had made that day by the wagon. He clasped her upper arms, lifted her aside and strode to the Swinton wagon. "Tom, get your rifle and come to the tent." He pivoted, and without so much as a glance in her direction, marched toward the crowd that had gathered. Thomas Swinton got his rifle and followed.

"What is it? What's wrong?"

Emma looked at Ruth climbing from the wagon with baby Isaac clutched in her arms, and gestured toward the tent. "Mr. Thatcher is telling them now." She hurried toward the people who had gathered, dimly aware that Ruth ran to walk beside her.

"—so I need you all to stay calm. Especially you

men." Zachary Thatcher's gaze swept over the people, touched hers and moved on. "Things can get touchy when you are dealing with a war party."

War party! Emma heard a gasp, glanced at Ruth's stricken face and laid a comforting hand on her arm.

"—I don't think they intend us harm. I think they were out hunting Pawnee or other enemies, spotted our wagons and decided to come see what we are doing. That does not mean they will not attack if they feel the booty taken will be worth the battle. That is why we must appear strong. The main body has stopped some distance away, but their scouts are looking us over."

"How do you know?"

"They're talking to one another. That quail whistle you heard a minute ago was a scout giving his position. The owl you heard was another scout answering."

An image of Zachary Thatcher's intent expression as he listened to the owls earlier flashed into her head. Emma shivered, felt those savage gazes upon her again. How could he be so calm? There was such quiet strength in his face....

"—Indians are not troubled by the morals of white men. To them stealing is a virtue...especially horses. All ours are to be brought inside and tethered to the wagon tongues." His gaze pinioned two of the men in front of him. "Ezra and Matthew, you'll help with that. Saddle up and report to Blake."

Traveler and Lady! She had not thought—

"The river will protect our left, the stock is to be herded in close to the wagons on our right. They will serve as a barrier between the Cheyenne and the women and children and our supplies. They won't be able to rush the wagons. Ernst, Josh, Seth, you'll help herd them in."

The men named ran for their horses.

"The rest of you—"

Emma swallowed hard, looked at the people standing quiet and tense waiting to find out what their role would be.

"I'm setting a double guard around the camp and the stock tonight. I don't have to tell you what will happen to us if they get stampeded and run off."

Emma's heart thudded. She closed her eyes. *Please, God—*

"All of you men will be assigned a time and place of duty. Stay alert. Indians are the best fighters you will ever encounter. They can hide behind a blade of grass, appear and disappear at will, move without sound. But they seldom attack a superior force, or one in a good defensive position. But bear in mind, when they do attack, they kill without compunction. For them, to kill an enemy is an honor." His gaze swept over them again. "You are their enemy. Don't forget it. Defend yourself. But I don't want any wild shots fired at something you hear or *think* you see. Be sure of your target. And remember, they yell like inhuman devils, but it's only noise to unnerve you and keep you from shooting straight and steady—ignore the yells. A bullet will kill them same as any other living creature. Now all you women go to your wagons and *stay there*. Should there be a battle, those of you who know how can load weapons or use them."

Once again Zachary Thatcher's gaze touched hers, slipped away. "John Hargrove, Tom Swinton—"

She stiffened.

"—James Applegate and Nathan Fenton. Your wagons are beside the river. You men will stay here and guard this area. If you spot any Indians approaching through the water, fire a shot to warn them off. If they turn back, let them go. Do *not* shoot to kill unless they keep coming. Keep a sharp eye out for diversions. Watch the water for Indians crossing while others draw your attention from them, and be ready to shoot. If they reach the trees along the riverbank they can sortie on the wagons from there and they will be hard to flush out. Hargrove and Swinton, you two take the first watch. Applegate and Fenton, rest while you can, but be ready. And douse this fire." His gaze swept over them once more. "You women, no lights in the wagons. An arrow can't find an unseen target. The rest of you men, come with me."

The women in attendance glanced at one another, then, faces set in grim acceptance of the situation, headed for their wagons. There was nothing to say. No comfort to offer. Things were what they were.

Emma watched Ruth Applegate hurry off beside her husband, baby Isaac clutched tightly to her chest. She looked at Pamelia Swinton hobbling along after Tom, young Edward beside her, and at Lydia Hargrove marching off beside John, at Carrie Fenton standing still as a statue beside her wagon. What would happen to all of them? And to all of the others on the train? What would happen to Annie? To her?

Annie. She had to protect Annie! Her stomach con-

tracted. A quivering started in her legs and arms, spread
to every part of her. She folded her arms across her torso
to try and stop the quaking and peered into the dusky
distance, fastened her gaze on Zachary Thatcher's rapidly disappearing figure. Somehow, though frightening,
it had seemed everything would be all right until he
strode away.

Chapter Nine

Zach edged up to the rock, molded himself to its form and studied the length of denser darkness on the ground ahead. Was it a ridge of stone—or a guard stretched prone on the ground? He scowled and edged a little closer. The darkness was an enemy that hid his foes. But the same darkness covered him. He stayed perfectly still, listened and watched a few minutes longer, then took a firmer grip on his knife, crouched low and inched his way toward the thick darkness near the top of the low, sandy rise.

Emma stared into the dark, listened to her sister's soft breathing. How could she sleep at such a time? It was worrying. Anne had not even been alarmed at the news of the Indians. Only irritated that she would not be left alone.

Emma released her grip on William's pistol, flexed her stiff fingers then reached up and rubbed her neck and shoulders. Never had a night been so long. Every muscle in her body was protesting her cramped position, demanding movement, but she dared not rise or stretch in the close quarters lest she bump something and knock it onto Anne.

She sighed and rested back against the side of the wagon, shifted slightly to ease the discomfort of the tense muscles around her shoulder blades, then wiggled her toes and feet to relieve the annoying prickles in her legs. The weight of William's pistol across her thighs hampered her movement. She lowered her hands, carefully felt for the weapon and again folded her fingers around the grip.

Hoofs thudded against the ground as the horses tethered to the wagon tongue changed position. Her heart lurched. Was an Indian stealing Traveler or Lady? Or had one crowded the horses over so he could climb into the wagon? She swallowed hard, lifted the heavy pistol with both hands and pointed it in the direction of the driver's seat. Should she issue a challenge to scare whoever might be there away? Or should she stay silent and shoot if someone tried to enter? *Could* she shoot? She supported her trembling hands with her raised knees and nodded. Yes. Yes, she could shoot someone to save Annie and herself. But then she would doctor whomever she shot.

Laughter bubbled in her chest, boiled up into her throat. The doctor in her recognized it as hysteria. She clamped her lips tight, fought the laughter down.

Some sort of night bird called. She held her breath and strained to hear if another answered. Oxen horns clacked together outside. She jerked her head in the direction of the noise, jerked it back toward the entrance over the wagon seat again at a soft whisper of sound. A horse swishing his tail? Or leather moccasins brushing against the wood? Tears smarted her eyes. Every normal night sound had turned into a threat. If only William were here. She so missed him and—

No! What a selfish thought. She did not want William to be in danger. And if he were here, he would be out there in the night doing whatever Mr. Thatcher told him to do. And Caroline and the babe she carried would be sitting here in this wagon with Indians prowling around outside.

Prowling around.

Moccasins are better for tracking. Her lungs seized. Is that what Mr. Thatcher had been speaking of? Tracking the Indians? Was he out there in the night sneaking up on the war party? An image of him as he'd stood listening to the Indians signaling one another by hooting like owls flashed into her head. There had been an intensity, a strength in his face that had both drawn and frightened her. What if— She shook her head, denying the thought. It was too terrifying. What would they do if something happened to Zachary Thatcher? Who would lead them to Oregon country? Who would get them safely across the mountains and rivers?

Emma shuddered, leaned her head back and closed her eyes, remembering how her wagon had slipped off the fording path in the Big Blue River and tipped sideways, how Zachary Thatcher had come and snatched her from the tilted seat as she was sliding toward the water. And of how safe, how *protected* she had felt with his strong arms holding her in front of him on his horse.

And, again, earlier tonight, when he had caught her and kept her from falling. When he had looked down at her and his arms had tightened around her…

Suddenly, with her whole being, she longed to be in his arms again. What if he didn't return? What if she never saw him again? Tears slipped from beneath her lashes and ran down her cheeks. *Please, Almighty God, please. Do not let Mr. Thatcher be harmed. Please keep him safe for…for all our sakes.*

She wiped the tears from her cheeks with her free hand and opened her eyes. She could see nothing in the inky darkness, but it made her feel more vulnerable to have her eyes shut. Her chest tightened. She forced her lungs to draw a deep breath, then expelled it slowly. It was so hard to be brave, sitting alone in the dark with a pistol in her hand guarding Anne while evil crept through the night.

Zach stretched out along the length of the ridge of rock and peered around the end. Five small fires burned at the bottom of the swale, the warriors around them dark silhouettes against the glow of their flames. So the Cheyenne were being cautious, but did not feel threatened. If there were Pawnee or other enemy tribes close by they would never light fires. And they were not preparing for battle. So, barring some fool mistake by one of the greenhorns, they had no plans to attack the train.

Relief eased his tense muscles. An owl hoot from behind him on the right drew them taut again. He turned his head, spotted a returning scout loping toward the camp and hugged the ground. The warrior's footsteps vibrated through the earth beneath his ear. The whisper of moccasins against the sandy soil grew louder. The scout was not being careful, which meant he felt secure this close to camp and would not be so alert. Perhaps he would pass by without spotting him. And perhaps not.

Zach tightened his grip on his knife, tensed his muscles to roll aside and spring to his feet to silence the brave before he could give an alarm. Grains of sand skittered along the dry soil between the sparse blades of grass and pelted his hand. He held his breath—waited.

The scout loped by the end of the rocky ridge. Zach lifted his head enough to turn it and watch the warrior into camp. He drew his legs up beneath him, chose his path and got ready to run if the brave raised a cry.

All stayed quiet below. The Cheyenne gathered around the fires continued to eat, some were sleeping. He could make out their forms at the edge of the firelight. Near as he could see there were close to fifty braves in the war party. More than double the number of fighting men he could field. And of the men he led, most were unskilled and untested in warfare.

Zach scowled, studied the area behind him, slithered back from the top of the rise, then crouched and ran toward the cover of a nearby tree. Best not to return on the path he had used to come to their camp. He would take a roundabout route back to the river.

"There are so many of them!" Emma straightened, wiped her brow and stole another look at the Indians sitting on their horses, a short distance beyond the massed herd. "There must be at least fifty of them!"

"Mind your skirt!" Lydia Hargrove gave her a little push back from the fire. "It's not Indians you'll be worrying about if you catch afire. And mind you don't burn that gruel. It needs stirring."

Emma nodded, bent and stirred the oatmeal bubbling in the iron pot over the coals. "How can you be so calm, Lydia? They look so…so…*savage!* Did you see their painted faces? And the feathers stuck in their hair? And they are fairly bristling with weapons." She straightened again. "Look at all those spears, and bows and arrows and shields! And now that the light is strengthening I can see hatchets dangling from their waists."

"Mayhap you would be calmer if you looked at what you are doing, instead of at the heathen. Remember, Mr. Thatcher said we are to act normal and not show fear."

There was tension in Lydia's voice, and her face was pale. She was not as calm as she pretended. Emma sucked in a breath and forced a smile. "I am acting normal. You are the cook, not I."

"True enough." Lydia laughed, but there was a strained sound to it. "That gruel is done."

Emma nodded, gave the oatmeal a last stir and pulled it off the fire. "What will happen to us, Lydia?"

"We will do as Mr. Thatcher says and break our fast as usual."

"And then?"

The older woman dumped the coals off the lid of the spider into the fire, lifted the pan out onto the grass and straightened. She wiped her hands down her apron and looked off toward the war party. "Most of our husbands and sons are shopkeepers or farmers, not fighters. What happens will be as God wills it."

The quiet words sparked a fire in her breast. Emma looked at her wagon, at her doctor's bag and William's pistol resting on the shelf beside the water barrel where she had placed them and shook her head. "I am not as accepting as you, Lydia. Life is sacred. And I will fight to preserve it—with my doctoring skills, or with a gun."

"You may soon have the chance."

Emma jerked her gaze toward the Indians, spotted the lone figure riding out to meet them astride the large roan with gray spots decorating its hip. Her lungs froze. She opened her mouth to call Zachary Thatcher back, but no sound came out. She commanded her feet to stay put, to not run after him. *Please, God! Please keep him from harm. Oh, please keep him safe. Keep us all safe!*

Her pulse thundered in her ears, throbbed at the base of her throat. She closed her eyes, afraid to witness what might happen, then opened them again in case she was needed. He had covered half the short distance and stopped. An Indian was riding out to meet him. She looked at the garishly painted face, the spear clutched in a powerful hand, whirled and hurried to her wagon. If something happened she was too far away. She had to get closer. She snatched up her doctor's bag and William's pistol and, mindful of Zachary Thatcher's order, forced herself to maintain a moderate pace as she walked toward the other end of the circled wagons.

Emma wrapped the pistol in the oiled cloth, slipped it into its leather bag and placed it back in the chest.

Weariness washed over her. She cast a longing look at the bed folded up against the wagon wall and sighed. She should try to sleep, but it was impossible. She was still too…unnerved. The Indians were gone. But so was Mr. Thatcher. He had ordered the wagons to remain in camp until he returned, then rode off in the same direction the Indians had taken. What if— No. She would not think about that.

She lifted the lap desk from the chest and closed the top. Writing letters had become her escape, her comfort. She would use this time to write home and tell them about the Indians. But she must make the telling amusing. She did not want to cause her family to fear for her and Anne. Her lips twitched. She would tell them about the tobacco and beads.

Laughter bubbled up and burst from her mouth. She sat back on her heels, wrapped her arms about her waist and rocked to and fro with the false hilarity. It was only a nervous reaction to the long hours of tension and fear. She knew that. There was nothing funny about those savages. Or about Mr. Thatcher riding out alone to talk with them. She had been so frightened for him. But still— *tobacco and beads?* That was all that was required to make those fierce warriors go away. But now…

The laughter died. Now he was out there somewhere. Alone. And if something happened to him… If he were wounded or hurt…or worse, they would never know. She would not be able to help him and he might… Tears welled up, spilled over and ran down her cheeks. She wiped them away, tried to stop the sobs building up in her chest, but they demanded liberation. She crossed her arms on top of the chest, placed her forehead on them and released all of her worry and fear for him in a torrent of tears.

Zach peered over the rim of the ledge and watched Gray Wolf and the rest of the Cheyenne ride down the length of the wash below and disappear around the rock outcropping on the other side. If the war party had intended to ride ahead and set an ambush for the wagon train they never would have ridden so fast or taken that direction. The wagons could not follow their path. And they had not left sentinels to watch and report on the train's progress.

The tension across his shoulders eased. He rose and trotted back down the hill. "All right, boy. We have trailed them long enough. Time to go back and get the wagons moving." He swung into the saddle, reined Comanche around and touched him with his heels. The horse leaped forward, then settled into an easy, ground-eating lope.

Zach scanned the area ahead and resisted the impulse to urge Comanche to greater speed. The Cheyenne were far from their normal haunt. This was Pawnee and Sioux territory. And Arapaho and Comanche roamed these parts, as well. It didn't pay to get careless. Hopefully, Blake would remember that and keep the emigrant green-horns alert and ready for an attack as he had ordered. But calm. They had to stay calm. His gut tightened. If other Indians happened upon the train before he got back, one foolish act, one careless shot on an emigrant's part could spark an all-out attack. And if that happened…

Images he didn't care to remember flooded his head. He thought about the women and children on the train, about Emma Allen. He clenched his jaw against the memory of the sight of her when he had turned back from meeting with Gray Wolf. He had ordered the women to stay by their wagons, but there she was, standing in the shadow of a wagon, watching the meeting, her face pale and tense, her doctor's bag in one hand and a pistol in the other. And when their gazes had met, he'd known from the look in her eyes and the set of her shoulders she would have used both to try and save him had he been in trouble. He had badly misjudged her. Emma Allen may have led a pampered life, but she had courage. And she took her doctoring seriously. And he'd never seen a woman as beautiful. If any harm came to her…

Zach shoved the thoughts away and again scanned the area as he rode toward the pass that led back to the river valley. It was dangerous to allow yourself to be distracted when— His heart jolted. Five mounted Indians stood atop the low ridge on his right. He kept his face straight ahead, watched them from the corners of his eyes. They turned their mounts and started down the hill on an intercepting path. He loosened his sidearm in its holster and judged the distance to the pass against the angle of the Indians' approach. It would be a close thing. Too close. Even with Comanche's speed. It would be better not to run and excite them with the chase. "Ease up, boy. We'd best meet these braves head-on."

Be with me, Lord. Give me wisdom. And, if need be, make my shots true. He reined Comanche around to face the Indians and halted. They galloped toward him. He leaned forward and patted Comanche's neck. "Be ready, boy. We may have a run ahead of us yet. But at least it will be a fair one with a chance you can win." The horse flicked his ears back, then forward again, tossed his head.

Zach straightened in the saddle, lifted his right hand palm out, and pushed it forward and back. The Indians slowed, trotted their horses a little closer and stopped. He could see them clearly now. Pawnee. And they were not painted. But that did not mean they would be adverse to a little "sport" with a white man. He fastened his gaze on the brave in the lead, raised his hands and locked his forefingers together in the gesture of friendship.

The Indian returned the sign.

But more than one soldier had died because of an Indian's treachery. Zach cast another swift glance over the surrounding area. He saw nothing alarming. "Okay, boy, let's go." Comanche snorted and walked forward. The brave walked his horse out to meet him.

Zach looked into the warrior's dark eyes. Their expression was wary, but not angry. "Do you speak my tongue?" There was no answer. He tapped himself on the chest, pointed at the brave and again linked his forefingers in the sign for friendship. The brave did not move aside to let him pass.

Zach again tapped himself on the chest, made walking motions through the air with his fingers, then drew his hand across his arm in the signal for Cheyenne and pointed behind him. The brave stiffened. Quickly, Zach, again, slashed his hand across his arm, then lifted his fisted hand to his forehead and turned it back and forth in the signal for anger. He held his hands forward and spread the fingers wide, clenched them, then repeated the process four more times. He pointed down to Comanche's tracks, then swept his arm back and pointed his finger. "Cheyenne war party...fifty strong."

The brave turned, shouted a guttural command. The other four Indians rode forward, one galloping off along his back trail. In minutes he reappeared, signaled the others to come. The four warriors raced off. Zach let out a long breath, heeled Comanche into a lope and headed for the pass. Things were happening too quickly. He had to get back to the train.

Chapter Ten

My beloved family,

I take up my pen to write you of the odd thing that has happened. Mr. Thatcher, being accosted by five Pawnee warriors, warned them of the presence of a large Cheyenne war party nearby. I believe this saved his life, for it seems though they are wild and savage, as evidenced by the bloody scalps dangling at their waists when they suddenly appeared at our wagon train a few days later, these Pawnee have their own code of honor. Those five warriors have escorted us safely through what Mr. Thatcher calls Sioux territory. During the past weeks, they rode ahead of us to discover the best path for our wagons, and to warn of any Sioux close by. And though we all were wary and distrustful of their intent, they proved to be excellent guides. They led us to the safest fording places and helped us to cross our wagons. We did not, during their time with us, lose one animal to the wilds or to ravening beasts thanks to their prowess.

There is so much I wish to share with you all. I have seen my first buffalo. Swarms of them! At the meeting of the North and South Platte rivers, the horizon was black with the beasts as far as the eye could see. There are elk there, also.

I do wish you could see this country. We have traversed plains, valleys and now hills that come down to the banks of the river and oblige us to climb the heights then curve around and again descend to the river below.

It is now late July, and tomorrow we will reach a place called Fort William where, Mr. Thatcher assures us, we shall stop for a day to wash, bathe, purchase available supplies, repair wagons, doctor ill or hurt animals and trade with Indians. Having brought us here, the Pawnee have now left us to return to their homes.

I am well. Anne is healed of her injuries but remains distant from everyone. How I wish I had news of you all. My concern grows for Caroline and the baby.

As ever, I am your devoted,

Emma

Emma addressed and sealed the letter, placed it atop the others she had written and rose to put the lap desk in her wagon. Dusk had chased away the sunlight and mellowed the heat of the day. A breeze played among the trees strewed along the riverbank and carried the voices of mothers calling to their children. She lifted her head and listened to the squeals and laughter of the playing youngsters echoing off the rocks behind the camp then smiled and returned waves as they came running in obedience to the mothers' summons—Gabe and David Lewis dragging in last, as always. The clamor quieted, stopped. From the direction of the river, a harmonica began a soft, languorous lament.

Emma glanced toward the herders bringing in the grazing stock and searched out the wiry form of the small, dark-haired man riding in a wide loop around the animals in the water to turn them back to land. Charley Karr said the beasts calmed when he played. But the music always brought an ache to her throat. She glanced toward Anne's wagon, noted the canvas flaps tied closed and sighed. It would be so lovely to have someone with whom she could visit while the other emigrants settled in for the night. Would Anne ever get over her grief?

A vague sense of failure gnawed at her. Had she left anything undone that might help her sister? She sighed and retrieved the oatcake she had saved from supper then headed for the horses grazing at the far end of the inner oval, mentally reexamining her treatment of Anne. She could think of nothing to do but continue to love her, even if she wanted to be left alone. Loneliness washed over her, creating a longing in her heart, a hollow feeling in her stomach. If only Mother and Papa Doc were here. Or William. They would know what to do for Annie.

Emma came out of her musings, stared at Traveler. He was growing gaunt since they had left the good grass of the prairies behind. And his feed was gone. Would he survive the arduous trek ahead over the mountains? Or would it destroy him? Tears stung her eyes. "I brought you an oatcake, boy." She fed him the treat and finger-combed snarls from his forelock and mane as he munched, noted the dull, lusterless condition of his coat and wished she had saved the other oatcake for him instead of eating it herself. Tomorrow she would—

"Sharing your supper?"

Emma jerked her head up, stared across Traveler's back at Zachary Thatcher. How was it possible a man of his size could move as silent as a shadow? She nodded. "A bit of it. I wish I had more to give him."

Understanding flashed in those bright blue eyes. He stepped closer, ran his hand over Traveler's proudly arched neck. "A journey like ours is hard on the stock. Mules fare better than horses. Especially when the good grass gives out when they are climbing the mountains."

That was not what she wanted to hear. Especially not with the sympathetic undertone of warning his voice carried. Would she lose Traveler? Her throat tightened so she was afraid to try and speak. She clenched her jaw and stared at Traveler's shoulder, fighting the urge to lean her head against him and cry.

"I saw you writing earlier and thought you might like to know if you leave your letters at the fort tomorrow, when someone passes through, headed east, they will most likely carry them with them."

She lifted her gaze to his face. "To St. Louis?" She snagged her bottom lip with her teeth to stop the trembling.

His eyes darkened, the rugged planes of his face soft-ened. He reached out his hand, lowered it to Traveler's back, close to where hers rested. So close she could feel the warmth radiating off it. "That is the end destination, yes. If they are not going that far they will pass the letters on to someone else." His thumb moved, brushed against the side of her palm, stayed.

She glanced down, fought the urge to slip her hand sideways, to know the feel of the warmth and strength of his hand covering hers. A strange reaction to his accidental touch, yet it remained. Grew. She moved her hand before she yielded to the temptation.

Zachary Thatcher stepped back and cleared his throat. "There is no guarantee the letters will make it back, you understand. There is a lot of rough, wild and dangerous territory they must pass through on the way."

She looked up, felt that same, strong draw when their gazes met and curved her mouth into a polite smile to hide behind. "Yes, I know, Mr. Thatcher. I have just come through that rough, wild and dangerous territory."

He nodded, held her gaze a moment longer then looked away. "So you have, Miss Allen, so you have." He touched his hat brim and walked off.

Emma stood and watched him go as silently, as quickly as he had come, feeling somehow cheated. It was only when the darkness swallowed him she realized night had fallen. Traveler nibbled at something and moved on. The horse's plight settled like a stone in her heart, drew her thoughts from Zachary Thatcher. What was she to do about Traveler? What *could* she do? "If I had known about the grass failing, I never would have brought you, boy. I am so sorry."

Tears blurred her vision. She blinked them away and

walked to the closest wagon she could see then made her way slowly along the circle toward her own in order not to startle the animals in the wagon corral. A spot of light flared ahead, steadied to a soft glow. She paused and stared at the small beacon, then moved forward more surely, guided by the light, trying to ignore the feeling of warmth stealing into her heart. She could be wrong…

She approached her wagon, looked around. There was only the empty night, and the welcoming light of her lantern. She picked it up and again searched the darkness, considered calling out to thank him in case he were near. But how foolish she would appear if she were wrong. Still…no one else knew she was out there in the darkness, alone.

Alone. But not as lonely as before. He had lighted her lantern and placed it on the water barrel shelf to see her safely to her wagon. The warmth around her heart grew. It was silly of her to feel so…so *cared about.* She was certain Mr. Thatcher would do the same for any of the emigrants on the train, but still… She climbed into her wagon, placed the lantern on top of the red box then pulled the canvas flaps into place and tied them closed.

She was safely inside. Zach stepped away from the rock he was leaning against and jogged off toward his campsite, the moonless night no challenge to his skill. Something he refused to identify coursed through him, bathed his heart in unwelcome warmth. She had smiled when she picked up the lantern. A small smile to be sure. One that merely played at the corners of her rose-colored lips. And it had not been directed at him, as she had smiled at Josiah Blake. No, she had smiled *because* of him. And that was better. There was no danger of his emotions becoming entangled that way. And there was a danger of that. No sense in fooling himself about it. There had been a moment tonight when she had looked at him....

Zach scowled, spotted the deep black of the fissure in the rock face and climbed to his bed on the shelf above. He had wanted to leap right over that horse and take her in his arms. He had touched her hand, hoping. But she had moved hers away. And that was for the best.

He stepped to the edge of the shelf, stood listening to the night, absorbing the normal sounds of the area so his senses would warn him if danger neared the train. Tonight had been a close thing. Too close. Dr. Emma Allen was like a magnet to him. He needed to keep his distance.

Chapter Eleven

"Annie, please come with me to visit the fort. I am certain you will find—" Emma stopped, stared at the russet-colored curls set swaying by the negative shake of her sister's head.

"You go, Emma. There is nothing of interest to me there. I shall stay here and rest."

Emma lifted her chin. "I will not go without you, Anne! There are Indians camped nearby and—"

"And Mr. Thatcher has set guards over the wagons and the stock. I shall be fine." Anne turned, focused her gaze on her. "I am not being difficult, Emma. I cannot— the children…the families…"

"Oh, Annie." Emma reached out her hand, took a step forward. Anne shook her head and turned away. Emma stopped, lowered her hand to her side. "All right, Anne. I will go without you. I must inquire as to getting my letters carried back to St. Louis." She cast a hopeful look at her sister's back. "Have you any letters—"

"No. None."

Anne's curt tone told her not to inquire further. She

held back a sigh. "Very well. I shall return shortly." She lifted her skirt hems out of the way and climbed from Anne's wagon, let the flaps fall into place.

"We're goin' to the Injuns' camp, Dr. Emma!" Gabe Lewis raced by, wheeled and ran back. "Pa says maybe I c'n trade my marble fer a bow and arrow!"

"Me, too!" Little David Lewis, never far behind his older brother, held out his hand and unfolded his pudgy fingers. A large amber-colored marble resting on his palm winked in the sunlight. He grinned up at her.

"Oh, my, that is a lovely marble!" She returned his grin, looked over at Gabe. "I wish you well in your barter." He flashed her a grin and raced off, David close on his heels.

"Gabriel and David! Do not go outside this wagon circle without your pa!" Lorna Lewis looked up at her and shook her head. "Those boys will be the death of me. Always runnin' off and gettin' up to some mischief!" She glanced toward the closed wagon flaps. "I come for your sister's laundry—sent Lillian to fetch yours. My wash water is heatin' down beside the river."

Emma ducked inside the flaps and drew out a pillowcase stuffed full of Anne's laundry. "Is Jenny using her arm normally, yet?"

Lorna chuckled and shook her head. "She's still tellin' the other kids it's her 'special hurt' arm. The little minx uses it to get her own way."

Emma laughed. "Very clever of her."

"Except she forgets now and again when they get to playin', so the kids are on to her high jinks."

"Will you be taking her and your other girls to the fort?"

Lorna glanced toward the palisade, then looked back at her and shook her head. "Mr. Lewis will buy what we're wantin' in the way of supplies. I aim to get the wash done, and the wagon emptied out and put to rights. Those young'uns make an awful mess of things. And then I mean to bake bread and biscuits enough for a week whilst there is light to see and wood to make a good fire. After that, I aim to bed down the children and enjoy the pleasure of sittin' still." She laughed and took the pillowcase from Emma's hand. "Tell Lillian to hurry on."

Emma nodded and headed for her wagon.

Emma stared at the fort. Indians roamed around the area, going in and out of the fort at will. So many Indians. She flicked her gaze toward the conical skin shelters dotting the grassy field. At least they were on the opposite side of this tongue of land formed by the Laramie and North Platte rivers. She drew her gaze back, lifted it skyward to the guardhouse overhanging the wide, gated entrance in the palisade wall. Surely they would watch and see her safely across—

"Dr. Emma! Dr. Emma!"

Emma whirled about. Mary Fletcher was running toward her. "What is it, Mary?"

"Ma says come quick!" The young girl clutched her side and drew in a ragged breath. "Daniel cut hisself bad...with the hatchet!"

"Where is he?"

"They're bringin' him…to…yer wagon."

"Stay here until you catch your breath!" Emma lifted the hems of her skirts and ran back across the inner oval toward her wagon. Charley Karr was climbing the slope from the river, young Daniel draped across his arms. Hannah Fletcher walked at his side, holding her son's hand. There was a bloody gash in the calf of the boy's leg, a gash so large it was visible even over the distance. She scrambled up to the driver's box of her wagon, gave a hard shove that folded the collapsible canvas overhang back against the first rib of the wagon body. Sunlight poured down on the driver's seat. She climbed over it, scooted across the red box behind it and yanked a sheet out of the chest.

"Where do y' want me to put him, Doc?"

"Here—on the driver's seat." She flapped the sheet open and spread it over the tops of the seat and red box.

Charley Karr hopped up onto the wagon tongue. "Y' might want to take that there sheet off, Doc. He's bleedin' pretty bad."

"I know, Mr. Karr. Please put him down."

The man shrugged, leaned forward and placed Daniel on the seat then stepped down.

Emma glanced at Hannah Fletcher. The woman's face was pale, but her grip on her son's hand was firm. "Please come up into the box, Mrs. Fletcher. I may need your help."

The boy bit down on his lower lip, stared up at her out of hazel-colored eyes that were clouded with pain and fear. The freckles marching across his nose and cheekbones stood out in stark contrast to the pallor of his skin.

Emma smiled, then fisted her hands, placed them on her hips and shook her head. "You are supposed to use the hatchet on firewood and trees, Daniel—not on your leg."

"I k-n-now, Dr. Emma. It s-slipped."

She glanced at his calf. "That's a nasty wound. I shall have to clean it, then stitch it up." The boy's face turned pasty white. He swallowed hard. She patted his shoulder. "But I promise you, you shall not feel it." She glanced up at Mrs. Fletcher, read the disapproval in her eyes.

"Daniel is eleven years old, Dr. Allen. He's old enough to know the truth."

"That *is* the truth, Mrs. Fletcher. Now, please sit down and let Daniel rest his head in your lap while I get things ready." She opened the red box, took out various stoppered bottles, a shallow bowl, suturing equipment, a pile of clean rags and a bandage roll. *Thank you, dearest William, for these supplies. And for your faith in me.*

She closed the top of the box, smoothed the sheet, placed the shallow bowl, the rags and bandage roll on top of it. The rest of the items she placed on top of the water keg. It gave her an excuse to turn her back so Daniel could not see her thread the needle. When she finished she placed the suturing material in the shallow bowl, opened one of the stoppered bottles and poured alcohol over it, then set the bottles on the box. *Almost ready.* She turned back to the keg and frowned. There was no time to heat water. Cold water would have to do. She dipped some water into her washbowl, pushed up her sleeves and scrubbed her hands and wrists with lye soap. *Thank you, Papa Doc, for teaching me to be a doctor. I wish I had more practice at this next part.*

Emma put on the long doctor's apron Ruth Applegate had made her, climbed from the wagon, walked to the front and climbed into the wagon box. Her patient looked up at her, his eyes dark with fear. She smiled down at him. "Do you remember I promised you you would not feel me stitching up your wound?" He bit down on his lip and nodded. "Well, this is the reason." Emma reached across him to the equipment on top of the red box, poured some alcohol into a small vial, opened one of the stoppered bottles and added some of the heavy, oily liquid to the alcohol. "This will put you to sleep. And when you wake up, it will all be over."

The boy's eyes widened. "For true?"

Emma grinned at him. "For true. Are you ready?"

He looked at his mother, then nodded.

"Good." Emma picked up one of the rags, looked at Mrs. Fletcher. There was fear and skepticism in her eyes. "I shall need your help, Mrs. Fletcher. I am going to pour this ether on this rag and hold it under Daniel's nose where he can breathe it. When he goes to sleep, I shall need you to hold the rag. If he starts to awaken before I finish stitching his wound, I want you to hold the rag back under his nose, until he again falls asleep. Can you do that?"

Mrs. Fletcher's face tightened. She looked at the rag. "It won't hurt him none?"

Emma shook her head and smiled. "I promise you it will not."

The woman looked down at her son, took a deep breath and nodded.

"All right then. I shall begin."

Emma poured the ether on the rag and held it under Daniel's nose. He took a tentative sniff, looked up at her and grinned. "It smells—" he took another, deeper sniff "—smells...kinda...funnnn..." His eyes closed, his body went slack.

"Well, I never seen the like!"

Emma smiled and handed his mother the rag. "There's no need to whisper, he cannot hear you. No!" She grabbed Mrs. Fletcher's hand and pulled it away from her face. "Do not sniff it. You will go to sleep, and I need you to watch Daniel." She reached for the alcohol, splashed some on her hands then poured some onto the cut, doused one of the rags and began to wipe the blood from his leg.

The day had slipped away. Emma frowned and placed her hand on her stomach. It still quivered with nerves. Not surprising as it was the first time she had used the ether on her own. Or on a child. She had thought it was safe. But she could not know for sure.

She took a deep breath, let it out slowly and blotted the notes she had made on Daniel's treatment. Her stomach added hunger pangs to the quivering, reminding her she had not eaten supper. Though she had watched the boy carefully all day, had stayed with him while he ate his supper and could detect no sign of any ill effects from the ether, her own stomach had rebelled at the thought of the meal Mrs. Fletcher offered.

She shook her head and tucked her medical journal back in her doctor's bag. In this instance, the patient had fared better than the doctor. Daniel had eagerly told his tale and showed off his bandage to all who had come around. Indeed, he felt so well, it had been difficult to make him stay quiet until he was settled for the night. She, however, had not enjoyed being the center of the excited furor that rose over her treatment of Daniel when the emigrants who had finished their work, or returned from the fort, gathered at the Fletchers' wagon. Not all of them were favorably impressed. Especially Mr. Hargrove. And she had little to offer them by way of explanation. There had been moments when she had wished for Mr. Thatcher's presence—when she would have welcomed his authoritative way. She latched the black bag, rested her hands on it and stared off into the distance. If anything should go wrong with Daniel's healing…

No! She would not think such things. She would write Papa Doc a report on Daniel. He would understand she had done what she thought best for her patient, and he would be thrilled to know the ether worked so well.

If he ever received the letter.

Emma looked out at the fading light, then glanced at the pile of letters on the dresser. She did not have enough courage to cross that broad expanse of field to the fort in the growing darkness. Tears welled into her eyes. She *so* wanted to send her letters on their way to her family. It would ease some of her loneliness for them by sharing a small part of what she was experiencing on this journey—by letting them know they were always in her thoughts and in her heart. The disappointment brought a choking lump to her throat. Perhaps Mr. Thatcher would grant her time to go to the fort and inquire about someone carrying the letters back to St. Louis before they started out in the morning. If not…well, Papa Doc would be proud of her. He always said a good doctor puts his patients first, before his own wants or needs.

Neighing and snorting and pounding hoofs intruded on her thoughts. She glanced up, saw the tossing heads and flowing tails of the horses the men were herding into the wagon corral where they would be safe from theft by the Indians. She wiped the tears from her cheeks and opened the crock of dried apples she had found when she was searching among the stores in Anne's wagon for something to feed Traveler and Lady. There was still light enough to visit the horses. She felt close to William when she was with his horse.

Emma climbed from her wagon and stood on the step looking over the corralled stock. Cold air touched her face and neck and hands. She shivered and started toward Traveler at a brisk pace. If the temperature dropped so quickly here along the river when the sun went down, how cold must it be in the mountains? She lifted her gaze to the massive wall of stone that barred their way west. The mountains looked cold, gray and impenetrable in the shadowed light of dusk. How would they ever get their wagons over them? It seemed an impossible task. But Mr. Thatcher had ridden off this morning to check the trail conditions for tomorrow's journey. Pray God, he returned safe. Myriad possibilities for harm to him flooded her mind. Fear knotted her already unsettled stomach. *Please, Almighty God, keep him safe.*

Emma yanked her gaze from the mountains, strode to Lady and fed her two of the dried apple slices then moved on to Traveler. The horse accepted her offering, then lowered his head to graze. She stroked his neck and listened to him chomping on the rich, thick grass. *A journey like ours is hard on the stock. Mules fare better than horses. Especially when the good grass gives out when they are climbing the mountains.*

Emma clenched her hands and took a deep breath. Zachary Thatcher had been warning her. But she would not lose Traveler. She would not! There had to be—

"Miss Allen…"

Emma whirled. "Mr. Thatcher! You are returned *safe.*" The words burst out of their own volition. Heat spread across her cheeks as she looked up at him. She had not meant to sound so…joyous. "I mean—I was looking at the mountains, and they seem so formidable…"

"They are that, Miss." A small, wiry-looking man, dressed in fringed leather, stepped out from behind Zachary Thatcher. "But Zach, here, is equal to 'em. He saved my bacon today! Them Blackfeet had me fer sure." The words were accompanied by a hefty thump on Zachary Thatcher's shoulder. "This the lady you was tellin' me about, Zach?"

Emma stared at the man's weathered and bearded face, looked into his alert, dark eyes. Why would Zachary Thatcher discuss her with him? She shifted her gaze back to Zachary Thatcher, let her eyes convey her puzzlement, but read reassurance in his.

"Miss Allen, this is Jim Broadman. One of the best mountain men in the country. He has business back East, and has agreed to carry your letters to St. Louis." A slight frown puckered his brow. "If you haven't made other arrangements, that is."

He had remembered about her letters! Emma's breath caught. "I have not. Thank you for your thoughtfulness, Mr. Thatcher." She smiled at the mountain man, who promptly yanked his stained and battered hat off. "How kind of you, Mr. Broadman. Thank you for—"

"No need fer thanks yet, Miss." The man frowned and clapped the dirty felt hat back on his head. "Them Blackfeet shot my horse plumb out from under me today. I can't go east 'till I get me another mount." He gave Zach a wry smile. "One that knows how to *run*. Not some sad excuse of a…er…of a horse like I had." He glanced back at her. "I'll get on over t' the fort an' see can I find—"

"No. Please wait, Mr. Broadman." She swallowed hard, glanced at Zachary Thatcher then looked toward the west, toward those high, rugged mountains. *A journey like ours is hard on the horses.* She lifted her chin, placed her hand on William's horse. Zachary Thatcher did not make a sound. He did not move a muscle. But, for some reason she could not define, she was certain he understood what she was about to do, and it gave her strength. She stroked the horse's shoulder, fought to keep her voice even. "This is Traveler, Mr. Broadman. I—I want to return him to my brother. Traveler is a swift runner, and I will loan him to you for your journey. In exchange, you must agree to deliver both Traveler and my letters to Mrs. Samuel Benton at Riverside, upon your arrival in St. Louis." She squared her shoulders and turned. "Do you find that agreeable, Mr. Broadman?"

The man nodded, stepped forward and ran his hand over Traveler's back. "He's a fine horse, Miss." His gaze locked on hers. "I'll take good care of him. Y' have my word on it."

Emma nodded and turned away. Zachary Thatcher stepped up beside her.

"Broadman, you go on to the fort. I will get the letters and bring them to you."

"And William's saddle." Her voice sounded odd, sort of tight and small, but she got the words out.

"As you wish. Now, come along, Miss Allen, there is no reason to delay."

Zachary Thatcher gripped her elbow with his strong hand and propelled her toward her wagon. She did not object. For once, she was thankful for his autocratic ways. And for the strength and warmth of his hand that supported and guided her.

Chapter Twelve

Wind rippled the canvas. Rain hammered on it with deafening force. Emma shivered and closed the dresser drawer, caught her breath as the yellow light of lightning flickered over the watery surface of the cover and flashed its brightness through the wagon. Thunder crashed, its fury vibrating the boards beneath her feet.

That strike had been close! Emma snagged her lower lip with her teeth and glanced down at the garment dangling from her hands. Perhaps she should stay in the wagon. "And then who would get the fresh water you and Anne need, Miss Coward? Garth Lundquist? He must keep the oxen calmed. Put on the cape!" Her voice was all but drowned out by the pounding rain.

She frowned, swirled the India-rubber cape around her shoulders and fastened the ties. How long ago the comfort of her life in Philadelphia seemed. Now there was nothing but storms and mountains and walking, walking, walking. "And do not forget being reduced to talking to yourself, Emma Allen."

She heaved a sigh, flipped the hood up to cover her

head then pulled the empty water keg to the back of the wagon and slipped the knot that untied the flaps. The wind tore them from her grasp, sucked her skirt hems out into the rain with such force she grabbed hold of the canvas to keep from being pulled after them. She turned and backed down the steps, wrestled the keg to the ground.

Water blew off the fluttering canvas and spattered against her face. She turned away from the wind and hurried toward the rock cliff beside her wagon, dragging the keg after her. Rainwater flowing off the rim of a deep ledge jutting out from the cliff formed a waterfall in front of her. She ducked her head and dashed through the deluge, the water splashing on her back chilling the India-rubber of the cape and making her shiver. The beating of the rain on her hood ceased. She shot a grateful glance at the ledge of rock that now formed a roof over her, then shoved the keg beneath the stream of water gushing out of a fissure in the rock wall and shook the raindrops from her hands.

Lightning sizzled and snapped. Thunder clapped and rumbled. She flinched, stepped closer to the wall of stone and looked around. The curve of the cliff and the overhanging ledge made a shelter of sorts, protecting her from the rain and the worst of the wind. What of the others? The storm had struck so fast it had caught the wagons ahead of hers strung out in a line along the ridge they were crossing. What if lightning struck one of the them? Or stampeded the oxen? And what of those behind her? Was Anne all right? She closed her eyes, tried to will away the frightening thoughts but they slipped into her mind like the cold, damp air creeping beneath her cape. What if night fell before the storm stopped, and they could not reach a place where they could camp and circle the wagons? There had been Indians watching them from the hills yesterday. Blackfeet, Mr. Thatcher had called them. Did Indians attack during rainstorms?

A shiver raced down her spine. She wiped the moisture from her face and stared toward her wagon but could see nothing through the pouring rain, could hear nothing but its drumming against earth and stone. It was as if she were alone in the watery world.

She drew her hands in through the slits in the cape and rubbed them against her skirt to warm them. Since they had entered the mountains, every day had become more difficult. In the broken terrain of the foothills, the grass had given way to sage and greasewood. Then the streams had turned bitter with alkali, making it hard to find a camping area. The poor animals bawled, neighed and brayed their misery throughout the nights. And every day the way became steeper and more rugged. Today's misery was the storm with its relentless, pouring rain. But, at least, she was able to catch the runoff gushing from the rocks. She would have sufficient good water for the oxen and Lady tomorrow if the alkali problem continued. Of course, tomorrow could hold a new trouble.

Take therefore no thought for the morrow: for the morrow shall take thought for the things of itself. Sufficient unto the day is the evil thereof.

Emma snorted, hugged herself against another chill. "I hear you, William, even if only in my memory. But I doubt you would quote that scripture so glibly, were you standing here with me."

Lightning threw flickering light on the water flowing off the stone ledge above her. She gathered her courage, drew the hood of her cape farther forward and grabbed hold of the filled keg and tugged. Water sloshed out and wet her shoes. She scowled, tipped out some of the water, then took a tighter hold and dragged the keg out of the sheltered area to the other side of her wagon. Rain pelted her, stung her face. She yanked the slipping hood back in place and bent to lift the keg. It did not budge.

"Hold on there, Miss Allen!"

Zachary Thatcher appeared like an apparition out of the watery gray. He slid from his saddle, hoisted the keg and dumped it into the large water barrel lashed to the side of her wagon.

She held on to the hood and tipped her head back to look up at him. "Thank you, Mr. Thatcher." The words were barely audible. She raised her voice to a shout. "I guess I overfilled the keg for my strength."

He nodded and leaned closer. "Where did you get the water?"

"There is a stream spurting from that wall of rock. I think it is overflow from the rain. Thank you again." She reached for the keg. He hefted it to his shoulder.

"Show me."

She led the way, conscious of him moving up to walk beside her, blocking the wind. And of his horse trailing behind. Surely the horse would not— She ducked under the water sheeting off the rock and turned. He would. Comanche followed his master into the sheltered area.

At least he came as far as possible. The water off the rock hit his broad rump and splashed every direction. Zachary Thatcher seemed not to notice. He carried the keg to the gushing fount.

"Here, boy." Emma took hold of the horse's bridle and turned him sideways, then stroked his wet, silky nose. "You are a very smart horse to come in out of the rain." She laughed and crowded back to give him room, bumped into Zachary Thatcher and bounced off. She might as well have hit the mountain for all the give there was to the man. She looked up, and the apology on her lips died. He was staring down at her, an odd expression on his face. "Is something wrong?"

"No…" He shook his head, frowned and removed his hat, slapped the water off it and settled it back on his head. "Comanche has never let anyone but me touch him."

"Oh." She looked back at the horse. "Perhaps it is because of the storm. He wants to please me so I will share my shelter." She smiled and ran her fingers through Comanche's mane, stroked his hard, heavily-muscled shoulder. The horse did not seem to suffer from the lack of good grass. "Why is Comanche not growing gaunt like the other horses, Mr. Thatcher?"

"He's a Western horse. And, as you said, a smart one. There are small patches of grass around little pockets of sweet water in these mountains. Enough for one or two animals. I set him free to roam at night and he finds his own grass and water."

She glanced up at him. "You do not worry he will get lost?"

He shook his head. "He doesn't range that far. He is always back before dawn."

"Truly? My, you *are* smart, Comanche!" The horse flicked his ears and tossed his head. She laughed, then sobered and lowered her hands to her sides. Zachary Thatcher's boots scraped against the stone. His bulk loomed beside her.

"Jim Broadman will take good care of Traveler, Miss Allen. His life depends on it."

There was sympathy in his voice. Zachary Thatcher was a perceptive man. Too much so at times. Emma nodded and straightened her shoulders. "I do not regret my decision, Mr. Thatcher. I am glad Traveler is being returned to William. I did not want to see him suffer. But I cannot deny I miss him."

"And your brother."

If that was an attempt to change the subject to make her feel better, it failed miserably. "Yes... And Mother and Papa Doc, also." Her throat thickened. She dipped her head, pointed. "The keg is full."

Zachary Thatcher nodded, grabbed Comanche's reins and dropped them to the ground, then turned and hoisted the filled keg to his shoulder.

She started for the wagon. His hand clamped on her shoulder.

"You stay here with Comanche, Miss Allen. No sense in us both going out in the storm."

She watched him go, grateful for the opportunity to get command of her emotions. She pushed the hood off, smoothed the wet strands of hair back off her forehead then put it on again and shook out her long skirts. The horse snorted. She laughed and did a slow pirouette. "I know…it is all foolishness. But it makes a lady feel better to look her best. Even in the midst of a storm."

"Talking to yourself or Comanche, Miss Allen?" Zachary Thatcher swiped water off his face and gave her a crooked grin. "It usually takes longer than a few weeks in the mountains for that to happen. Besides, you've no need to be worrying about such things. I've never seen a time you didn't look pre—fine." He stepped past her and shoved the keg back under the spouting water.

What was she supposed to say to that? She ignored the warmth his comment spread through her and turned her back and braced a hand against Comanche's shoulder. Zachary Thatcher's grin was having a queer effect on her knees. "Thank you for your kind words, Mr. Thatcher."

"It wasn't kindness, it was the truth."

The softness in his deep voice stole the remaining strength from her knees. She grabbed for the saddle horn.

"This Papa Doc? Is he the one that taught you to be a doctor?"

"Yes." She took a breath, launched into the safe subject. "Billy…William…was run over by a carriage when we were orphans and lived on the streets in Philadelphia. Mother, well, she was not our mother then, of course, she adopted us later. Anyway, Mother and Papa Doc saw the accident and took us to her home. Billy had a broken leg and a head wound." She stared at the rain, remembering her fear when her big brother would not wake up and talk to her. "Papa Doc treated Billy's injuries. He made him better." Something of the wonder she had felt then returned. She smiled, stroked Comanche's neck. "That was the beginning of my desire to be a doctor. I loved Mother, but I adored Papa Doc. I followed him all around the orphanage when he came to treat the other children." She gave Zachary Thatcher a sidelong glance. "Mother turned her home into an orphanage. And then, when she and Papa Doc married, they took William and me and Annie to live with them in Papa Doc's house." Her throat tightened again. She drew a deep breath.

"He must have been a good teacher. I've never heard of a doctor putting someone to sleep before working on them the way you did Daniel Fletcher. I'm sorry I missed seeing that."

His quiet, matter-of-fact tone drove the threatening tears away. Was he approving of her work? Or merely curious about the ether? She looked up. Their gazes locked, held. Rain fell outside the small, sheltered area. Lightning flashed and thunder crashed, but, suddenly, it did not matter. Something in his eyes made her feel safe. And more. She lowered her gaze and stared at his boots, wishing he would take her in his arms. The boots moved toward her. She caught her breath, looked up, lost it again. His eyes had darkened to the color of blue smoke. Something flickered in their depths. He sucked in air, pivoted on his heel and stepped over to Comanche.

"It seems everyone who comes out to Oregon country has a dream, Miss Allen. I'm guessing yours is to be a doctor." He looked down, swiped water off his saddle.

Heat burned in her cheeks. Obviously, that moment had not shaken him as it had her. She drew her hands inside the cape and pressed them against her stomach to stop its quivering. "You have guessed wrong, Mr. Thatcher. To be a doctor *was* my dream. I have learned that is impossible. Men want a male doctor to care for them and their families. And no one can be a doctor without patients."

"You have patients."

"For now…yes. But I do not delude myself. The men on the wagon train permit me to treat their families only because there is no male doctor available. And there are those who still refuse to acknowledge my skill." The old bitterness rose. Zachary Thatcher was one of those men. The thought steadied her when he again looked her way. "It is not my dream that brought me on this journey, Mr. Thatcher, it is Anne. You see, William was to teach at the Banning Mission in Oregon country, and when his wife became too ill to make the journey, Anne declared she would take his place. As she had been recently injured in the carriage accident that killed her husband and child, I could not let her make the journey alone and without care."

Her words called forth a vision of her empty future with disturbing clarity, and suddenly, she knew what she would do. "Oregon country holds nothing for me. When Anne is settled at the mission, I shall travel on to Oregon City and take a ship for home." An unexpected sadness washed over her. She forced a smile. "And what dream brings you west, Mr. Thatcher? Do you hope to found a town and build an empire?"

He shook his head, threw the trailing reins back over Comanche's head. "Like you, Oregon country holds nothing for me. I'll leave the founding of towns and empire building to Hargrove and Applegate and the others. It is these mountains that call to me. All I want is to be to be free and unfettered to roam them as I will."

She nodded, smiled through an unreasonable sense of loss and disappointment. "I wish you well in your travels, Mr. Thatcher."

He looked at her.

Her smile faded. That queer weakness overtook her again. She grabbed for the saddle horn and found his hand waiting. His fingers curled around hers, rough and warm and strong. That smoky look returned to his eyes. Her heart faltered, raced. She stared up at him, shy and uncertain, unable to breathe as he stepped close, lowered his head. Rainwater dripped off his hat brim. His lips, cool and moist, touched hers. She closed her eyes, swayed toward him. His arm slid around her, crushed her against him. His mouth claimed hers, his lips heated, seared hers. And then it was over. He released her, stepped back.

She stared up at him, her heart pounding.

"I've wanted to do that since the day you stood on the deck of that ferry, fear and fury in your eyes, and told me you had no husband." His voice was husky, ragged. "Now it's done." He turned, hoisted the keg onto his shoulder, ducked under the water and headed for her wagon. Comanche plodded after him.

His words were as rough against the exposed tenderness of her heart as his work-hardened hands had been against her skin. Emma touched her fingers to her lips. She drew a deep breath, lifted her hands and yanked her hood up, then squared her shoulders, ducked her head and walked out into the wind and rain, defying her emotions that were as raging and turbulent as the storm.

Fort Hall was a disappointment. The few log buildings hiding behind the high log wall enclosure had no windows, only a square hole cut in each mud-covered roof. And in the bastion were a few portholes large enough for guns only. But, as the captain explained, it was not meant for comfort. Its purpose was to afford the inhabitants protection from the frequent attacks by hostile Indians.

Emma pushed her bonnet back to allow the breeze to cool her face and looked up at the hill above the path the wagons were obliged to take to cross over the waterfalls below. Blackfeet Indians had been watching them every day. And they made no effort to hide the fact. Whenever you looked up, they would be there. It was unnerving. They put her in mind of a cat stalking a mouse.

She stepped around a rock following the ruts the wagons ahead were cutting into the ground, then stopped and looked back. Anne was riding the mule that had belonged to the captain's wife at Fort Hall. The woman had been happy to trade the mule for Lady. Emma sighed. Another connection to William was gone. But it was for the best. There was abundant grass at the fort for Lady, and the mule seemed docile enough. Even if it were not, it would find its match in her sister. Anne was an excellent rider, with gentle hands and a firm seat.

Emma grinned. It had not always been so. Annie had often been thrown from her pony. But one day after Pepper threw her, she had stood up, dusted off her skirts, gripped Pepper's reins and led him back to the mounting block, her russet curls bobbing with her every determined step. Anne had never been thrown from a horse again. Mother insisted it was the red curls.

Emma stared at Anne, her faltering hope for her sister strengthening. Anne still had red curls. She would get over her grief. She only needed something to rouse her strong, fighting spirit. Perhaps Anne would find that something when she began teaching at the mission.

Emma faced forward and started walking again. When Anne was settled, she would be free to return home and…and what? Content herself to help Papa Doc? It was as close as she would come to her dream of being a doctor. Tears stung her eyes. Anger drove her up the steep grade. If God did not want her to be a doctor, the least He could do was take this desire to be one out of her heart and give her a new dream!

The storm, the half cave and Zachary Thatcher's kiss slipped into her mind. She set herself firmly against the thought. That was no dream! The kiss had meant nothing. He had told her his dream was to be unfettered and free to roam the mountains at will. The kiss had only been something he had to do, like…like when she had jumped off the roof of Uncle Justin's stable onto the hay pile. The idea had taunted and tempted her. But once she had made the jump, it was done. She had never been tempted to do it again. And that is what Mr. Thatcher had said, "Now it's done." And so it was. And she was not foolish enough to think or hope otherwise. She had only reacted so strongly because she was lonely and frightened of the storm. Zachary Thatcher had offered a moment of safety and comfort. That was all.

She huffed the last few steps to the top of the hill, stopped to catch her breath and look at the small valley a short distance below. There was a meandering stream, trees scattered here and there and grass for the animals. It would be a good camp tonight. She sighed, shook her head and started down the descent. How strange life was. Everything she had known had been stripped away from her. Her comfort, her *life,* now depended on those three things—water, wood and grass.

"Dr. Emma!"

Emma lifted her gaze from the stony ground and looked down the hill. Mary Fenton was running toward her, waving her hand in the air. The girl stopped and cupped her hands around her mouth. "Miz Hargrove says can you come, she needs you. She says hurry!"

Lydia? Had there been an accident? Emma lifted the front hem of her skirt and ran.

Chapter Thirteen

"I am here, Lydia!" Emma put her foot on the bottom step, stopped and stared as Lydia Hargrove shoved aside the canvas flaps over the tailgate of her wagon. "What is wrong? Are you—"

"I'm fine, I—"

A moan, quickly broken off, came from the wagon's interior. Emma glanced toward the sound, then looked back up at Lydia Hargrove.

"It's Ruth Applegate." The older woman's voice lowered. "I thought it best to keep her here 'till Mary found you." She climbed out of the wagon, turned and held out her arms. "Come to Auntie Lydia, Isaac." She lifted the toddler out, held him close. "Time for me to start the cook fire. I'll keep Isaac with me while you talk with his mama."

Emma nodded, read all the things the woman left unsaid in her expression and climbed in the wagon. Ruth Applegate was sitting in Lydia Hargrove's small rocking chair, clutching her abdomen. The young woman's face was pale, her mouth compressed into a thin line.

Emma picked a path through the various trunks and household items and knelt in front of her. "Are you in pain, Ruth?"

The young woman nodded, gave a soft hiss and rubbed her hands over the fabric covering her stomach.

Emma watched Ruth's eyes close, noted how she clenched her jaw to hold back an outcry. "Is the pain constant? Or does it come and go like cramps?"

"Like cramps." Ruth released a breath and opened her eyes. "I—I think it's the baby. It feels like when Isaac started to be born."

Emma nodded, kept her expression serene. "When did the cramps begin?"

"Not long ago. When I was carrying Isaac up the grade. The pain doubled me over and I had to put him down. Lydia saw me when their wagon came by and they stopped. She took Isaac and bid me sit in her chair. I asked her to send someone for you." Ruth's eyes filled with tears. "I don't want to lose my baby, Dr. Emma."

Emma reached out and squeezed her hand. "I cannot promise that will not happen, Ruth. Babies have a way of choosing their own destinies. But I will promise you I will do everything I know to help you." She looked the young woman straight in the eyes. "Will your husband let me come to your wagon to care for you?"

Ruth looked down at their joined hands on her stomach and shook her head. "I'm sorry, Dr. Emma. You saved Isaac when he had the measles. And even told me what to do for James when he got them so bad, but he—he won't…"

"I understand, Ruth. Here is my first instruction." The

young woman's gaze shot to her face. Emma smiled. "Do not distress yourself. It is very bad for the baby. We shall manage." *But how?* She thrust the worry aside. "My second instruction is this…no more work."

"But—"

"There can be no buts, Ruth. You must go to bed and rest. You will do no more cooking, no more walking. You cannot lift or care for Isaac."

Ruth's eyes filled with tears. "Dr. Emma, that is impossible. James will nev—"

"Nothing is impossible, Ruth. It may be difficult, but not impossible. I will give it some thought and—ah!" Emma clapped her hands together and smiled. "Olga Lundquist prepares my meals and Anne's. I will simply give her more supplies from our stores and have her cook them for your family." *And increase her pay.*

"And I will care for Isaac." Lydia Hargrove stuck her head and shoulders into the end of her wagon and grabbed hold of a large iron spider.

"Oh, Lydia, I cannot—" The tears slipped down Ruth's cheeks. "Isaac is getting so…rambunctious." There was worry, but also a touch of pride in her words.

Lydia snorted. "I'm not so old I can't handle a toddler. He's settin' out here, quiet as you please, diggin' in the dirt with my spoon. The matter is settled. Caring for your little one pleasures me. And I will cook your meal tonight."

"Oh, but I—how will I ever repay you both!" Ruth covered her face with her hands and sobbed.

"Bosh!"

Ruth jerked her head up.

Emma gaped at Lydia.

"You stop that nonsense, Ruth Applegate! Our husbands drug us along on this journey, and it's up to us to help each other survive it! There'll be no talk of repayin'!" She withdrew her head and shoulders and disappeared.

Emma laughed, she couldn't help it. Lydia Hargrove looked as if she would like to use that spider on her husband and James Applegate, instead of cooking with it. If only Ruth had some of that spunk. She turned back to her patient.

"All that remains is to get you to bed."

Ruth put her hands on the rocker's arms and started to rise.

Emma shook her head. "I said no walking. I will go find your husband."

"And everything will be all right if Ruth goes to bed?"

Emma met James Applegate's skeptical gaze. "I did not say that, Mr. Applegate. But she will almost surely lose the baby if she does not."

"Almost." The man's brows drew down into a frown. "How long does she have to stay abed?"

"I cannot answer that question with any certainty."

"Seems there's not much you *can* say for certain. Too bad there's not a *real* doctor here."

Emma clenched her hands, fought to keep her voice calm and pleasant. "Not even a man doctor could answer your questions, Mr. Applegate. These things are a matter of nature."

"Not havin' a man doctor handy, it's hard to know the right of that." He raised his hand and stroked his beard, looked off to the west. "With these steep climbs, the extra weight will be hard on the teams." He looked at her again. "She can stay abed three days."

"Three—"

"But if the way gets too steep, an' the teams start to struggle, she will have to walk."

Emma clenched her hands, fought to keep her voice even. "If you are agreeable, Mr. Applegate, there may be a solution to your problem. Ruth can stay in my wagon, where I can watch over her." She tried to hold them back, but the words popped out anyway. "My brother bought extra teams."

She need not have worried about her acerbic comment. He merely nodded and stroked his beard. She could almost see him weighing his dislike of her against his team's well-being. At last, he lowered his hand and deigned to look at her. "All right. I will be along shortly to carry Ruth to your wagon."

Emma lifted a small pile of clean rags out of the red box, closed the lid and turned to look down at her patient. "Are you more comfortable now?"

"Yes. The cramps have stopped." Ruth gave her a hopeful look. "Perhaps I should go back to my wagon."

Emma shook her head. "I do not want to dishearten you, Ruth, but I also do not wish to give you false hope. It happens this way sometimes. The cramps stop, and then start again. I am hoping that if you stay abed for a few days, things will be fine."

Ruth nodded, fingered the ribbon adorned with embroidered rosebuds that separated the bodice from the skirt of the nightgown she wore. "This is fine work. Too fine. My shift—"

"Is not warm enough for these cold nights. I do not want you taking a chill." Emma placed the rags on the dresser to have close at hand should they be needed for spotting, then set a pail close by for discards. "You should cover up."

Ruth pulled the blankets and quilt that covered her legs up to her chin. "It sure feels strange goin' to bed without cleanin' up supper and puttin' Isaac down to sleep. I hope he don't give Lydia trouble. He can be stubborn…"

"I am quite certain Lydia is equal to the task."

"Yes. I'm sure she is…"

Emma studied Ruth's unhappy face and reached for her wrap. "I am going to see if Anne needs anything before I retire. I shall check on Isaac on my way." She gave the worried mother a smile and glanced toward the tailgate. She could not get by the bed to open it. She stepped to the front of the wagon, scooted across the lid of the red box and climbed out onto the driver's seat. Moonlight flooded the world in silver. A shiver coursed through her. The night air was cooling fast.

She closed the flaps tight, then climbed down and hurried toward the Hargrove wagon. She was almost there when Zachary Thatcher came striding out of the night toward her. Her stomach fluttered. She stopped and pulled her wrap more tightly around her shoulders, ignoring, as best she could, the betraying quickening of her pulse at the sight of him. He stopped in front of her, dipped his head in greeting.

"Matthew Hargrove said you wished to speak with me, Miss Allen."

"Yes." She braced herself for his reaction. "Ruth Applegate is with child and a problem has developed. She is in danger of losing the baby." She gave him an imploring look. "She must have rest, Mr. Thatcher. We cannot travel tomorrow. Or—" She stopped, stiffened at the shake of his head.

"I'm sorry, Miss Allen. But the wagons form up and travel on tomorrow at dawn, same as always."

Emma stared at him, disappointment and anger churning in her stomach. "Mr. Thatcher, as a *doctor,* I am telling you that being bounced and jolted by that wagon will almost certainly cause Ruth Applegate to lose her baby. Perhaps even her life. I am asking you—"

"Have you seen the Indians on the hills, Dr. Allen?"

She stared up at him, taken aback. "The Indians? Yes. But—"

"There are over three hundred of them. There—" he jabbed his finger in the air to their right "—there—" another jab behind them "—and there."

The last jab was to their left. She peered beyond the circled wagons into the darkness, her heart pounding.

"They surround our camp every night. The only way open is west."

The quiet, factual way he spoke was terrifying. She shuddered, looked up at him.

"They do not attack the train because I have assured

them we are only passing through their territory. They are watching to see if what I say is true." He stepped closer, locked his gaze on hers. "If these wagons do not roll west tomorrow morning, Dr. Allen, Mrs. Applegate, her baby and every other member of this wagon train will be in grave danger. If we travel on, at least she and her baby have a chance. Now, if you will excuse me, I have guards to post." He touched the brim of his hat, turned and walked off.

Emma stared after him until he disappeared, then looked around the inner oval. The animals were settling down for the night. Here and there the red embers of dying cook fires shimmered against the dark, or a lantern showed as a dull circle of gold on the canvas of a wagon. Voices, muted and indistinct, floated on the air as men and women finished chores and bid one another good-night. Did any of them know of the danger that lurked out there in the night, waiting to pounce on and destroy them?

There was no lantern light showing in the Hargrove wagon. Little Isaac was asleep. And little Jenny…and Gabe and David… Mary… Emily and Susan and Amy… So many children.

Emma turned and forced her trembling legs to carry her back to her wagon. Ruth was waiting to hear about Isaac. Ruth, who was in danger of losing her unborn baby and, perhaps, her life. And she was helpless to do anything about it.

She climbed to the driver's box, took a deep breath and fixed a smile on her face. Ruth must be kept calm.

She could not let her guess… She ducked beneath the canvas flaps to tell Ruth Isaac was sound asleep.

Zach moved from guard to guard under the cover of the darkness, checking their positions, making sure they were alert without alarming them. Thus far the Blackfeet had kept their word, but their presence was a constant threat—one that weighed heavily on his shoulders. He had not told Emma Allen the whole truth.

He scowled, detoured around a rock outcropping and headed for the far side of the herd. The hard truth was, the Indians were driving them the same as they were driving these oxen and mules and horses. And if they did not move, that open-ended circle would close about them, they would be overrun by the multitude of fierce warriors and his few unskilled, untrained fighting men would die quickly in battle. It would be different for the women and children on the train. His gut knotted. It had been bad enough seeing the horrors visited on women and children he did not know. To think of Emma Allen and—

Emma. She was so beautiful standing there with the moonlight bathing her face. And the way she had looked at him as he walked toward her… For a moment he'd thought…

The knots in his gut twisted tighter. Zach took a firmer grip on his knife and slipped through the night toward his camp. What he had thought had no bearing on the truth. Or on his job. He had to keep this train moving. Now more than ever.

Chapter Fourteen

"Ugh!" The jolt slammed her back against the dresser, her breath gusting from her lungs. Emma clamped her lips together to stop a moan, pushed herself back onto her knees and resumed her gentle kneading of Ruth's abdomen. The baby was lost, but the bleeding had not stopped, and she refused to lose Ruth, too. She simply *refused*.

Ruth's sharp intake of breath alerted her. The flesh beneath her hands went rigid, relaxed, went rigid again. *Please!* Emma stopped the kneading, checked the rag between Ruth's legs. At last! She folded the rag over the expelled birth matter, slipped a clean rag in its place, then dropped the dirty one in the pail. The tension in her shoulder muscles eased. Ruth should be all right now. If… No! She would not think that way. *Sufficient unto the day…*

"The bleeding should stop now, Ruth." She pulled the nightgown back down over Ruth's legs and tugged the covers up over her. "I want you to stay well covered. You have lost blood and will take a chill easily." She sat back on her heels and looked down at her patient. "I am sorry about the baby, Ruth."

"I know you tried your best, Dr. Emma. And you were right. The cramping and spotting did stop after I went to bed last night." Ruth turned her face away. "It was the bouncing around this morning that started it again."

"Yes, but—" Emma raised her head. "Listen!" Chains rattled, hoofs stomped. The very distraction she needed for Ruth. She looked back at her. "Mr. Lundquist is unhitching the oxen. We must have reached our camping spot. It seems dusk comes earlier every day, and our travel time grows shorter and shorter." She rubbed her upper arms, chilly now that she had stopped working on Ruth. "But it is good that you will be able to have a long night of rest."

Ruth nodded, plucked at the quilt. "James worries about the weather. It is already so cold at night ice forms on the water in the barrel. He's afraid snow will catch us in the mountain passes."

From the sound of Ruth's voice, James was not alone in his concern. In truth, she had thought about that possibility herself. How could she not with Mr. Thatcher issuing dire warnings of such an occurrence, or of Indian attacks, whenever she asked him to have mercy and stop the train for her patients' sakes. Emma shoved away thought of the Indians and gave Ruth a wry look. "I am sure the snow would not have the temerity to defy Mr. Thatcher. He will bring us safely through to Oregon country."

The comment brought forth the smile she was seeking, albeit a weak, listless one. She pushed to her feet and slipped by the bed to peek out of the tied flaps.

"What do you see?"

"We are stopped on a low plateau, very near a river below. I suppose it is still the Snake River." She undid a tie and tugged the flaps farther apart. The cool September air rushed in. She shivered, closed the flaps and turned back to Ruth. "There are three islands in the river, side by side. Rather like this…" She folded her index finger down with her thumb, spread her extended fingers and held out her hand where Ruth could see it.

"That should make James happy. It will mean plenty of good water, and maybe grass, for the stock."

"The islands are too small and rocky for grazing. But they are almost on a level with the water. It should make things easier if we are to ford across tomorrow."

"Dr. Emma…"

"Yes?"

"Where are my clothes, please?" Ruth boosted herself to a sitting position. "I'm grateful for all you've done, but there is no reason for me to stay now. I would like to go back to my own wagon." She swallowed, cleared her throat. "I want to see Isaac. And I—I have to tell James about the baby."

Emma bit back her objection and lifted Ruth's clothes off the top of the chest and handed them to her. "You must go right to bed, Ruth. Do not lift or carry Isaac, and do not get chilled."

"I'll be careful, Dr. Emma. I'll keep Isaac in bed with me." Ruth stood, removed the nightgown and pulled on her shift. "James will not—" She looked away, put on her dress and busied herself with the buttons. "I will be happy to sew you another dress to pay you for all you have done for me."

"Another dress would be wonderful, Ruth. You do lovely work." Emma smiled and helped Ruth into her shoes. "We will talk about it when you are stronger." She picked up a blanket and handed it to Ruth. "Put this around your shoulders while I untie the flaps and open the tailgate, and then I will help you to your wagon." *And see you settled in bed.*

"But Isaac—"

Emma shook her head, untied the flaps and slid back the latches on the tailgate. "I will go and get Isaac from Lydia, *after* I help you to bed. Now, take these rags for the spotting, and let me help you down these steps."

Things had quieted. The children had been called to their wagons for the night. Emma turned her lantern low and peeked out of the flaps. There were no curious youngsters running about who might follow her. She put on her wrap and picked up the small, towel-wrapped bundle she had put on the floor beside the chest out of Ruth's sight. An image of the tiny baby, of her minuscule hands and feet, filled her head. She forced the image away, put the bundle in the empty pail and climbed from the wagon. Her flesh prickled. She scanned the area ahead as she walked away from her wagon, visions of wild savages with feathers in their hair filling her head, fear quickening her steps.

Moonlight lit her way to the spot she had noticed earlier. She went down on her knees, placed the tiny bundle in the small hollow at the base of the large rock, then gathered up nearby stones to seal off the opening. The smooth cold surfaces numbed her fingertips as she wedged the stones firmly in place.

There. It was done. She dusted off her hands and rose to her feet, then stood looking down at the rock, unable to simply walk away. "I wish you were here, Mother. You would know the right words to say." She sighed and closed her eyes. "Almighty God, this baby did not grow to know life on this earth. May it know eternal life with You. Amen."

There was a soft, rustling sound. Her heart lurched. She snatched up the pail and ran for her wagon.

"…that current is mighty swift."

"The rain has swollen the river, but we should make it across all right. If need be, we will lash the wagons together…"

Emma jerked to a halt. That was Zachary Thatcher talking with Axel Lundquist. He must be making his nightly round of the wagons. Had he discovered her missing? She frowned and headed toward the other end of her wagon. Zachary Thatcher was the last person she wanted to see at—

"Miss Allen…"

Too late. She turned. He was coming toward her, a scowl on his face. "You know the rules, Miss Allen. No one is to go off by themself at night. Especially a woman."

Emma lifted her chin. "Yes, I am aware of your rule, Mr. Thatcher, but—"

"There are no exceptions, Miss Allen." He glanced

down at the pail dangling from her hand and his scowl deepened. "You were dumping trash? Why didn't you do that with the others earlier, when it was safe?"

She clamped her jaw together and moved to the tailgate of her wagon. His hand closed on her arm, preventing her from climbing the steps—bringing back the memory of being in his arms.

"You cannot put the other members of this train in danger because of your whims, Miss Allen. From now on—"

She jerked her arm free and whirled about. "It was not a *whim* that took me off by myself, Mr. Thatcher, it was a *baby*. A tiny, little baby girl that will never know life because I could not save her! The least I could do was bury her." Her voice broke. She whipped back toward the tailgate. His hand closed on her arm again. She braced herself against his touch.

"If there is fault to be borne in this circumstance it is mine, Miss Allen." His deep voice flowed over her, bringing the tears she was struggling to hold back dangerously near to flowing. "I am the one who ordered the wagons to move on in spite of your warning as to the likely consequence. I am sorry for the outcome, but—"

"The fault is not yours, Mr. Thatcher." She turned and looked into his eyes. "As guide and leader of this wagon train, your task is to keep its members safe. You succeeded. As a doctor, my task is to preserve life. I failed."

"Miss Allen—"

She shook her head. "Please, do not say more." She

looked down at his hand still holding her arm and took a breath to steady her voice. "Please release me, Mr. Thatcher. I would like to retire."

He didn't move.

She stared at his hand, afraid to look at him, afraid to say more for fear the tears that were so close would escape her control. She willed herself to wait, to stay still, when everything within her yearned to step into his arms and cry out her despair in the one place she had felt safe since this wretched journey had begun.

His fingers flexed, lingered. She heard him draw in a quick breath, and then he released his hold.

Cold replaced the warmth where his hand had been, traveled deep inside her. She stepped to the water shelf and hung the pail on the hook on the underside hoping he would not notice the trembling in her hands. When she returned to the back of the wagon he was gone.

Emma gripped the sideboard of the wagon and stared at the roiling, foaming water in front of the oxen. The three fords of the swift-flowing water in the channels between the islands had been frightening. *This* was terrifying! She looked from Garth Lundquist, who was calming the nervous beasts, to the two wagons that had already made it through the maelstrom to the opposite bank of the river and sucked in a deep breath. William's wagon was well built and Garth Lundquist was an excellent driver. She would be safe. And Anne. *Please let Annie be safe.*

Wind flowed down off the surrounding mountains and whipped across the river valley, its cold breath stinging her face and hands. She drew her wool wrap closer about her shoulders, then wiped her clammy hands on her skirt. Her wagon was next.

She took another, firmer grip on the sideboard and watched the pantomime of motions as Zachary Thatcher spoke to Josiah Blake and John Hargrove. The wagons moved away from the riverbank, then, once again, Zachary Thatcher rode upstream and urged Comanche back into the river. The horse struggled against the strong current, his head bobbing on the water, his tail floating at a downstream angle from his body as they drifted diagonally toward the island. When they reached the solid ground at the upper point of the island, man and horse surged free of the water.

Emma focused her attention on the roan, and, less obviously, on his rider. Zachary Thatcher's belt encircled his neck and one broad shoulder, his holster rested high on his chest. His boots, pants and the lower half of his tunic were sodden. He leaned forward and stroked Comanche's neck, his mouth moving, his words swallowed by the roar of the rushing water. After a minute or two, he straightened in the saddle. Her stomach flopped. It was time. She faced front, her heart pounding.

Comanche's hoofs beat against the stony ground, drew closer. Zachary Thatcher rode by on the other side of the wagon and took up a position to the left front of the oxen. Garth Lundquist talked with him a moment, then nodded and ran back, climbed into the seat and took up his whip. He snapped it over the oxen's broad backs. Comanche plunged into the foaming water, the oxen lunging after him. The wagon lurched and rolled off the island, the roiling water swirling around the floorboards, washing up against the sides and splashing over the sideboard to soak her skirts. She gasped at the touch of the frigid water against her skin. Zachary Thatcher must be—

A rush of water hit them, swept over the oxen. The wagon quivered and slewed sideways. Zachary Thatcher urged Comanche close, plunged his hand into the water then straightened in the saddle, pulling the lead ox's head up out of the water by a horn. The beast lurched forward, the other oxen following. The wagon straightened, shook and shuddered, buffeted by the water. The old fear rose, clutching her throat, squeezing her chest.

The lead oxen's shoulders cleared the water, step by plodding step they rose slowly out of the water. They were through the maelstrom! They were safe.

She took a long, slow breath and released her death grip on the seat and sideboard as the wagon broke free from the sucking water and rolled up the sloping bank.

Zachary Thatcher waved them on toward the other wagons, then rode off upstream.

What a mess! Emma swept her gaze around the circled wagons. Women and children were carrying barrels, boxes and cloth bags of food stores, mattresses and bedding, chests, trunks and household items and clothes out of the wagons to dry. The canvas covers on several of the wagons were rolled up on the sides to let the wind blow through and perform the same service. The frosty wind that made wet or damp clothing torture. There would be colds and sore throats, frostbitten fingers and toes to treat from this day's work. Thank goodness William had purchased all those medical supplies.

She slid her gaze to her wagon, then brought it to rest on Anne's. Guilt nudged her. For no good reason. It was not their fault William had the wagon beds shiplapped and caulked so watertight the only place river water had oozed through was around the tailgate. It was their blessing. Still—

Lydia Hargrove chuckled. "Stop borrowin' trouble, and give these pots a stir, Emma. Making soup to feed everyone was a good idea, but the soup won't be any good lest you rile the pots every once in a while. Too bad we don't have one big enough pot!"

"How do you know I was 'borrowing trouble,' Lydia?" Emma smiled at the older woman. "Perhaps I was daydreaming."

"No, you was borrowin' trouble. You had your doctor face on."

"My *doctor* face? Gracious, I was not aware I had one! I shall have to be more careful." Emma laughed, lifted her arm to protect her face from the smoke and swirled the liquid in the pots with the wooden spoon. In spite of her precaution she got a strong whiff of smoke and started coughing.

Lydia Hargrove straightened from dividing the dried green beans young Amy had brought as the Fletchers' contribution among the four large iron pots hanging close over the flames and wiped the tears from her eyes. "It's sure tryin' to cook on a fire with the smoke blowing in your eyes an' makin' them smart so as to blind you."

"And while shivering so with the cold it's hard to hold

on to things." Olga Lundquist dipped a cup into the bag at her feet and scooped out rice to add to the pots.

"That is the reason for the soup, Olga. It will help warm everyone." Emma squinted her eyes against the smoke and leaned over to peer into the pots. "Should I get you more bacon?"

"No. You brought a good, generous chunk."

Emma nodded, pulled her wool wrap higher up around her neck and smiled at the young girl running toward them. "Hello, Susan."

"Hello, Dr. Emma. Ma sent some carrots, and Mrs. Applegate give me some onions to bring for the soup." Susan Fenton handed the small sacks of desiccated vegetables to Lydia Hargrove, then hunched her shoulders, wrapped her arms around herself and turned her back to the wind. "Ma says do you need me I can stay an' give ya a hand. She's sortin' through the stuff the water soaked to dry it out."

Lydia shook her head. "You go back and help your mother, Susan. We have already sorted out and repacked our wagons. It's—"

"Dr. Emma! Y' gotta come quick!" Nathan Fenton ran up and skidded to a stop beside the fire.

Emma's stomach flopped. She dropped the spoon and hurried toward him. "What is it?"

"Edward Swinton fell in the river. Mr. Thatcher got him out, but he's not wakin' up."

No! Not another child! Emma lifted her skirt hems and ran toward the river, Nathan running along beside her. *Please let him be alive, please—*

"Dr. Emma, help me!" Pamelia Swinton sat on the

ground beside the river, holding Edward and rocking to and fro and sobbing.

Emma dropped to her knees and reached for the little boy's wrist. A slow throb pulsed against her fingers. Too slow. His flesh was icy cold, his skin blue. *What should she do? How could she—*

"Thomas and Mr. Thatcher got the water out of him, but he—" Pamelia's voice choked "—he won't wake up. So they sent Nathan for you. Edward's dead, Dr. Emma! But they have to get the wagon out—The Indians—"

Emma grabbed Pamelia's shoulders and gave her a quick shake. "Stop it, Pamelia! Listen to me! Edward is *not* dead. He is only cold." *Too cold.* "We must get him *warm*. Help me get these wet clothes off him." She jerked the shoes and socks off Edward's small feet, started tugging at his sodden pants.

Pamelia released her hold on Edward and yanked at his shirt.

A whip cracked. Hoofs thumped the ground behind her. Edward's pants came off in her hands. Emma threw them on the ground, grabbed the hem of Pamelia's skirt and folded it up over Edward's legs and feet. "When you get Edward's shirt off, wrap him in this." She yanked off her wool wrap and dropped it beside Pamelia. "I will be right back." She stood and raced to the wagon being pulled up the riverbank. "Mr. Swinton, I need a blanket for your son. Hurry!"

The man looked down at her, turned and dived into the wagon.

She looked out at the river and froze. Zachary Thatcher was back in the water, swimming Comanche toward the stock bunched at the opposite riverbank waiting for the herders to start them across. She stared at the wet hair clinging to his bare head, the soaked tunic stretched across his broad shoulders and her heart trembled with fear for him. In this frosty wind… *Please*— She lifted her gaze upward, gasped. The plateau behind the herders was covered with Indians sitting their horses and watching. So many Indians. Hundreds of them. Watching. If they attacked while the men of the train were split by the river… While Zachary Thatcher was caught in between—

"Here!"

She shifted her gaze, caught the blanket Thomas Swinton threw her, stole another quick glance at Zachary Thatcher then ran back to Pamelia and Edward. She was a doctor. She could do nothing about the Indians or the weather or any of the other terrible, frightful hazards of this journey. But she might be able to save young Edward's life.

For how long?

Emma set her jaw, dropped to her knees. She wrapped the doubled blanket around Edward, took him into her arms and started up the slope. *For as long as I am alive to fight!*

Pamelia scrambled to her feet and reached for her son.

Emma shook her head. "I will carry him, Pamelia. Your gown is soaked from Edward's clothes, you will wet his blanket. Run ahead to the fire and dry your clothes before you take a chill." She glanced at Pamelia's face and firmed her voice. "Do not waste time in argument, Pamelia. Edward needs you well to care for him." Thought of the Indians watching from the plateau sent a shudder through her. A silent prayer rose from her heart. *Please, Almighty God, grant that it might be so.*

Chapter Fifteen

Emma propped her pillows against the sidewall, placed the lantern on the water keg and quickly withdrew her hand. Everything was cold to the touch! She snatched up the extra blanket and draped it around her shoulders, then lifted the covers and sat on the bed, tucking her dressing gown around her legs and pulling the covers over them. The toes of her stocking-clad feet ached from the chill of the floorboards. She wiggled them deep into the downy softness of the feather mattress and leaned back.

Cold air, radiating off the canvas, sent a shiver down her spine. She jerked forward, tugged the blanket around her shoulders higher around her neck and rested back against the pillows again. What would it be like when they reached those snowcapped elevations? It seemed every day's climb brought colder weather. And the days were growing shorter, the cold nights longer.

She frowned, picked up the lap desk and put it on her legs. She was beginning to understand why Mr. Thatcher had been pushing them so hard and fast. And why he found her an…annoyance. But she had to fight for what was best for her patients, even if that ran afoul of his wishes.

She looked down, absently ran her fingertip over the small scar on the desk, then sighed, blew on her cold hands, rubbed them together and lifted the top. The letters she had written since leaving Fort William stared up at her. Had her other letters reached home yet? Traveler was a strong, fast horse, and Mr. Broadman would not be slowed by traveling with a wagon train. How excited Mary would be to receive them. She smiled, arranged things to her satisfaction and dipped her pen.

My beloved family,
I pray this finds you all in good health. Anne is still withdrawn, but we are both well. The weather is deteriorating. Many of our fellow travelers have colds, coughs and sore throats from the wetting they received during our fording of the Snake River. I wrote you of that eventful day. Little Edward is recovered from his near drowning, though he must still be protected from the cold.

We passed Fort Boise today without stopping, as our path was a long, steady climb that took until nightfall to accomplish. Our camp is by the Powder River. The Indians that have been trailing us left us today as we approached the fort. There is great relief among us all.

Mr. Thatcher has been pushing us to greater effort than before. Not that we see him. He rides off at dawn to discover our path for the day and choose our next camp. Mr. Blake now makes the nightly rounds of the wagons and relays Mr. Thatcher's orders. We are approaching the Blue Mountains, and the air grows more chilly with every climb. Do not be concerned, Mother. I have my winter cape.

I would be remiss, William, if I did not tell you that your wagons are holding up admirably to the journey. Neither Anne nor I have been troubled with the need for repairs. And our wagons do not leak when fording the rivers, save for a little water coming in at the tailgate. That is a blessing that Caroline will be truly grateful for, should you continue to pursue your dream and someday make this journey. I warn you, it is arduous beyond belief! Yet, Anne and I fare well.

My dearest love to you all,

Emma

Emma slipped the letter back into the desk, corked the ink bottle and set the desk aside. She would take care of it tomorrow, when it was warmer.

She tugged the blanket off her shoulders, shivered at the rush of cold air and hurried to spread the blanket over the bedcovers. Her fingers prickled. She cupped them over the lantern chimney a moment, relishing the heat, then extinguished the flame and crawled under the covers, curling up in the warm spot where she had been sitting. Mr. Thatcher had no wagon. Where did he sleep? Most likely out in the open on the hard, cold ground.

He seemed impervious to things like weather and frigid water.

She frowned, burrowed her head deeper into the feather pillow and covered her exposed cheek and ear with the edge of the blanket. He had been thoroughly soaked diving in the river to rescue little Edward Swinton, yet, in spite of the biting wind, he had continued to work to get the stock and herders across safely. She had feared he would sicken, but he was working harder than ever. He no longer came near the wagons, but spent all his time in the saddle searching out their best route. Or was he roaming the mountains "free and unfettered"? And why should she care? It was good that someone should achieve their dream.

She yawned, turned her thoughts from Zachary Thatcher and determinedly focused them on her plans to travel on to Oregon City and take ship for home. Anne's injuries were healed and she neither needed nor wanted her now. There was no reason to stay....

The fatigue dragged at him. His legs felt wobbly as a newborn foal's. Zach mustered determination in place of his usual strength and slid the saddle from Comanche. Whatever was wrong with him was getting worse. Fear flashed through him. He scowled, tamped it down.

Maybe Miss Allen would have some medicine— something to make him feel better, stronger. He rested a moment, then removed the saddle blanket, draped his arms over Comanche's broad back and leaned against him trying to absorb his body heat. He couldn't go to Miss Allen. The woman would probably demand he stop the train and rest! He couldn't do that. There wasn't time. He could smell snow in the air.

The fear pounced again, stronger. He had to get these people out of these mountains before the snow started. He *had* to! Or they would die. He lifted his shaky hand and wiped a sheen of moisture from his forehead. At least the Indians had kept their part of the bargain he had struck with them and left when the train reached this valley. 'Course, that was not to say they wouldn't be back. A frown creased his forehead. He couldn't be sick! He had to fight his way through this weakness. Maybe if he rested…

"No rubdown tonight, boy." He took a breath to ease the growing tightness in his chest, coughed at the rush of cold air then winced at the stabbing chest pain the cough produced. Chills chased one another through him. He forced himself erect, stepped back and went to his knees.

Comanche tossed his head, gave a soft nicker.

Zach waved his hand in the air. "Go on, boy. Dismissed!" He reached for his bedroll. A fit of coughing took him. The pain in his chest stabbed deeper. He braced himself with his hands on the ground, hung his head and struggled to breathe. The moonlit earth whirled. *Give me strength, Lord. Help me. These people need me.* He dragged the saddle blanket to him, dropped onto it, grabbed the edge and rolled. It wasn't big enough to cover him, but it would have to do.

Comanche plodded close, lowered his head and snuffed. The horse's breath was warm on his face. And then there was only the darkness…

* * *

"Dr. Allen!" A heavy fist thumped the side of the wagon. *"You awake?"*

Emma dropped the lap desk, jerked upright and bumped her head on the lid of the chest. It slammed closed as she bolted to her feet. "I am coming!" She grabbed her wrap and shoved open the canvas flaps above the tailgate, stared down at Josiah Blake and Charley Karr. "What is it?"

"Somethin's wrong with Zach. We need you to come with us."

Her heart lurched. Bile surged into her throat. Charley Karr was leading a horse. She swallowed and nodded. "Lower the tailgate. I will get my bag." *Please, please let him be all right!* She whirled, grabbed the black leather satchel off the dresser, turned back and climbed from the wagon. "Where is he?"

"Up there." Josiah Blake gestured toward a small rise to the left of the circled wagons and started walking.

It was too far. What if they did not reach him in time? What if she were not a good enough doctor to help him? The thoughts tumbled through her head in time with the half-running steps she was taking to keep up with the men's long, determined strides. She looked at the horse and the rifles, at the men's grim faces and the bile surged again. *If a bear, or wolves, or—* "Has Mr. Thatcher been attacked by an animal? Do you have to kill—"

"His horse."

No! Horrid pictures flashed into her head. "Comanche is…injured?" *Could she help him?*

"No." Josiah Blake shot her a sidelong look. "The

fool animal won't let us near Zach. Just keeps circlin' him and gnashin' his teeth at us, like some mare with a colt. Ain't never seen anything like it! We gotta put him down to get to Zach."

"Oh, no, Mr. Blake! Mr. Thatcher would never want that."

The man's face tightened. "We got no choice."

Comanche has never let anyone but me touch him.

Until that day in the storm. Her pulse raced. "Let me go first, Mr. Blake." She shot him a pleading look. "Let me try to calm Comanche."

He stopped, faced her and shook his head. "No tellin' what that fool horse might do. He might come at y', Dr. Allen."

"I am not afraid of that, Mr. Blake. Please, for Mr. Thatcher's sake, let me try."

He frowned, rubbed his thumb back and forth on the rifle barrel. She held her breath. Finally, he nodded. "All right, Dr. Allen. We'll stay out of sight. But we'll be ready, should you need us. You'll see the horse when you get up top. Zach's on the ground beside him."

"Thank you, Mr. Blake." She took a deep breath and ran ahead. The climb was steeper than it appeared. She breasted the top of the rise and stopped, her heart leaping into her throat. Zachary Thatcher was sprawled on the ground, a horse blanket half covering him. Her body twitched with the desire to run to him. She made herself concentrate on the horse standing beside him. "Hello, Comanche. Remember me?" She started forward.

The roan tossed his head, thudded his hoof against the ground then trotted around his master.

She stopped. *Don't do this, Comanche! Please! Let me pass.* "You do not mean that, boy." She held her voice low and calm, took a slow step forward. "You know me." Comanche's ears flicked. Was that a good sign? She took another step. "And you know all I want is to help your master. I love him, too." She jolted to a stop, stunned by what she had said. Could that be *true?* Of course not. It was ridiculous. She pushed the thought aside and took another step. "Please, boy, let me help him." She stretched out her hand.

The roan gave a low whicker, tossed his head and stepped toward her. "Good boy, Comanche." She rubbed his silky muzzle, then rushed to Zachary Thatcher and dropped to her knees beside him. His wrist was cold, his pulse rapid but strong. She placed her hand on his forehead. Hot—in spite of the cold weather. A chill shook him. She jerked off her wrap to cover him, then spotted his bedroll a short distance away and jumped up to get it. One quick yank on the leather thongs and the groundsheet and blanket unrolled on the ground beside him. She dropped to her knees, reached over and gripped the front of his tunic and tugged with all her strength. On the third try, she rolled him onto the bedding.

He coughed, winced and opened his eyes. "Troops, *dismissed!*"

Comanche wheeled and thundered off.

The men ran up to stand beside her.

"Heard him yellin' about troops. He must be 'dreamin'"

She shook her head. "No, Mr. Karr, he is delirious." She grasped the edges of the bedding and covered him.

"I can do nothing more for him here. We must get him to my wagon."

"I'll get my horse."

Emma nodded, watched Charley Karr run to get his mount and sat back on her heels, holding back tears.

How would she get him warm? She had every blanket and quilt in the wagon piled on him, but he needed to be warm *now*. Emma jerked open the chest that held the linens, dropped to her knees and pawed through the piles of towels and sheets. There had to be a bed warmer…or a soapstone…or a—

A stone!

She bolted to her feet, glanced at Zachary Thatcher then scrambled over the red box and ducked through the canvas flaps onto the wagon seat. Josiah Blake was standing by the fire, talking with the men of the train. He looked at a loss. She cupped her hands around her mouth. *"Mr. Blake!"*

He looked up. There was something close to panic in his eyes. He ran to her wagon. "Is he…"

"He is the same, Mr. Blake. But I must get him warm. Please have some of the men gather flat stones and warm them in the fire, then bring them to me. And hurry!" She didn't wait for his answer. She turned and crawled back into the wagon, grabbed the iron teapot from her medical supplies in the box, added some herbs then closed the box, set the teapot down and placed a pile of towels beside it. *Please let it work—*

"Squad, right!" Zachary Thatcher jerked upright, coughed.

"Lie down, Mr. Thatcher! You must stay covered." Emma grabbed his shoulder.

"They're coming around our flank!" He shoved her hand away, tried to rise and fell back, his entire body shaking with a chill. He coughed, coughed again. His face went taut with pain. His eyes closed, and he went still.

She pulled the covers back over him, tucked them up around the sides of his head, his face hot against her hands. His breath wheezed from his lungs. She brushed the damp hair off his forehead and her doctor's mien crumbled. If only she had seen him during the past few days, she could have— Her breath caught. She stared down at him and pressed a hand against the sudden sick feeling in the pit of her stomach. Was that why he had not come around the wagons? Because he was ill and wanted to avoid *her?* Did he think that little of her skill? Or was it her personally he derided?

"Dr. Emma… I have stones for you. Ma had some at the edge of her fire."

Emma blinked tears from her eyes and turned back to peer out the front of the wagon, once more the doctor. "Please bring them up to the driver's seat, Matthew."

The young man hopped up onto the wagon tongue, leaned down and lifted a pailful of the heated flat rocks to the seat, then leaned down and lifted another.

"Thank you, Matthew." Emma dumped the stones out of the first pail onto the lid of the red box, tossed in the iron teapot and the bags of herbs and reached for the other pail. "I shall need more when these cool."

He nodded. "They're gatherin' 'em now. I'll bring

'em soon's they're hot." He grabbed the pails and hopped down.

"And Matthew, please tell your mother and Olga Lundquist I need some good, strong meat broth for Mr. Thatcher. And also, some summer savory and sage tea. The herbs are in the pail." Emma closed the flaps, covered one of the stones with a towel and carried it to the bed. She lifted the covers, tucked the wrapped stone next to Zachary Thatcher's shivering body and hurried back for the next one. *Please let this work. Please…*

The prayer rose in a continual stream from her heart as she concentrated on wrapping the heated rocks and placing them around Zachary Thatcher as quickly as possible, her ear tuned to the sound of the air whistling in and out of his lungs, his hard coughs and his feverish mutterings. She closed her mind to the word pressing against her will. Not even in her thoughts would she admit Zachary Thatcher had pneumonia. Or that it might already be too late to save him.

Chapter Sixteen

Emma glanced up at the sound of someone climbing to the wagon seat, caught a glimpse of Lydia Hargrove's face, then skirts being shaken into place. She smiled when Lydia poked her head through the opening of the canvas flaps.

"Here is the tea, Emma." She set the towel-wrapped iron teapot on the lid of the box and started to climb in.

"No, Lydia, do not come in!" Emma scurried from her place on the floor beside the bed to stop the woman from entering. "Mr. Thatcher is contagious, and I do not want you to sicken." She grasped the teapot and placed it on the top of the dresser out of the direct draft. "Thank you for making the tea so quickly, Lydia." She poured a bit of the hot liquid into a cup.

"It's little enough to do. The broth is cooking." Lydia glanced at Zachary Thatcher. "How is he?"

Emma hesitated, then took a breath and shook her head. She could not lie. "He's not well."

"His breathing sounds labored."

"Yes."

Lydia fastened her gaze on her. "He looks fevered."

Do not make me say it, Lydia! She nodded, went to her knees on the floor and set the cup down to lift Zachary Thatcher's head and shoulders. He was too heavy for her. She could not hold him *and* the cup. Tears smarted at the backs of her eyes. She bit her lip to keep them from flowing, and tried again. Fabric rustled. Lydia Hargrove's skirts appeared, ballooned out as the woman knelt beside her and slipped her arm beneath Zachary's raised head and shoulders. "I'll hold him. You give him the tea."

Emma shot her a grateful look, grabbed the cup and raised it to Zachary Thatcher's mouth. He turned his head away, rolled it side to side. "Draw sabers!" He jerked his arm from beneath the covers, raised it. "Charge!" His arm dropped to the bed, and he went limp.

She touched the cup to his mouth again. "Drink this, Mr. Thatcher. It will help your cough and your fever." There was no response. She tipped the cup so the tea touched his parched lips. They parted. She poured a little of the liquid in his mouth and he swallowed, then swallowed again, and again. He burst into a fit of coughing, grabbed at his chest. "Lift him higher, Lydia!" She put down the cup and rubbed his back as Lydia raised his shoulders. When the paroxysm passed, she fluffed his pillow, piled the extra pillow on top of it and they lowered him to rest against them. He was shaking with chills. She tucked his arm back under the covers and pulled them up close around his head.

"How long has he been like this?"

Emma looked at Lydia, then averted her gaze. Knowledge of Mr. Thatcher's dire condition was in the woman's eyes. "I cannot say. He was like this when they found him this morning." She rose, stepped to the keg and ladled some of the cold water into the wash bowl.

"Fool man! Why didn't he come get help when he come down sick?"

Because of me. The pain stabbed deep. She had fought him for her patients' sakes, and because of that Zachary Thatcher was…was— Emma swallowed hard, tossed a cloth in the water, wrung it out and folded it. Fortunately, judging from the tone of her voice, and the look of disgust on her face, Lydia was not expecting an answer. She fixed her professional doctor's expression on her face and carried the cloth to the bed and laid it on Zachary Thatcher's forehead. He muttered something unintelligible and turned away.

"Ain't a man born got the brains God give a goose when it comes to takin' care of hisself!" Lydia frowned down at Zachary Thatcher, then lifted her gaze. "I expect that's why God made us women. Though it sure is worryin' for us."

It is indeed.

"I'd best be gettin' back to help Olga with the broth an' such." Lydia fixed an assessing gaze on her. "We'll send along some good, nourishing soup an' biscuits for you. You're lookin' a mite peaked." She rose and stepped to the red box.

"Lydia…" The woman looked back at her. "My Papa Doc taught me to always wash my hands when I left a patient. He said it keeps the illness from spreading."

She smiled at the older woman. "Thank you for your help. You will find soap and hand balm beside the washbowl."

The day passed in a blur of worry and work. Emma wrapped heated stones, coaxed spoonfuls of soup and swallows of tea into Zachary Thatcher and searched her memory for every tiny crumb of information Papa Doc had given her on treating someone with his disease.

She remembered Papa Doc's story of how he had discovered the benefit of fresh air for the patient with straining lungs while he had been caring for the then Laina Brighton, and dived into the dresser to find her Augusta spencer in bottle-green velvet. She put the short jacket on beneath her doctor's coat, tucked the covers more snugly around Zachary Thatcher and opened the canvas flaps a bit to let the brisk September air blow through the wagon.

She folded her extra sheets into a bundle, enlisted Matthew's help to lift Zachary Thatcher's head and shoulders, and slipped the bundled sheets beneath his pillows to further elevate his torso and stretch his chest to aid the expansion of his lungs.

Nothing helped. In spite of all she did, Zachary Thatcher's condition worsened. During the night his fever climbed. His cough deepened. His chills became so severe they shook his entire body, and his lungs rasped and wheezed with his efforts to breathe.

She tried to maintain a professional detachment, but with every passing minute her fear increased. She was losing the battle. Zachary Thatcher could die, and it would be her fault. She was the reason he was so sick, and she was not a good enough doctor to save him. Guilt warred with reason. Fear undermined determination. And finally, tears overcame her will. She buried her face in her hands and sobbed out her misery. "Oh, Papa Doc, I wish you were here! If only you were *here*."

We are doctors, Emma…not God. Never forget that. And never fail to pray for your patients.

Anger shook her. She jerked her head up and swiped the tears from her cheeks. "I *prayed* for Annie's baby, Papa Doc. I did! I begged God to let her live, but she died. Little baby Grace died in my arms! And I prayed Caroline would get well so William could have his dream of coming to Oregon country. I prayed and prayed, but she did not. I prayed Annie would get over her grief. She has not! I—"

Trust Me.

The words rang through her spirit. Emma caught her breath, clenched her hands and stared at the canvas arching over her head. "No, God. Not anymore. I am afraid to trust You."

Zachary Thatcher coughed, coughed again. He arched his back, his lungs struggling to draw in air, then went limp.

She leaned over him, clutched his shoulders and gave them a violent shake. "Mr. Thatcher! Mr. Thatcher, *breathe!*" Her lungs strained to suck in life-giving air for him. His remained silent, deflated. Panic took her. She collapsed to her knees, sobbing into her hands. "Oh, Heavenly Father, there is nothing more I can do. You are the source of life. Please…*please* breathe for him…"

A soft, rasping whistle broke the silence. It was the most beautiful sound she had ever heard. She held her breath, listened. It came again. She lifted her trembling hand and placed it on Zachary Thatcher's blanket-covered chest, felt the slight rise and fall as his lungs filled to their impaired capacity then emptied. She did not know if it were answered prayer or mere coincidence. But she knew what William and their mother and Papa Doc would say…and do. She closed her eyes, allowed her heart to open to her shattered faith. "Thank You, Heavenly Father. Thank You." Peace washed over her. A peace she had not felt since she turned away from God in anger.

She stayed there a few minutes watching Zachary Thatcher breathe, then lifted the cloth from his forehead and wiped the sheen of sweat off his face. His skin was cooler against her hand. His shivering abated. She studied his face. He was sleeping normally. The crisis was over.

If a patient with pneumonia survives the crisis, it is most likely that, with proper care, he will live.

With proper care. She would see to that…somehow. In spite of Zachary Thatcher's disdainful feelings toward her. She rose on her shaky legs and stepped to the front of the wagon to tell the others she would need no more heated stones. Dawn was lightening the eastern sky.

Emma shifted the pail to her other hand and made herself slow her steps. Lydia was with him. He was sleeping normally. He would be all right. Unless he did something foolish and caused a relapse.

She sighed and smoothed the tabs at the hem of the spencer over her knotted stomach as she started up the rise. This urgent need to be with Zachary Thatcher, to reassure herself he was still alive and on the mend, was foolishness. But it had been such a close thing she still could not believe it. And telling herself it was so did not help. But her feelings and needs were not important. The best thing she could do for Zachary Thatcher right now was to take care of Comanche.

She smiled and looked down at the pail as she crested the low hill. How fortunate that William loved oatmeal with honey for his morning meal. She had found a large bag of rolled oats and a sealed crock of honey among the food stores in Annie's wagon. Comanche should—

A low nicker greeted her. She looked up, relief making her knees go weak. She had not realized until that moment how afraid she was that the horse would not have returned. "Hello, Comanche. I brought you a treat." She held out the pail.

The horse stretched his neck, snuffed then drew back and tossed his head.

"Ah, so you want to be coaxed, is that it?" Emma laughed and tipped the bucket toward him. "You know you want the oats and honey. You might as well give in."

The roan snuffed, drew his head back and thudded his hoof against the ground.

"Hmm, stubborn are you? All right. I will set the bucket down. But I will not go away." She placed the pail on the ground at her feet. "If you want the treat, you must come get it."

The horse jabbed his nose toward her, then stepped back, dragging his feet.

"I know…you want me to leave, but I am staying right here." She sobered. "You cannot outwait me, Comanche. You are too important to your master. You might as well make friends."

The horse flicked his ears, took a step forward.

"Good boy, Comanche." She kept her voice low, confident. "Take another step."

The roan stepped toward her, stuck out his head and snuffed at the bucket.

She stood perfectly still.

He stuck his nose in the pail, then lifted his head and crunched the mouthful of sweetened oats. A minute later, he shoved his nose back in the bucket.

"Good boy, Comanche." Emma lifted her hand and stroked the horse's hard, heavily muscled shoulder. His flesh rippled beneath her hand, but he did not move away. She slid her hand up. "You have got tangles in your mane." She scratched beneath the long, thick hair, then ran her fingers through it. Comanche crunched on. She smiled and began finger-combing out the snarls.

Zach came awake, his heart pounding. Something was wrong. He felt as weak as a new fawn. He stayed perfectly still, listening, smelling, assessing his situation before he moved. Had he been wounded? He mentally searched his body for pain, found nothing but the incredible weakness. And thirst. His mouth felt dry as dust, and his body was screaming for a drink of water. He ignored the need. The greater need was to know what had happened to him. Where he was.

There was a hint of golden light against his eyelids. A lantern turned down low? So it was night. A soft breathing to his right alerted him to the fact he was not alone. He pressed his fingers down slightly, expecting hard earth, finding a yielding softness. Soft weight held him in a cocoon of warmth. Where was he? Wind moaned. There was a sound of fabric rippling. He inched his hand to the side beneath the warm weight, found cold wood. Floorboards? He was in a wagon. Whose? And how had he gotten here?

Zach opened his eyes a slit, waited. When they had adjusted to the dim lantern light he slid his gaze to the right. His heart jolted. Emma Allen was sitting on the wagon floor, leaning against a pillow that was propped against a dresser. She was wrapped in a quilt, only her head showing. Her long lashes lay like smudges against her skin. Her lips were parted slightly in slumber, and tresses of her hair trailed along her cheek and curled onto the quilt. Emma Allen. *Doctor* Emma Allen. Memory flashed. Yes. He had been sick. *Very* sick. That would explain the weakness. And the tiredness. And the doctor. And— It was *her* wagon! He should not be here. Did the woman give no thought to her reputation?

Zach scowled, considered waking her, but the exhaustion overrode his need for answers. Tomorrow would be soon enough. For now he would go to his camp. He shoved against the floorboards, found no strength in his arms. He lifted his head, tried again. The effort exhausted him. He dropped back against the downy pillows and closed his eyes to rest and gather strength for another try.

Emma took another peek from under her lashes. Zachary Thatcher had succumbed. His eyes were closed, his face relaxed. The rise and fall of his chest under the blankets was slow and even. The weakness from the pneumonia had defeated him. He was fast asleep.

She frowned and fully opened her eyes to study him. What was the man thinking, trying to get up and leave? In the cold of the night? To go where? Back to his camp to roll up in a horse blanket? He could relapse and die. Why would he do such a thing? Was his desire to avoid her that strong?

Hurt washed over her. She called up anger to fight it. Zachary Thatcher was an arrogant, stubborn, ungrateful man! Yet her fingers itched to touch him, to take his pulse, to feel his forehead and be certain he was all right. Perhaps that made her a good doctor, but it also made her a very foolish woman.

Chapter Seventeen

Emma had not stomped her foot since she was a very young girl, but she was close to doing so now. She looked at Lydia Hargrove for support, read the "let it be, they will not listen" look in her eyes and took a calming breath. "Mr. Thatcher, you are not a well man. You need rest and—"

"And this wagon train needs to get moving." His voice was quiet, implacable. But not nearly as strong as normal.

She watched him set his breakfast plate aside and stand, did not miss the shiver he tried to hide, nor his careful movements that betrayed his weakened state. At least there was no sign of recurring fever. She clenched her hands at her sides to keep from placing one on his forehead to be sure. She looked at his set jaw and turned to the others. "Mr. Hargrove, you are the leader of this wagon train. You can order—"

"Thatcher has full say. And he is right. The train has to keep moving. We've already lost a full day's travel and more." The older man gave her a piercing look. "You don't understand the importance of our decision, Miss Allen, and—"

"Mr. Hargrove, I fully understand the import of your decision." She looked straight into the portly man's deep-set eyes. "It is you, sir, who do not understand. Tell me—" she swept her gaze over Joshia Blake, Charley Karr and back to John Hargrove "—who is going to lead us out of these mountains if Mr. Thatcher has a relapse and dies? Do any of you know the path we must take to reach Oregon country?"

She swallowed back the lump of anger rising to clog her throat and looked at the subject of her fear. There was no sign of yielding. "Will you at least wear a coat and do all in your power to keep yourself from taking a further chill, Mr. Thatcher?" She jutted her chin in the air. "I assume you have a coat as you are so concerned about the snows in the mountains! I can only hope your concern for the welfare of these people lends itself to your deigning to obey my instructions that far!"

She pivoted on her heel and stormed off toward her wagon, too furious, worried and afraid for Zachary Thatcher to watch him leave camp.

Zach guided Comanche through the stand of pitch and spruce pine at the foot of the hill, choosing the best path for the following wagons, snapping off branches to point the way when he changed direction. The wagons would have a hard time of it coming down that steep descent. It had taken all his strength to stay upright in the saddle. He rode out into the open, shivered as the air sinking off the mountains touched his neck with its icy fingers and chased down his spine.

He reached up and pulled the collar of his sheepskin-lined buckskin coat higher. He hated to admit it, but Miss Allen was right. He was not well. He was still weak and easily chilled. He frowned and tugged his shrunken hat down lower on his forehead. His body had betrayed him. He had figured he would get stronger as the day wore on, the way he always did. The opposite was true. Fatigue such as he had never known pulled at him. He found himself slumping in the saddle. But the air smelled of snow. He had no choice but to push on. If the wagons were caught here in the mountains…

Who is going to lead us out of these mountains if Mr. Thatcher has a relapse and dies?

Zach deepened his frown to a scowl. Emma Allen had struck straight at the heart of the matter. The choices were the same as always—stop and rest for her patient's sake, or push on. But this time there was a huge difference. *He* was the recovering patient. And if she was right and he sickened and—

Zach gave his head a sharp shake, glared up at the darkening, overcast sky. He wouldn't die. He couldn't. These people's lives depended on his staying alive. He leaned forward and patted Comanche's neck, shifted his gaze to the lofty snowcapped heights that surrounded the circular Grande Ronde plain. There was not time enough to continue on today. Those mountains were the worst of the journey. They would likely have to double the teams to haul the wagons up, maybe use block and tackle…and again to hold them back on the steep descents. As weary and worn as the animals were, that forced rest because of his illness might have been a fortuitous thing. And an early stop tonight would help, as well.

He straightened in the saddle and glanced around. There was dried grass and a good mountain stream for water. Plenty of large timber for wood. They could camp here tonight and make the long climb out of the plain tomorrow when the animals were fresh off a night's rest. When he had rested.

He scanned the surrounding mountain walls, found what he was looking for and urged Comanche forward.

The spot was perfect. The stone curved along the narrow ledge, providing protection from the worst of the wind. He glanced up at the slight overhang above him. It was deep enough to shield him from falling snow if he crowded his bed close against the rock wall. He turned in the saddle and looked out over the basin below. There was a clear view of the entire area, he would be able to see if trouble threatened. If the Blackfeet returned.

A flash of white through the cluster of pines on his back trail caught his eye. Josiah Blake rode into view, followed by the first wagon. Zach gave a shrill whistle, waited until Blake spotted him on the ledge, then stood in his saddle, lifted his arm and circled his hand over his head. Blake turned toward the following wagons and repeated the signal. The first wagon entered the plain and swung out to the right.

Blake could handle things now. Zach urged Comanche over to the rock wall and slipped from the saddle. He removed his gear, brushed the saddle blanket over

Comanche, then stood back and slapped the spots on the horse's rump. "All right, boy, our work is done. Dismissed!"

The horse tossed his head, nudged him in the chest and trotted off. Zach dropped to his knees, yanked the ties and spread out his bedroll. He would rest until the wagons were circled and the herd massed. Time enough then to go down and set the guards in place for the night. He placed the extra blanket he had taken from the supply wagon on top of his groundsheet and stretched out on it, grateful for the added barrier it provided between him and the cold stone. The other blanket brought a warm comfort to his chilled legs.

He closed his eyes, let his mind drift. That feather mattress had sure been warm and comforting last night, not like the stone beneath him now… He shifted his weight, tugged the hatchet at his belt out from under him. Not as comforting as Emma Allen's hand on his forehead though. Or the quiet prayer for his healing she had been whispering. She certainly had soft hands. And a gentle touch. He hadn't wanted her to move her hand. Had stayed still, barely breathing, until she moved away. A man could get used to that kind of thing. And to the soft yielding of her lips beneath his, the way she felt in his arms…

A gust of wind whipped around the stone barrier, picked up dust and dirt off the ledge and swirled it through the air. He frowned, tugged the collar of his coat higher around his ears. That kiss had been a mistake. A big mistake. He had thought it would satisfy him to hold her, kiss her. Instead it had made it worse. Emma

Allen was a woman from a wealthy family who had stated her desire to return to the pampered life she had always known. And she was a doctor. She cared for all her patients. He'd seen that. The gentleness in her touch meant nothing special. Nothing at all. Nor did he want it to. He wanted no ties to her or any other woman. He had valleys to roam and mountains to explore. Still…

He scowled, rejecting the thought, tried to summon a vision of the valley where he wanted to build his trading post. But all he could see was the look of hurt and anger in Emma Allen's eyes when he had refused to rest as she advised. He had no need to worry about an entanglement with her. She wanted no part of him. But all the same, he'd never seen such beautiful eyes…

Every ridge had gotten higher, steeper and more difficult to climb, every chasm deeper and more frightening to descend. And the trees! So many trees the men had to cut a way through them. But it was over now. Emma donned her blue wool cape, climbed from her wagon and walked toward the group gathered around the fire by the head wagon. Zachary Thatcher was there. She had seen his tall, gaunt frame from her wagon. He had lost weight since his illness. He should—

She frowned, broke off the thought, ignored the worry and fear that haunted her for him. Zachary Thatcher did not want her advice…or anything to do with her. He had made that abundantly clear. And in a few more days he would be out of her life forever. If he accepted her offer to take Anne to the Banning Mission and then escort her on to Oregon City.

That sick, hollow feeling struck the pit of her stomach again. She paused, took a deep breath, and then another to gain control. It would not do to let her emotions show. The last thing she wanted was for Zachary Thatcher to guess how she felt about him. What was wrong with her anyway? Why was she so foolish, always desiring what she could not have? And why should she care so deeply about someone so arrogant, so… So competent and brave. And right.

She looked up at the falling snowflakes, sparkling like diamonds in the moonlight. If he had agreed and halted the wagons for the quarantine, or the other times she had asked, this snow would have caught them deep in the mountains. And she knew now how terrible and costly that could have been. The snow and ice on these dreadful, twisting trails was dangerous. But deep drifts in those narrow gaps would have trapped them…

She shuddered, started walking again. It did not matter now. Soon they would make the last mountainous descent to the Columbia River Valley. Then the emigrants had only to choose the place where they would begin building their town. She and Annie would travel on. Annie to the Banning Mission, and she to Oregon City to board a ship for home. Tears stung her eyes. She would miss these people she had grown so close to over the past months. The hardships they had endured together had formed a closeness she had never known in her friendships at home. Lydia and Pamelia and Olga and Lorna and— She would never see little Jenny and Edward or the other children grow. She would never know if Pamelia's baby—

She stopped again, blinked the tears from her eyes. She must focus her thoughts on family and home. But they seemed so far away... And Annie would be here. And if William brought his family to Oregon country next year, she would be on one of Uncle Justin's ships docking at Philadelphia when he was starting out from St. Louis. She would not see him, or Caroline or their baby if— *Please, Heavenly Father, let William's baby live. And please watch over these people. Please keep them safe and—*

"Dr. Emma! Joseph was about to come fetch you. Come join us."

Dr. Emma. She would never be called that again. She looked across the remaining distance at Lydia, swallowed the lump in her throat and hurried to the fire, automatically scanning faces for signs of illness, looking for any visible injury. "Is there a problem?"

"Yes." John Hargrove cleared his throat, glanced around the people assembled then fixed his gaze on her. "We have been discussing our new town and the needs—"

"Fire that bullet straight, Hargrove—'for the target in yer sights gets away!'"

There was a roar of laughter at Axel Lundquist's taunt. Emma shot a glance at him. The grizzled farmer winked. She stiffened, shocked to her toes. She looked at Lorna Lewis who wore a huge grin. And Pamelia—

"We have taken a vote, Miss Allen, and—"

"Oh, for goodness sake, John! We want you to stay and be our doctor, Emma! The men will all help build you a cabin. And our boys will keep you supplied with

firewood. We'll all share our garden bounty with you."
Lydia rushed around the fire to her. "Will you?"

Emma stared, her mouth gaping open. Then all of the
women were crowding around her, urging her to say yes.
She looked from their anxious faces to the men. Axel
Lundquist winked again and nodded. Joseph Lewis gave
a sheepish nod. Thomas Swinton actually smiled and
nodded. And the others—they had voted for her to stay.
Her heart swelled. She kept her gaze from straying to
Zachary Thatcher. He had no part in this request, or her
decision. He would be off roaming the mountains…free
and unfettered. That thought stole her elation.

"We should like an answer, Miss Allen."

Emma looked over at John Hargrove, took in his
frown. Poor Mr. Hargrove, obviously he disapproved.
But the others… She cleared her throat and nodded.
"Yes. My answer is *yes*."

"I told them you would!" Lydia gave the other women
a smug smile. "They were afraid you would say no, seein'
as how we haven't much to offer you." The women, who
had stood silent and staring, broke into speech.

"Hush, ladies! We have business to conduct." John
Hargrove glared across the fire at them. "Your chatter-
ing will keep us all standing out here in this snow! Now
then—" He turned toward the men. "Thatcher, we can't
offer much by way of recompense, but we want you to
stay on, as well."

Hope surged in her, vibrant, intense, unbidden. Emma
caught her breath, lifted her hand beneath her cape and
pressed it against the sudden, wild throbbing at the base
of her throat. She turned and looked Zachary Thatcher's

way. He turned his head. Their gazes met. She lifted her chin and turned away for fear he could read her desire that he stay in her eyes.

"—At least until we get the town built up and are settled in. You know how to deal with Indians. And we'll need your skills to lead hunting parties. We're running low on supplies."

"I appreciate the offer, Hargrove. But my job was to bring you to Oregon country. I'll be moving on."

His deep, rich voice killed her hope. She lowered her hand to press against that sick, emptiness in her stomach, looked at the women and forced a smile. "If you will excuse me, ladies, I want to go tell Anne what has happened." She hurried away, refusing to let her emotions overcome her.

Chapter Eighteen

My dearest William, Mother and Papa Doc,
I write exciting news. We have arrived in Oregon
country! I confess there were times I did not
believe we would make it here as the journey
is fraught with dangers, not the least of which
is making almost perpendicular, snow-and-ice-
covered ascents and descents such as we experienced on our last days in the Blue Mountains.
At Mr. Thatcher's direction, the men hitched up
extra teams and used block and tackle attached to
trees to help the poor teams that were struggling
to maintain their footing haul the wagons uphill,
then slowly played out the rope to keep the wagons
from sliding forward and overrunning the teams
going downhill. It was harrowing and frightful,
especially when there were no trees near. The men
would then hitch teams to the back of the wagons,
and, often, themselves grasp hold of the ropes to
hold the wagons back. It was very treacherous footing and many took hard falls, including the women

and children, who, of course, could not ride in the wagons because of the danger. Hannah Fletcher fell and broke her wrist. Thankfully, the break was in a fortuitous position and I was able to splint it.

I can never adequately thank you, dearest William, for the medical supplies you provided. Or for praying for me. God has heard and answered your prayers. The emigrants have asked me to stay with them and be their doctor! My dream is coming true, as you said it would. I believe the Lord will bless you and make your dream come true, as well.

We are encamped by a river at the base of the Blue Mountains on a range of small, low hills covered with a growth the farmers among us call bunchgrass. They say it will provide excellent grazing and help the weary, trail-worn animals quickly regain their strength. Beyond these hills, as far as the eye can reach, are plains and mountains. Timber, well suited for building, is in abundance on the mountains. Mr. Hargrove says many back East are desirous of moving West and a town situated to "welcome" them to Oregon country will prosper. The women simply want to have this journey end. Several of the men are exploring today in hopes of finding the most advantageous location for our town. Wherever the town is placed, its name will be Promise.

Anne does not wish to tarry until the town's location is settled. Mr. Thatcher, too, has no desire

to stay with our company. He will take Anne on to
the Banning Mission. I shall miss her.

Emma stared down at the words, blinked to clear her
vision. And Mr. Thatcher. She would miss Zachary
Thatcher. She took a deep breath against the heaviness
in her chest, wiped the nib, stoppered the inkwell and
set aside the lap desk. It was time. But she had promised
Anne...

She rose and climbed from the wagon, brushed the
hair back from her face, shook the long skirt of her red
wool gown in place and looked toward her adopted sister's wagon. Anne was on the driver's seat facing straight
ahead, her slender frame draped in her black widow's
garb. Zachary Thatcher was hitching Comanche to the
rear of the wagon. She lifted her chin, turned and started
up the low rise behind her wagon. She had promised
Anne she would not come and say goodbye, but she
would not simply let her ride away.

The sound of mules braying and wagon wheels rum-
bling spurred her on. She reached the top of the rise
and turned. Zachary Thatcher sat beside Anne, the
reins held in his hands. Hands that had once held hers.
She swiped at her tears, wrapped her arms about her
torso and watched the man who held her heart drive her
adopted sister away. She watched until the hills hid them
from her sight, and then she turned and started back
down the hill, a horrible empty ache where her heart
had been.

"Look what I found, Dr. Emma!"

She started out of her thoughts, looked down at

David's pudgy hand and forced a smile. "What a lovely stone, David."

"Yeah, it looks kinda like a heart." His hand lifted. "You c'n have it, Dr. Emma. I'll find another one." He thrust it into her hand and raced off.

Emma opened her hand, looked down. A stone heart to replace the one she had lost. She lifted her gaze to David, who now squatted beside his brother, examining something on the ground in front of them. *Dr. Emma.* She was a doctor. Her dream had come true. It was enough. She would *make* it enough. She blinked, blew out a long breath and continued down the hill.

Emma pulled the desk onto her lap and unstopped the well. She had to hurry now. The men would be leaving soon. She kept her gaze from the words she had already written, dipped the pen in the ink and continued the letter.

I have learned much and, I pray, gained wisdom on this long, grueling journey. I believe I am the stronger for it. I know my faith has grown. How could it be otherwise? God has answered my prayer to be a doctor in a way I could not imagine.

A few of the men are going to ride to Fort Walla Walla and there hire Indians with canoes to take them down the Columbia River to Oregon City for needed supplies. They will carry with them my small bundle of letters to send on their way to you. I wonder often if Mr. Broadman carried my first bundle of letters safely to St. Louis. I hope that my letters have reached you and that Traveler is safe and well and waiting for you, dear William, at cousin Mary's. Shall I confess to you the terrible selfishness I have discovered in my heart? Having made this long, punishing journey, and thus being well acquainted with the deprivations and dangers thereof, my heart still longs for you to come to Oregon country next year. I do not, for one moment, wish you or yours harm, and my best advice would be that you stay home. But, what joy it would give me to see you again!

Now I must close for the men are ready to leave. I pray one of Uncle Justin's ships will have reached port during our long journey and there will be letters from you all waiting for me. My heart aches with loneliness for all of you. I long to receive news of you.

My dearest love always,
Your Emma

Emma addressed the letter, affixed the wax seal and placed it with the others. A length of narrow blue ribbon from the dresser tied them into a neat bundle. All was now ready for the men's departure. She placed the lap desk back in the chest and climbed from the wagon.

Controlled chaos greeted her. Once again, the women were taking advantage of the day off from traveling to clean their wagons, their clothes and bedding. Washtubs steamed over fires strung out along the river. Furnishings, clothing and food supplies littered the area around each wagon.

Except for hers.

She glanced at her wagon and an odd sort of dissatisfaction, a sensation she had never before experienced, gripped her. The extent of her cleaning was the quilt and blankets she had hung out to air over the boxes, crates and barrels of supplies off-loaded from Anne's wagon and stacked in the driver's box. A woman alone did not require the prodigious amounts of supplies and possessions that cluttered and crowded the wagons of those with a family. A woman alone did not make a mess. And a woman such as she did not know how to clean, or cook, or do the wash or any of the other myriad tasks these other women, some much younger than she, did so effortlessly.

She frowned, wrapped her arms about herself and stared at the other women. She had agreed to stay and be the doctor in their town. And she was alone. She had better learn how to take care of herself. Because, other than her doctoring and shooting skills, she was useless here on the frontier.

I will observe, or I will ask. I may be a pampered woman, but I am not unintelligent, only untaught in these matters. And I will rectify that very quickly.

The words she had spoken to Zachary Thatcher the night he had pointed out her ineptitude for life on the wilderness journey brought a flush to her cheeks. They were brave, challenging, *empty* words. She had not tried to learn the skills she needed for survival on the journey or here in Oregon country. She had merely paid others to care for her and Anne, the same as the servants at home had done for them all their lives. No wonder Zachary Thatcher found her worthy of…of disdain.

Emma squared her shoulders and scanned the women. Zachary Thatcher was out of her life, but she still had her pride! And a need to survive. *Cooking first!* As soon as she gave her letters to Josiah Blake she would go to Lydia and ask her to teach her.

Zach tightened his grip on the reins of the packhorse he was leading and urged Comanche to a faster walk. He wanted to be out of these rolling hills and into the Blue Mountains before nightfall.

He topped a rise and scanned the surrounding area, searching for the wagon train as Comanche crossed the elevation. He didn't want to come upon them accidentally. He had made a clean break and he wanted to keep it that way. His last job was done. He had escorted Anne Simms to the Banning Mission four days ago. There was no need for further involvement with the emigrants. He had his fee and his bonus money, less what he had spent on supplies for wintering in the mountains. He was free. And he intended to stay that way.

There was no sign of the wagons. He stopped Comanche, took a closer look around. Nothing. A thread of worry wormed its way into his thoughts. He had told them to keep close by the river. Of course, they could have followed the north branch. Perhaps he should ride over that way and—

No. The emigrants were no longer his concern. Not… any of them.

Zach frowned, forced the image of Emma Allen from

his mind and guided Comanche on a straight path to the thick growth of pine at the base of the mountains. There was no need for caution now, and he had no time to waste. If he pushed forward every minute of daylight of every day, he could reach the valley where he wanted to build his trading post before the blizzards started.

He slowed Comanche, peered into the dusky light beneath the trees then ducked beneath a feathery branch and began to wend his way up the wall of mountain. He had it all planned. He and the horses would live in that huge cavern he had found. And he would spend the winter cutting down trees and trimming and notching logs. In the spring he would start building…

Emma poured the saleratus into the palm of her hand, dumped it onto the flour in the crockery bowl, stirred it in and added a wooden spoonful of lard. "Tonight, Lydia, my biscuits will be as light and fluffy as yours."

"Not if you use that spoon. You work the dough over-much."

"Is that what I am doing wrong?" Emma dropped the spoon on top of an upturned barrel serving as a "table," lightly fingered the mixture until the lard was well distributed then added a small amount of potato water to make it all hold together.

A cloud of smoke rose from the stone-encircled fire and made her nose burn. She wiped her tearing eyes with the back of her hand, scooped up some dough and gently patted it into a circle. She would need eight of them to fill the spider she had greased with lard. "Do you expect Matthew and Charley with a load of logs for your house tonight? Or are they staying on the mountain to fell trees with the others?"

"They'll stay the night." Lydia carried her filled spider to the fire, grabbed the small iron rake and pulled a pile of hot coals forward. She sat the spider over half of them, and used the rest to cover the rimmed lid. When she finished she stepped back and fanned her heat-reddened face with the long skirt of her apron.

Emma lifted her gaze to the Blue Mountains, raised it to the snow-whitened pinnacles. Was he up there? Alone? Was he ill or injured or— Her finger poked a hole in the last biscuit. She pushed the edges together and put it in the spider, carried the heavy, iron frying pan to the fire and put the coals under it and on the lid to start the biscuits baking.

"Here's more wood fer your fire, Mrs. Hargrove. Mrs. Lundquist and Ma have got all they need." Daniel Fletcher grinned and dumped a bucket of large wood chunks on their already big pile. "Ma says Pa and Josh are choppin' the notches out of the logs fer houses so fast she an' Mary an' Amy are gettin' buried by 'em!" The young boy's chest swelled. "Pa and Josh let me help."

"Well we need every hand if we're to get our homes built before winter sets in."

The boy nodded. "Pa says it don't take long to get the houses up when everyone helps. I got to get back to work!" He ran off.

Emma stared after him, listening to the sound of the bucket bumping against his leg as he ran, of axes biting deep into wood. Was Mr. Thatcher close enough to hear the men cutting down trees? Or was he already high in the mountains on his way to his valley? The memory of those treacherous ice-covered slopes lifted her gaze toward the sky. *Please keep Mr. Thatcher safe, Almighty God. Please keep him healthy and safe.* She picked up the spoon and stirred the soup simmering in the iron pot hanging over the fire. Bits of browned bacon floated among chunks of potato and diced onion and corn. The men here would be eating good, hot food tonight. What would Zachary Thatcher eat?

The fish was good. He would save what was left for his breakfast. Zach moved the pan and added another piece of broken branch to the fire. He would not be able to do that much longer. He was almost to Indian territory. He leaned back against a rock, tipped his hat low over his eyes and listened to the tethered packhorse grazing. Were the emigrants adding to their dwindling supplies by fishing? Had they settled on a site for their town yet? Had they started building their homes? Emma Allen's home? They'd better. If winter caught them…

He frowned, watched the fire flare as the branch broke apart and fell against the hot coals. How cold did it get in Oregon country anyway? Did they have blizzards? Or ice storms? If they did, and Emma Allen was still in her wagon…

Zach surged to his feet, yanked off his hat, ran his hand through his hair and tugged his hat back on. The sun was setting, hiding its face behind the tall mountain peaks, shooting warm, red-and-gold streaks into the western sky. He should get his bedroll. He turned, faced east. The sky was a cold gray with black encroaching along the far edge. He stood and watched the sky growing darker by the minute, feeling the cold seeping into his heart and spirit.

What was he doing? Why was he riding toward that darkness? There was nothing for him there. There was no excitement, no anticipation to this journey. He had been forcing himself to go on each day. His dream of building a trading post, then roaming the mountains free and unfettered was as cold as that eastern sky. That life had no appeal for him now. Everything he wanted was back at the wagon train, wrapped up in one feisty, slender, blond-haired, brown-eyed woman. Somehow, somewhere along the way on their journey west he had fallen in love with Emma Allen.

But what was he to do about it? She was a doctor and he had withstood her every request, effectively destroying any personal regard she might have held for him. Of course, he was a soldier. And if there was one thing he knew how to do, it was to win a battle…

Chapter Nineteen

"I got me a bad hurt, Dr. Emma!"

Emma set aside her writing desk, rose and peered over the side of the driver's box. Gabe Lewis looked up at her and held out a bloody forearm for her inspection. David was at his side, as always. The boys could have been twins but for their age difference. Both had black curly hair, dark blue eyes and grins that made you want to hug them, no matter what mischief they had been up to. She nodded and stepped back. "Perhaps you had better come up here and let me look at your arm."

Gabe flashed one of those wicked grins at David and both boys charged for the wagon tongue, Gabe a half step ahead. Before she could even turn around he was scrambling over the front board into the box. Obviously, the wound was not causing him great pain. He inched toward her, making room in the box for his brother. She planted her feet more firmly and motioned David onto the seat.

The five-year-old hopped up to the spot she indicated, then dropped to his knees, peering at her lap desk. "What's this thing?"

"It is a lap desk."

Gabe turned and looked at it. "What's it for?"

"It is for writing letters and other things. Such as accounts and party invitations."

Gabe stretched out his hand to touch it, stopped and put his hand behind his back instead. "That what you was doin' when we come?"

His voice reflected the wonder in his eyes. Her heart squeezed. She should have thought— "Yes. I was writing a letter to my brother. He lives in Philadelphia." *Perhaps she could send one of the men to the mission to get a few slates and readers...*

"That one of them big, back East cities with people crowded all over one another I heard about?"

Her lips twitched at his description, but she managed to stem the smile. "Yes. Philadelphia is a very large, important city. It is where the Declaration of Independence was signed."

Both boys frowned, swiveled their heads in her direction, their eyes alight with curiosity. "What's that?"

William, my dear brother, how you would love this moment. She sought for an explanation they would understand. "Well...a 'declaration' is when you state something very firmly."

"Like Ma telling Pa he ain't goin' to smoke his nasty-smelling pipe in her clean wagon?"

So that was why Joseph Lewis sat outside by the fire alone at night! Emma coughed to control the laughter bubbling up into her throat at Gabe's example. "Yes.

That is correct." The boy's face lit up as if she had given him a piece of candy. She smiled down at him. "And 'independence' is—" *Oh, my. This could be dangerous, heady information for a seven-year-old.* "—it is when one is *old* enough and *wise* enough to manage one's own affairs."

The boys looked at one another, gave sober, sage nods. "Like Pa tellin' Ma he'll have the say of where he smokes his pipe."

Oh dear. Emma cleared her throat. "Let me see your arm, Gabe." It was covered in both fresh and drying blood. "I shall have to cleanse that before I can see what harm has been done." She picked up the lap desk. "Sit down. I will get my things."

A conspiratorial look flashed between the boys. Gabe grinned and plunked himself down on the seat. *What was that look about?* Emma tied the canvas flaps back, set the desk on the red box, slid it out of the way and climbed inside.

Gabe twisted around, perched on his knees on the seat and looked at her. "Are ya gonna give me some of that sleepin' stuff an' stitch me up like ya did Daniel?"

Ah! So that was it. "I will not know if your wound requires me to put you to sleep while I make the stitches until I clean the blood away. I will make my diagnosis after I see the wound." She bit down on her lower lip to keep from laughing and dipped water out of the keg into the washbowl. Now to teach these little schemers that doctoring was not for fun. She set the desk aside, opened the red box and removed a bottle of alcohol, the shallow bowl, her suturing equipment and a roll of clean, narrow cloth bandages. She placed them all in full view on one end of the red box, then donned her doctor's apron, tugged the cork from the bottle of alcohol and splashed a little into the water, enough to cleanse with only a little sting. She wanted to teach him a lesson, not torture him. "I believe I am ready now."

Gabe did not look quite so happy about the situation as he had a few moments ago. She fixed a sober look on her face, tossed in a clean rag and handed him the wash-bowl. He scooted back off the seat out of her way and she climbed outside, took the bowl. "Sit down, Gabe."

The boy swallowed hard, did as she bid. David's eyes looked wider, rounder...scared. She wanted to hug him. Instead, she placed the bowl on the seat beside Gabe, squeezed out the cloth and began to gently clean away the dried blood. It was only a surface abrasion. With bits of bark clinging to it.

"You have been climbing trees again." One glance at his sheepish face told her she had made a correct diagnosis. It was also the most likely reason he had come to her, instead of going to his mother, who was continually warning the boys to stay out of trees. He did not want to give her proof of her warnings. She was quite sure the "being put to sleep" idea was an afterthought. She rinsed the rag and began again. What would it be like to have sons like these? Adorable boys, full of curiosity and energy, that explored the world with such enjoyment and zest. Zachary Thatcher would father such sons.

The thought brought heat rushing to her cheeks, tears welling into her eyes. She blinked the tears away and continued her work. She would never know if that were true. Zachary Thatcher wanted only to be free of all entanglements. Most of all he wanted to be free of *her*, and her stubborn insistence on having her advice for her patients obeyed. He had been gone almost three weeks. Had he reached his valley?

She fixed a smile on her face and looked up at her young patient. "This will not need to be stitched, Gabe. It will heal fine if you will only keep it nice and clean." She dropped the cloth into the water, spread some salve on the scrape and wound Gabe's arm with the clean bandage.

A good doctor puts his patients first, before his own wants or needs.

How many times had she heard Papa Doc say those words? How many times had *she* said them? Sincerely, but blithely said them. She tied off the bandage and patted Gabe's hand. "I am finished. You may go now. But you come back if your arm turns red or starts to hurt you. Promise?"

He grinned up at her, nodded then climbed over the side of the driver's box, dropped to the ground and ran off. David followed.

She lifted her hand and rubbed to try and ease the pressure in her chest, but there was nothing she could do to make it stop. It was her heart that hurt. And only having Zachary Thatcher's love could stop the ache. Zachary Thatcher...who was lost to her because of her calling to be a doctor. She threw out the bloody water, pushed the bowl through the opening and climbed inside to take care of her things. Tears slipped down her cheeks as she went down on her knees, opened the red box and placed the alcohol and her suturing equipment inside. She stared at all the bottles and crocks and herbs and bandages, then slowly closed the lid, sat back on her heels and covered her face with her hands.

"I did not know, Lord." The hot tears ran down her fingers, mixed with the soft sobs, the warm, hesitant breath carrying her words, and dripped off her wrists onto the red wool covering her lap. "I truly did not know how much being a doctor could cost...until now."

"I cannot thank you enough, Mr. Thatcher, for your consideration in taking the household furnishings and the apple seedlings off of my hands. I have no desire to stay in this wretched backwoods country without Mr. Canfield. Indeed, I had no desire to come here at all. But Mr. Canfield fancied himself a nurseryman of great talent. A woman's lot is a hard one." The Widow Canfield sniffed delicately into her embroidered lace handkerchief, stepped closer and looked up at him from beneath her lashes. An extremely coy look from a woman so recently bereaved.

Zach took a step back and gave a small, polite bow. "I am sure it is the Lord's hand that has made your need to leave Oregon country, and my need to stay here, meet in such a fortuitous way, Widow Canfield. I wish you a safe and pleasant journey." He turned away from the cloying woman and gripped the hand of the big, white-haired man walking with them toward the ship waiting on the Columbia River. "And to you, sir, I offer my sincere thanks for agreeing to store the furnishings here at Fort

Vancouver until my home is built. I give you my word it will be a matter of a few months only."

"'Tis not a problem, Mr. Thatcher. There is no need to be rushing the building. We have plenty of room here for storage of such items." The chief factor of the fort lifted a big hand and clapped Zach's shoulder. "Welcome again, to Oregon country. I'll look forward to hearing how those apple trees fare, when next you come to visit."

"I shall do all in my power to make that report an excellent one, sir."

Zach turned and headed for the barn, his steps long and eager. All he had set out to do had been accomplished. And without traveling all the way to Oregon City as he had thought would be necessary. He shook his head, smiled. *Those apple seedlings...* A turn he had not planned or expected. Surely God was blessing his endeavor. He entered the dusty, dusky barn and marched to the far stalls.

Comanche neighed, bunched his shoulders and hopped then lowered his head and kicked the back wall of the stall.

Zach stepped to the door, reached across and scratched under Comanche's dark forelock. "I know, boy. I'm sorry I had to put you in here. Let me get this travois packed and we will be on our way."

The roan whickered his displeasure. Tossed his head and pawed at the door with a front hoof. "At ease, Comanche!" Zach gave him a last pat, stepped to the back wall and knelt down to load the apple tree seedlings onto the piece of canvas stretched between the two long poles leaning against the wall.

He pulled the first crate toward him and carefully lifted out the fragile seedlings to pile them on the travois. Each had a narrow blue ribbon tied around them. The corresponding blue crate was labeled Sheepnose. He grouped them together and reached for the red crate labeled Winesap. The last group had green ribbons on them and were labeled Pippen. They might better have said Blackfeet, Sioux and Comanche. He would have understood that.

He stood, moved to the corner and picked up the large piece of burlap he had placed there last night. He spread it overtop the apple seedlings and tied it in place with leather thongs to hold the seedlings secure on the long ride, then stared at his handiwork. Was that the right thing to do? Would it hurt to cover them? It was the only way he could think of to protect them. He removed his hat, shoved his hand through his hair and scowled down at the bundled sprigs. "I sure hope I'm right and this is Your plan for me, Lord, because I know nothing about growing apples!"

He tugged his hat back on, leaned down to pick up his packs and noticed a small, green-covered book in the blue crate. He picked it up, thumbed through it and grinned. It was full of information about growing apples, written in a neat, careful hand. Seemed as if everything was working out fine. He chuckled, a low, confident sound that came from deep in his chest, lifted the book toward the ceiling and snapped off a sharp salute. "I hear You, Lord."

He stood there for a moment in the quiet, then tucked the book in one of the packs and carried them to the opposite stall to load on the packhorse. He had his battle plan and his weapons. And he was certain now the Lord was blessing his efforts. He couldn't wait to get back and lay siege to Emma Allen's heart!

Emma threw off the covers, sat up and pulled the quilt around her. She could not sleep. She felt hemmed in, restless. How wonderful it would be to have someone to talk to when worry stole your sleep, and your peace. She stood and stepped to the front of the wagon, listened for any unusual sounds. Anything that might indicate danger. All she could hear was the river's whisper as it brushed along its banks on its way. She untied the end flaps, peeked outside. Bright moonlight lit the landscape, turned the distant mountains silver.

She gathered up the dragging edge of the quilt and crawled outside to sit on the driver's seat. The air was frosty. It nipped at her cheeks, her ears and toes. She drew her feet back under the quilt's protection, folded the top edge high on the back of her neck, then grabbed both front edges and tucked her covered hands under her chin. They were well into October now. How long before winter would arrive? How would it come? With snowstorms? Ice storms? Or would it be gray and over-cast and soak them with frigid rain? It was strange not to know what sort of weather to expect.

She lifted her chin, blew out a long breath and watched the small gray cloud appear. The air touched its cold fingers to her exposed throat. She shivered, tucked her chin back into its warm spot between her covered, fisted hands and looked toward the mountains.

The highest peaks were white with snow. Was it so deep it had closed off those narrow passes? Not that it mattered. She knew he wasn't up there. He would have traveled beyond that distance long ago. Still, she liked to look at the mountains. It made her feel close to him. Fear clutched at her heart. She hoped he had an extra blanket.

It was done. Zach smoothed the rough edges where his knife had gouged the board, blew off the tiny bits of wood and slowly ran his hand over the surface to test for slivers. There was no roughness anywhere. He turned the board this way and that studying his work in the moonlight, then smiled and shoved the board in his saddlebag. Time to sleep.

A sharp yank on the ties freed his groundsheet and blanket. He stretched out and spread the cover over his legs. Cold air kissed his cheek. He frowned, looked up at the streaming moonlight. It was a clear night with a chill in the air. It could get down to a frost level before morning. He shoved off the blanket and put more wood on the fire, gathered up a few more pieces littering the ground under a nearby tree and carried them back to have close at hand. He didn't want anything happening to those apple seedlings. He took hold of the double poles and pulled until the loaded end was near the fire. That should protect them.

He stretched out again, linked his hands behind his head and stared up at the sky. Where were the wagons? If he knew where Hargrove and the others had located their town, he could figure the best place to plant his orchard.

And build the cabin. A nice one with two rooms, a lean-to kitchen and a loft. And a stone milk house. That would do for a start. He would build her whatever she wanted later on. There was plenty of timber on the mountains. And rocks for chimneys.

A frown drew his brows together. Would it be good enough? She was from Philadelphia. And judging from her clothes, and her sister's and the way her brother had outfitted his wagons, they were wealthy. What if she refused him?

He scowled, flopped onto his side and closed his eyes. That was enough of thinking. No soldier should ever go into battle thinking he was going to be defeated. He would win Emma Allen's heart. Nothing less was acceptable.

Chapter Twenty

Emma put her plate, cup and flatware in the small chest, tossed out the dishwater and set the small tub back on the shelf that had held the water barrel. That item, no longer needed with the river only a few steps away, had been upturned to use as a "table." She dipped her fingertips into the small crock beside the chest on the shelf and rubbed the soothing balm into her hands, then lifted them and stroked them over her cheeks. The hint of lavender scent made her smile. In her next letter she would ask Papa Doc to send at least a dozen crocks of the hand balm with William—if he decided to come to Oregon country next year.

She frowned at the rush of hope and excitement that thought caused her, removed her long apron and hung it on the nail by the shelf. She had not yet overcome her selfishness in wanting her brother to make that dangerous journey; the loneliness made it difficult. And it was harder than ever with Annie gone to teach at the Banning Mission and the emigrants all spread out on their selected parcels of land. She had become accustomed to having the children racing around the wagons playing games and getting into mischief, and now they had new homes and this vast land to explore. And the women—

Stop! You are being pathetic. Emma made a wry face and walked to the fire to place the iron pan in which she had cooked the piece of beef that, along with yesterday's cold biscuit, constituted her supper, onto the hot coals to clean. One small piece of beef cooked by herself, *for* herself, on her own small fire *was* pathetic.

The sound of children's laughter floated to her from the direction of the Lewis family's new home. No doubt Gabe and David were up to some high jinks. If so, there was a good chance she would see them soon. They were her most frequent patients. She laughed, grabbed her wrap off the sideboard of the driver's seat and walked beyond the front of her wagon toward the plains so she could see beyond the Hargrove and Swinton homes to where the river emerged from the rolling hills. Joseph Lewis had decided to build there so the fall of water coming out of the hills would drive the blades of his sawmill.

She walked a few steps farther and peered through the dimming light. Yes, his wagon was standing outside their front door, waiting for tomorrow's leave-taking. What a blessing it would be for everyone if he found the ship carrying his saw blades had arrived when he reached Oregon City. Everyone was hoping and praying it would prove to be so. They were all eager to have cut boards available to finish their homes. They were using split logs now for the roofs. She frowned and pulled her wrap closer about her against the growing chill. It made

her wince every time she saw them lifting those heavy
logs into place. If one of those ropes broke—

She shuddered and shifted her gaze higher. Black dots
that were the emigrants' oxen, mules and horses grazed
on the rolling hills under the watchful eyes of the night
guards. It would not be so when barns were erected.

She shook her head and looked again toward the river.
Change had come so rapidly. The men had divided into
crews, some to fell trees on the mountains and cut them
to the needed lengths, others to haul them to town and
still more to trim and notch them. All worked together
to raise the houses. Even the children, who were so eager
to help, had been given tasks according to their abilities. She had written a long and careful accounting of
the building to William, had even drawn a map of the
homes' locations.

The first, up against the rolling hills, was the Lundquist farm. Soon to be two farms when Garth's betrothed
arrived next year. And standing on the riverbank, the
Lewis home and the spot where the sawmill would soon
stand marked by wooden stakes. Next—she shifted her
gaze down the silvery ribbon of water—the Applegates'
home and cornerstones for the future mill. And then—
again, a short distance downriver—the Fentons' home
and blacksmith shop.

Her gaze drifted over the empty space left for a school-
house and any businesses that might come to their town,
skimmed over the Swintons' combination home and general store, the Hargroves' combined home and bank,
and stopped on her wagon. Beyond that, at a distance
too far to see in the deepening dusk, was the Fletcher

farm. And then the Suttons' and Murrays'. Those three families were still in wagons. But the Fletcher cabin was to be raised tomorrow.

She glanced up at the darkening sky, rubbed her chilled hands together and walked back to light her lantern. She knew how now, thanks to Mr. Thatcher. She pushed the thought of him away, placed the end of a long, slender twig against the dying coals of her fire, blew gently and when it burst into flame, held it to the wick in the lamp. She adjusted the flame, set her clean iron pan up on the surrounding wall of stone and rose.

A tiny thrill of anticipation zinged through her. This was where her home and doctor's office would be. Soon. After the homes of the Fletchers and Suttons and Murrays. She had insisted her home be the last one built. She did not have a husband or children to make a home for, and the wagon was sufficient for a woman alone, though it would be wonderful to have walls and—

A slow rhythm, so scarce she wasn't sure she heard it, echoed faintly through the night. Horse hoofs. More than one perhaps… *How far away?*

Her heart lurched. She held the lantern close, spun down the wick to extinguish the flame and turned toward the west, every fiber of her being straining to detect the sound she had heard in the distance. It came again, the sound of hoofs striking against rock. Slow, steady… Closer now. Indians?

Her mouth went dry. The dark pressed in on her. She pivoted and swept her gaze toward the emigrants' homes. Without glass windows for candle or lamplight to shine through, they were invisible in the dark. Her fire!

Had the stones hidden it from view? She snatched up the small hoe and dragged dead ashes over the glowing coals.

The hoofbeats had stopped. She cast a longing glance toward the Hargroves' log cabin, torn between her desire to run to them for safety, and her need to stay outside and listen so she could give warning should danger come their way. Would any hear her cry? She tightened her grip on the iron hoe and inched her way back toward her wagon. She would go and alert John Hargrove. But if danger rode at her out of the night, she wanted William's pistol in her hand.

Zach slipped from the saddle, let Comanche's reins dangle to the ground then led the packhorse to the river and tethered him to a tree. That was lantern light he had seen ahead. He was sure of it, though it had been quickly extinguished. He shoved the travois beneath the low, feathery branches of a pine for protection, lifted off the packs and hurried back to Comanche. A quick dip into his saddlebags produced his moccasins. He tugged off his boots, laid them across his saddle and laced the moccasins on.

Comanche turned his head and nudged him in the chest.

"Sorry, boy, but I can't let you roam until I know what's out there." He gave the strong shoulder a commiserating pat and jogged off into the night, following the river.

The smell of a smoldering fire led him to them. He stared across the river at the wagon cover, a leaden gray in the lightless night. The log cabin black beside it. And there was another. He'd found them.

He stomped down the impulse to splash across the river, find Emma Allen and kiss her senseless. That day would come. First, he had to show her that his opposition to her advice on the trail was of necessity, not desire. He had to convince the woman of his respectful regard for her position as a physician. Because any man that wanted to marry Emma Allen had to court the doctor, too. That much he knew for a certainty. The woman was a she-bear when it came to fighting for her patients. It was one of the reasons he loved her. He had to convince her of that. And he would start tomorrow. He grinned, turned and loped back the way he had come.

Emma dried her face, smoothed on some cream and scowled at herself in the small mirror. She had made a fool of herself last night, rushing to the Hargroves' with a pistol in her hand and warning of "hoofbeats" in the night. Mr. Hargrove had warned the others and set guards, but it had all come to naught. And now John Hargrove thought her "hysterical." And several of the men thought the "hoofbeats" she heard were only in her imagination.

Emma sighed, brushed a tendril of hair back off her forehead and pulled her Augusta spencer on over her red wool dress. The velvet fabric gave warmth without the bother of a wrap. And she wanted to look her most sensible and efficient after last night's disaster. The frown reappeared in the mirror. She shoved the mirror back in the pocket on the canvas cover and climbed from the wagon. She had been *sure* she heard hoofbeats!

Like now.

Emma turned toward the sound, stared through the morning mist along the river at the imposing figure atop a roan with distinctive spots on its hindquarters. Her heart stopped, lurched into a wildly erratic beat.

Mr. Thatcher had returned.

No. That could not be. Perhaps she *was* imagining things. She closed her eyes, took a deep breath and opened them again. The man wore a fringed buckskin shirt. And he was leading a packhorse. But there was no mistaking that erect posture and those broad shoulders. It was Zachary Thatcher.

He rode closer, began to wend his way through the trees along the river.

Emma pressed her hand over the throbbing pulse at the base of her throat and stepped out of sight behind her wagon. She couldn't let him see her. Not like this. Not while she was so…undone.

He stopped, tethered the packhorse to a tree branch then guided Comanche into the river. Water splashed around the big roan's hoofs, rose to his knees, his belly then dropped again. Man and horse surged up onto the bank, headed her way. She stood frozen, willing Zachary Thatcher to not see her, begging God to blind his eyes to her presence. He looked straight at her, impaled her on the gaze of those bright blue eyes that peered out from beneath his broad-brimmed hat. Eyes that looked straight at a person, noticed everything about her— She squared her shoulders, lifted her chin.

He stopped, smiled. "We meet again, Miss Allen. Could you tell me where I might find Mr. Hargrove?"

She nodded, found her voice. "That is his cabin next door."

He dipped his head, touched the brim of his hat and rode off.

She sagged against the wagon and watched until he disappeared around the corner of the Hargrove's cabin.

"Haw! Haw!" A whip cracked, cracked again.

Matthew Hargrove! The first load of logs for the Fletchers' cabin was on its way. And she had not even started her cook fire. She pushed away from the wagon, walked to the fire and used the hoe to scrape the ashes off the banked coals. A few handfuls of dry pine bark and some gentle blowing brought flames leaping to life. She added some small chunks of wood from her pile and went to the wagon to get the things she needed to start a pot of soup.

Zach stood in the doorway of the Hargrove cabin and watched the wagon come. He looked over his shoulder at John Hargrove who was pulling papers from a small chest. "Matthew is coming with a load of logs." He couldn't resist the temptation to bait him a bit. "You adding on to this cabin already?"

"No, no." Hargrove shook his head and spread one of the papers out on the top of a dresser. "Those logs are for the Fletcher cabin. He's downriver. Figures the plains will be good for farming. The Suttons and Murrays are downriver, too."

Zach nodded, turned to face the dim interior of the cabin. "And Miss Allen's cabin? Will she be next to you? Where her wagon now sits?"

"That's right. Though I wish it were not! I dislike hysterical women." The older man smoothed out the creases in the paper. "Now here—"

"Hysterical?" Zach frowned. The word had come out a bit too sharp. Lydia Hargrove had stopped making biscuits and looked at him. He slouched back against the wall.

"Yes. As hysterical as I've ever seen!" John Hargrove's gray, bushy eyebrows drew together in a deep frown. "Last night, she came running over here in the middle of the night carrying a pistol and raving about some imagined 'hoofbeats' she heard coming our way. Got everyone stirred up."

"It was not the middle of the night, Hargrove." Zach gave him a cold look. He did not care for men who exaggerated the truth. "And it was not 'hysteria.' It was me."

"You!"

"That's right. I camped a short way downriver last night. But even if it hadn't been me, Miss Allen did the wise thing in raising an alarm. Had it been someone bent on evil, delay could have brought disaster. It's better to lose sleep than your scalp." He gestured toward the dresser. "Is that the map you were looking for?"

"Yes. If you will show me the land you are interested in, I'll mark it off as taken."

Zach nodded, strode to the dresser, looked at the map

and pointed. "That's the section I want." *The one behind Emma Allen's lot. Where she will see me every day.*

"Across the river?"

"That's right. From this bend in the river all the way to the Blue Mountains."

The banker gave him a sharp look. "That's a big parcel, Thatcher."

"I've got big plans, Hargrove. Mark it as taken."

"The men got the Fletcher cabin well started today."

Emma glanced over at Lydia and nodded. She didn't feel like chatting. She was exhausted from being around Zachary Thatcher. She had tried her best to avoid him, but every time she carried water to the working men, he called for a drink. And he had been in her line when she had ladled out her soup. And…and every time she saw him or heard his voice she tried to think why he had returned. And to prepare herself for his leaving. Her breath caught. He could not possibly be intending to cross those mountains now, could he? Not after all the warnings he had given them about the snows closing the mountain passes and trapping you— Is that why he had that packhorse and that—that *trundling* thing it was pulling? Were all those supplies in case—

"Emma! I asked you a question."

She stopped, looked at Lydia. "I beg your pardon. I—"

"Was not listening to a word I said." Lydia gave her a searching look. "Are you feeling all right, Emma?"

"I am perfectly fine. Only a little weary." She turned

away from Lydia's perusal and started walking. "What was your question?"

"I want to know if you will come by in the morning and help me make dried apple dumplings for tomorrow's meal for the men? Olga and Hannah are making stew."

Tomorrow. How would she face tomorrow? If he were here, it would be torture to be around him. And if he were gone— Yes. It would be easier if he were gone. The emptiness would be unbearable. But at least she would not have to pretend she did not love him. She looked down to hide her face from Lydia, stared at her empty hands and flexed her fingers. He had offered to carry her kettle home for her, and when she had made an excuse to linger, he had smiled and taken it from her anyway. Oh, yes. It would be much easier if Mr. Thatcher were gone tomorrow.

"Of course I shall help you, Lydia. I will come by first thing in the morning." She fixed a bright smile on her face, lifted her hand in farewell and walked to her wagon. She climbed to the driver's seat and went inside. She did not want to see where he had put her kettle. She did not want to look across the river to see if he was still there. She *would* not!

Her resolve lasted until she had prepared for bed. By then she could resist no longer. She turned the lamp down low, braved the cold to open the back flaps a crack and peered out. There was enough moonlight to spot the grazing horses immediately. And then she saw him. What was he— He was digging for something. It looked as if there was a *hole—*

He stopped, leaned on the shovel and looked her way.

She jerked her head back and snapped the flaps closed. Surely he had not seen that tiny crack of light? But then, with that penetrating gaze of his bright blue eyes, perhaps he had. She dared not look out again.

She shivered her way to the bed and crawled under the covers. He was not gone. She sighed and closed her eyes. *Almighty God, please exchange my weakness for Your strength. Please help me to be strong and hide my love for Mr. Thatcher if he is still here tomorrow. Or help me to accept the emptiness that will be in my heart if he is gone. Amen.*

Zach stared at the wagon cover. The slit of lamplight was gone. She had closed the flaps up tight. Had it been an accident they had been open a crack? Or had she been looking out? At him? He smiled and turned back to his digging. There was no way he could know for certain. But the possibility that his plan was working gave him pleasure enough to warm his heart all night. If Emma Allen was curious enough to spy and try and see what he was doing, she must care about him. At least a little. He would do his best to make her curiosity and her caring grow.

Chapter Twenty-One

Her cheeks and nose were red from the cold. Emma flexed the stiffness from her fingers, pushed the combs into her hair then tied the length of dark blue ribbon around the base of the thick coil at the crown of her head to hold the tendrils from escaping. Her hands shook from the shivers coursing through her as she put away the hairbrush and mirror. The nights had been growing steadily colder, but last night had been frigid! No matter how many blankets she had piled on, she could not get truly warm. How she had longed for the fireplace that graced her bedroom at home in Philadelphia!

She frowned and drew her thoughts away from the past. She must look to the future. She would have her cabin soon. There would be no cold air slipping beneath a canvas cover to nip at her exposed skin then. No floors from which the cold rose to chill her limbs in spite of the extra wool petticoat she wore. She would have a fireplace that would warm her as she performed her morning toilette, and warm water always ready on the hearth.

She glanced at the water in the washbowl, shivered at the memory of its frosty touch. There had not been ice on the water in the keg, only the thin skin promise of the winter yet to come. She must remember to write and warn William and Caroline of the weather. If her ink wasn't frozen!

She stared in disgust at the small crock she had opened. Her hand balm was hard. She loosened a bit with the tip of her scissors, then held it in her palm to soften before she rubbed it in. Her Augusta spencer added warmth her blue wool dress alone could not provide. But even it was not enough this morning. She put on her long apron, then lifted her fur-trimmed wool cloak out of a dresser drawer and swirled it around her shoulders, tugged the hood in place. The fur lining of the hood felt wonderful against her cold ears and cheeks.

She reached up to the lamp that dangled from a hook in one of the hickory ribs that supported the wagon cover and extinguished the flame, then stepped to the front of the wagon and untied the canvas flaps. Cold air rushed at her. She glanced at the Hargroves' chimney. There was smoke rising like a gray column toward the lightening sky. She secured the flaps, climbed from the wagon and hurried toward the warmth of their cabin.

Not once did she allow herself to look across the river. She reached to pull aside the blanket that served as the Hargroves' door, heard a deep, rich voice and jerked her hand back. *He was there.* She spun about to go back to her wagon.

Who shall abide in the Lord's tabernacle, children?

He that sweareth to his own hurt and changeth not. If you make a promise, you must keep it.

Lydia was expecting her. Emma clenched her hands and gritted her teeth. Why had her mother been so diligent in teaching them God's Word? Why could she not ignore it? She took a deep breath, turned back and stepped inside. The fire was burning. But it was the look in Zachary Thatcher's eyes as he looked her way and rose to his feet that brought warmth to her. She was suddenly thankful for the cold that had turned her cheeks red. It would mask the blush that was making them burn. She lifted her chin.

"Come in, Emma. I have already started soaking the apples."

"Coming, Lydia." She glanced at John Hargrove, who, as usual, did not bother to hide his displeasure at her coming. "Forgive me if I interrupted your conversation." She stepped into the room, gave a polite nod of greeting in Zachary Thatcher's direction and removed her cloak. She hung it over the back of Lydia's rocking chair and joined her friend. "What shall I do, Lydia?"

"You can help me make the dough to wrap the apples in." The older woman dumped some flour in a large crockery bowl and reached for the saleratus. "That other bowl is for you to use."

"—Fletcher cabin will be finished today, Thatcher. It's taking longer because it's a big one. The Sutton and Mur—"

"Make the dough the same as for biscuits, Emma. Only use a bit more lard."

She nodded, turned her back toward the men and

dumped some flour in the bowl, trying not to pay attention to their conversation, but unable to avoid hearing bits and snatches of it in the close quarters of the room.

"—my guess is six or seven days. We can start on yours—"

Her hand jerked. *"Yours?"* The word escaped. There was no choice but to turn and face him. "I could not help but overhear, Mr. Thatcher—though I believe my ears deceive me. I thought I heard Mr. Hargrove say you were going to build a cabin. A strange occupation for a man who wants no *fetters*."

His gaze held hers. "As is making biscuits for a doctor, Miss Allen."

"You've got a mite too much saleratus in there, Emma."

She turned around, saw Lydia's curious gaze and looked down. "Yes. I—it was an accident." She picked up a spoon and scooped out some of the saleratus to save for the next batch of dough. Zachary Thatcher's deep voice rumbled in the background. She abandoned politeness and tilted her head to better hear.

"I'm not sure I want—"

"We'll be rolling it out thin."

Oh, Lydia, please do not talk!

Lydia grabbed a handful of flour, sprinkled it on the table, then scraped the dough out of her bowl on top of it. "Joseph Lewis made this table out of our wagon's tailboard and some sturdy pine limbs. You should have him make one for you when you are in your cabin, Emma. It works fine."

"—to Fletcher's and start working." Zachary Thatcher's

voice raised. "I will look forward to eating some of those apple dumplings at supper, ladies." There was a soft swish and a draft of cold air as he lifted the blanket and stepped outside.

The conversation was over, and still she did not know if he would stay or go. He had not answered her query. She dusted the table with flour, dumped out her dough, made a fist and thumped it—hard.

She was so beautiful. His heart had almost stopped when he looked up and saw her standing there in that fur-lined cloak. Zach frowned, wrapped the rope around the split log and tied it off. He had almost blurted out the truth right then. But he had caught himself in time. Still... "Haul away!" He stepped to the side and prepared to steady the log as Nathan Fenton urged the oxen to pull. Something of what he was feeling must have shown on his face the way her eyes had widened, and that proud little chin of hers had lifted. She had been more cool than normal to him after that. Still, she was curious as to his intent. Perhaps more than curious. He had seen her back stiffen when Hargrove mentioned him building a cabin. And he had seen the flash of frustration in her eyes when he evaded answering her query. But there had been a challenge in her question—and hurt. It was not time to declare himself openly. He would continue working his plan until— "Whoa! That's far enough, Nathan!"

Zach slid out on the ridge beam, yanked on the rope end to undo the knot and dropped the rope to the ground. It took a little maneuvering but he finally got in position to wrap his arm about the half log and lift the end enough he could slide it into the notch. That was the last one. They could put the roof planks on now. Then tomorrow they could start building the Sutton cabin. It could not be soon enough for him.

He slid back off the ridge beam and went hand over hand down the climbing rope to help get the first roof plank in place. Tonight, he would finish planting his apple seedlings. And tomorrow night he would show her he was a man with a future.

"Is there something wrong, Emma?"

"Wrong?" Emma lifted the last apple dumpling in the pan onto the large ironstone platter and shook her head. "No. There is nothing wrong. Why do you ask?"

"You seem quiet, but...touchy." Lydia fixed an assessing gaze on her. "Like you were when you were around Mr. Thatcher yesterday."

"Why, that is—" She looked at Lydia's raised eyebrows and gave a little laugh. She could not let her guess how she truly felt about Zachary Thatcher. She did not care to be an object of pity. "All right, I confess. I find Mr. Thatcher's low opinion of me...annoying." She pushed the emptied pan to Lydia's side to be refilled with the raw dumplings they had made and piled in the middle of the table. Now for another. She grabbed the hem of her long apron, leaned down and removed the lid from another pan on the hearth to see if the dumplings were done.

"Hmm. He's mighty quick to speak up for you for someone who holds you in low regard."

"Whatever are you talking about?"

"I'm talking about yesterday, when John named you 'hysterical' to Mr. Thatcher. He told him how you come runnin' over here in the middle of the night carryin' a pistol and ravin' about imagined 'hoofbeats' and gettin' everyone all stirred up."

Emma drew up straight as an arrow and looked at the older woman. "It was *not* the middle of the night!"

Lydia grinned. "That's what Mr. Thatcher told John. And he told him you weren't hysterical either." She nestled the raw dumplings close together in the pan, poured in a bit of boiling water from her iron teapot. "He said it was him you heard riding in. And that you were wise to raise an alarm, 'cause it was better to lose sleep than to lose your scalp." The lid of the iron spider clanged against the rim of the pan.

Emma stared at her, the dumplings she'd been checking forgotten. "He said I was wise?" She frowned when the older woman smiled and nodded. "Well, I cannot imagine *why*. He certainly did not think I was wise when we were coming west! He opposed my every request for my patients."

Lydia nodded, glanced down. "The dumplings in that pan done?"

Emma flushed, put down the lid she held and lifted the pan to the table. "It was obvious that Mr. Thatcher shared most men's disdain for women doctors." The spoon clanged against the pan as she lifted out a dumpling to put on the platter.

"Or that he was only trying to do what we hired him to do, keep us all safe." Lydia raked a fresh batch of coals out onto the hearth, set the refilled spider on them and covered the lid with more coals. "If I recollect right, when little Jenny Lewis injured her head so severe you said the joltin' around of ridin' in a wagon would kill her, it was Mr. Thatcher that come up with the idea of that 'swing' bed that made it possible for her to ride without being hurt."

Emma stared at her. "I—I had not thought of it that way. I thought…"

"That Mr. Thatcher was fightin' you because of you bein' a woman doctor."

"Yes."

Lydia wrapped her apron hem around her hand, reached across the table and pulled the iron pan to her side of the table. "It appears to me, he respected your doctorin' skills so much he figured out a way to follow 'em and still move the wagons forward like needed to be done."

Could that be possible? Emma searched her memory, trying to find a flaw in that argument.

"Same as when baby Isaac come down with the measles, and Mr. Thatcher held that meetin' tellin' everyone about your idea for a movin' quarantine to keep people from gettin' sick." Lydia lifted a dumpling to the platter, scooped up another. "When Tom Swinton challenged your sayin' Isaac had measles when he didn't have spots, Mr. Thatcher told him that him and anyone else that didn't believe you had to leave the train and not come back. And he was right rigid about enforcing that movin' quarantine. Seems to me he wouldn't have done all that if he didn't respect your doctoring."

Yes, but the moving quarantine was because he would not stop as she—

"Seems to me, you two worked hand in hand to make that whole nasty situation come out right well."

Hand in hand. A sick feeling hit the pit of her stomach. *Had she been so angry and close-minded because of the way men sneered at her for being a doctor, she hadn't seen the truth?*

"You gonna let them dumplins burn?"

"What?" Emma looked down at the pan Lydia was refilling. *The dumplings!* "No. No, of course not." She whirled to the hearth, snatched hold of the end of her apron and lifted a lid from one of the pans.

Emma cut the pans of corn bread into generous squares, then placed the knife on the table and walked away. The preparation for today's supper was finished, and she needed to be alone.

She hurried up the path being worn into the grass-covered plain. By the time the Sutton and Murray cabins were finished, the wagon wheels and the people's footsteps would have turned the path into a road, one that sandwiched the cabins between it and the river. Already it had the look of a village.

Promise.

But perhaps not for her.

Tears stung her eyes. She blinked them away and hurried on to her wagon, went to the stone circle that held the banked coals. She needed the comfort and warmth of a fire to chase away the shivers that trembled through her.

Could she have been so wrong? Had she seen Zachary Thatcher's actions through the haze of past disdain and scorn, through the hurt of rejection? Had she unwittingly destroyed any personal regard he may have felt for her by her stubborn insistence on having her doctoring skills acknowledged? Had her calling as a doctor cost her the possibility of a shared love?

She went to her knees, heedless of the fine dusting of gray ash on the ground beneath her, and breathed the fire to life. She fed the flames wood until they leaped with unrestrained joy and threw sparks of celebration into the growing dusk.

She stared into the flames and shivered. What was she to do? Every time she saw Zachary Thatcher the ache in her heart grew more acute. And now, it seemed, he was going to stay in Promise. He was going to build his own cabin, on his own land.

I'll leave the founding of towns and empire building to Hargrove and Applegate and the others. It is these mountains that call to me. All I want is to be to be free and unfettered to roam them as I will.

She rose and looked across the river to the plain where his packhorse grazed, then turned and looked up at the rugged Blue Mountains. What had changed? Why had he returned? Why—

The thud of Comanche's hoofs against the ground warned her.

She closed her eyes and clenched her hands. There were miles and miles of river. Why must he cross here? She squared her shoulders, arranged her features into a cool, polite expression and turned.

He had dismounted and was standing behind her. So close. If she lifted her hand she could touch him. Her fingers twitched with the memory of clinging to his shirt when he saved her from sliding into the river, of the feel of his hand holding hers. Her heart raced with the knowledge of the warmth and strength of his arms holding her close. She swallowed the swelling lump in her throat and blinked her eyes.

Comanche gave a low nicker, stretched his nose toward her. She reached out and stroked his velvet muzzle, turned to slip her hand beneath his dark mane. *Bless you, Comanche. Bless you for giving me a reason to turn away.*

"He likes you. He's never been like this with anyone but me."

Zachary Thatcher's deep, rich voice flowed over her. She took a breath to steady her own. "He likes the oats and honey I fed him when—" *Oh dear!* She swallowed again. Took another breath. Kept her face turned toward Comanche's side. It didn't work. He walked around to Comanche's other side, rested his hand on the saddle. She could feel his gaze on her face. She did not dare look up.

"When what?"

"When you were ill."

"You did that?"

She nodded, dredged up a smidgen of courage and looked up at him. Her knees slacked with that odd weakness at the blue, smoky look in his eyes. She grabbed the edge of the saddle.

"Why?"

The word felt like a caress. "Because I—" She stopped, horrified by what had almost slipped out. She gave a small shrug. "You had told me Comanche grazed on his own, but always returned to you. I was responsible for your not being there. I wanted to give him a reason to keep coming back so he would be there if—when—you returned." *Dangerous ground. Do not speak of that time.* "The oats and honey were a bribe."

"I don't think the oats and honey are what brought him back. He let you pet him when we were getting water during that thunderstorm on the mountain."

She looked up, saw his eyes were darker still and jerked her gaze away. *Do not think about that day. Do not think about those moments—*

"He trusts you."

"I shall try to be worthy of his trust."

"You already are."

She could take no more. She had to stop this. Send him away. She drew on all of her professional training to mask her emotions. "Mr. Thatcher—"

"I gave him one of your apple dumplings."

She was so shocked by the rapid change of subject and tone she lifted her head and stared at him. He grinned. A slow, lopsided grin that had her clutching the edge of the saddle again.

"He liked it. So did I." He tipped his hat back, crossed his arms on the saddle and rested his chin on them, gazing down at her. "I didn't know you could cook like that."

"I learned."

He grinned.

She lifted her chin. "I did not know you could build log cabins like that."

His grin widened. "*I* learned."

She caught her breath, thrown off guard by this teasing, charming side of him she'd never seen before. "Mr. Thatcher—"

"I know how to carve things, too."

"I am certain that is very useful, but—"

"I made you a present."

"Me?" He had done it again. Thrown her completely off balance. She hoped her lack of equilibrium did not show.

He nodded and walked around Comanche to stand beside her. He reached in his saddlebag, pulled out a good-size piece of wood and handed it to her. "For your cabin door."

Her fingertips felt ridges and grooves on the underside. She turned the board over.

Doctor Emma.

"Oh." Tears welled. She blinked and blinked, ran her fingertip over the letters, the vines that curved around each corner. "Thank you, Mr. Thatcher. I—I will treasure this always. But…I do not understand."

His fingers curved beneath her chin, lifted. She had nowhere to look but at him, unless she closed her eyes. Her heart lurched at the memory of what had happened the last time she had done that. She swallowed and met his gaze.

"We had some rough times over your patients on the journey here. I wanted you to know that I never doubted your doctoring skills…Dr. Emma." He leaned down, touched his lips to hers then turned, swung into the saddle and rode off.

She stood there staring after him, feeling the warmth of his mouth on hers, long after the sound of Comanche splashing through the river had faded away.

Emma washed and creamed her face and hands, brushed her teeth, then donned her rose-embroidered cotton nightdress and dressing gown. She removed the combs and brushed out her hair, let it fall free around her face and shoulders for warmth, then slid under the covers and picked up Zachary Thatcher's gift. Her movements were all slow and deliberate, because she felt brittle. As if a quick movement would make her break.

She ran her hand over the beautifully carved sign, then pulled it beneath the covers and hugged it to her chest. The question she had been asking herself since talking with Lydia this morning had been answered. Lydia was right. She was wrong. Zachary Thatcher had respected her as a doctor from the beginning. She held the proof of that in her hands. But what did that quick, gentle kiss mean? Was she wrong in her thinking there, also? Did he hold her in high regard as a woman, or not? Perhaps so. But that was not what she wanted from Zachary Thatcher. Not anymore. She wanted his love.

Heaviness settled over her, drove her deeper under the covers. But there was no place to hide from the pain. She had said yes when the emigrants asked her to be their doctor. She had "sworn to her own hurt." Because Zachary Thatcher did not return her love was not a reason to break her word. She would have to stay in Promise and pray she did not see him often.

God had answered her prayer. He had given her her dream. She simply had not realized what her dream would cost.

Chapter Twenty-Two

"Can you open your mouth and stick your tongue way out for me, Edward? Like this." Emma looked down at young Edward and stuck out her tongue and crossed her eyes.

Edward giggled and tried to mimic her. He broke into a barking cough, struggled to catch his breath. His eyes widened with fright. He began to wheeze.

"Let me help you sit up, Edward." She slid her arm beneath the little boy's shoulders and lifted him to a sitting position. "Now, do as I say. Breathe very…slowly…" She smiled and gently rubbed his back. He calmed. His breath came easier. "There, you see. You need not fight to breathe. You are all right. Now, let me put this pillow here—" she propped it against the wall "—and you lean back and rest."

She rose and smiled down at him. "I am going to give your mama some things that will help you feel better. I want you to do as she says." She walked to the front of the room.

"What is wrong with Edward, Dr. Emma?"

"He has the croup, Pamelia." She glanced back at the little boy. "He should improve in two or three days. Meantime, it is frightening for him because he feels he can't breathe. I want you to keep him calm and help him to relax when he has a coughing attack, as I did. Keep him sitting up, it makes it easier for him to breathe. And give him some sage and savory tea regularly. A warm poultice on his chest may help." She took a tighter grip on her bag. "His condition will worsen at night, so be prepared by resting during the day. I do not want you becoming ill. The croup is very contagious, so please do not let others come to see him, especially children. And wash your hands every time you take care of him."

"I will do as you say, Dr. Emma." Pamelia smiled. "And this time Thomas told me he will come to your office and pay your fee." She laughed. "I believe that means your wagon."

Emma smiled. "For a few more days. They are cutting the logs for my cabin today." She stepped to the blanket that covered the doorway. "Send Thomas for me if you are concerned for Edward."

"Yes. Thank you for coming, Dr. Emma."

She nodded, swept the blanket aside and stepped out into the sunshine. It was a lovely day, surprisingly warm after the cold weather they had suffered. She hoped it lasted until her cabin was built. And her fireplace. Carl Sutton and Luke Murray were adding fireplaces to the cabins that were being raised so quickly. The Hargroves' fireplace had been the first.

She glanced at the wide stone base that tapered upward to the narrow chimney as she walked by the Hargroves' cabin. Their fireplace was lovely and warm on cold days. She wanted one like it. And a table made from her tailgate. She would ask Joseph Lewis to make her one the next time she saw him. She would need a good, sturdy table for any operations. And a cupboard to hold her medical supplies. And a door. She was tired of canvas flaps and blankets. Could Joseph make her a door from the wood of the wagon? And perhaps shutters for windows? How lovely it would be to have windows again! Where did one purchase glass in the wilderness?

He will come to your office. She sighed and turned into the open area where her wagon sat. Perhaps one day she would have an office. For now, people would come to her home. She *did* have her first furnishing for the office. She had a sign. Her Doctor Emma sign from Mr. Thatcher. She would use it always.

She stood looking at the open area where, tomorrow, her cabin would sit, then looked down at her feet and smiled. Someday, this would be a wooden sidewalk. Or, perhaps, brick or stone. Someday.

She walked to the wagon, climbed to the wagon seat, pushed the flaps out of the way and crawled inside. Yes. It would definitely be lovely to have a door again! She put her doctor's bag on the dresser and looked around. There was not much to furnish her cabin.

The mattresses were in a good, sturdy wood frame. Perhaps Joseph Lewis could make legs to raise it off the floor. And she had the dresser. And the chests. And the long red box. She would keep that always. It had held so many treasures for her on the long journey. And the sign. Her symbol of success as a doctor, and failure as a woman. Which would become more important as the years went by?

She drew a long breath and stepped to the rear of the wagon, opened a slit between the canvas flaps and looked out across the river to Zachary Thatcher's land. He would build his cabin there. Perhaps that had something to do with his mysterious digging. They would be neighbors. Every time she looked out her windows, or walked outside, or went to the river, she would see his home. And she would wonder.

When would he bring a wife there? For surely that would happen. How would she bear meeting her, seeing her around town over the years? How could she bear watching her grow large with his children? And then see them playing and exploring, hear their shouts and laughter? How could she bear watching him grow older and never share his joys and sorrows? Would this feeling of fragility, of…shattering frailty…lessen? Would she ever stop feeling empty inside?

"Dr. Emma?"

She dropped the canvas, whirled, her heart pounding. She had not heard him come.

"Dr. Emma?"

Finally. The acknowledgment of her doctoring skills she had sought. But it was not the name she wanted on his lips when he called to her. "Yes, I'm coming."

She wiped the tears from her cheeks, hurried forward and climbed out into the driver's box. He had dismounted, and was standing beside the wagon, Comanche behind him. She could see him out of the corner of her eye. She shook the long skirts of her red wool dress into place, arranged her face in her "professional doctor's look" and gathered her courage to look at him. "Is something wrong?"

"No." He tipped his hat back and took her gaze prisoner. "I have something I want to show you. Will you come with me?"

To the ends of the earth. "Yes. Of course."

He held up his hands.

Her heart stopped. *She couldn't…shouldn't…* She moved to the side of the seat, felt the strength of his hands circle her waist and leaned forward to place her hands on his hard, broad shoulders.

She never touched the ground. He lowered her until her waist was level with his chest, turned her back to him and caught her against him with one strong arm. He swung into the saddle and urged Comanche forward still holding her tight against him. The way he had held her once before. He had saved her then. She was dying now.

Comanche splashed through the water, surged onto land and walked to the small copse of trees that clustered on the riverbank. His camp was there, hidden from view. A stone fire circle, the packhorse equipment and a small tent. He dismounted and grasped her waist, lifted her down, looked at her. She turned and hid her face from him.

"Is this what you want to show me?"

"No. It's this way." He gestured toward the open plain.

She nodded and started walking toward nothing,

needing to put space between them. He moved up beside her, adjusted his long stride to match her shorter one.

"Over here." He took her elbow, turned her to the left, walked forward a few feet and stopped. There was a small circle of disturbed soil with a long, skinny piece of twig sticking out of it. He touched the twig and looked at her. "This is an apple tree. A Winesap apple tree. There are twenty of them here." He swept his hand forward.

She saw them then. All the small circles of raw soil with twigs sticking out of them. "This is what you have been digging!" She glanced up at him for confirmation, saw his smile and knew her error. She had just admitted she had been watching him. Heat crawled across her cheekbones. She ducked her head, touched the twig. "It looks dead."

He chuckled, a low, manly sound that made her want to turn and step into his arms and place her head against his chest to hear the rumble of it inside, before he set it free.

"I thought the same when I first saw them, but they are only dormant, ready to wait out winter and grow in the spring."

She looked up at him, the question in her eyes.

"I've been reading up on growing apples. Over here—" he led her to another twig "—are twenty Sheep-nose apples. And there—" he gestured farther to their left "—are twenty Pippen apples."

"You must like apples." It came out more droll than she intended. He threw back his head and laughed and the sound brought joy bubbling into her heart. She turned and looked up at him and his laughter died to a grin.

"I like apple dumplings."

Oh dear. She whipped back around toward the open plains. "Are there any more dormant twigs out there?"

"No. But there is space for more, if these do well. And on the left, all the way to the rolling hills, there is space to grow grain to sell and to feed the cattle and horses that will graze those hills. I figure the world can use more Comanches." He stepped up beside her, pointed to one of the lower, flatter hills close to the plains. "I see the barn right there."

There was an odd, fluttery feeling, a *knowing,* growing in her stomach. She took a deep breath and looked up at him. "I thought your dream was to roam the mountains free and unfettered."

He nodded, took her gaze captive. "A man can change. *Hearts* can change. When I left here, I started back to my valley to build my dream. But every step I took got harder to take. Every mile became a chore. There was no excitement, no anticipation, no pleasure in the journey and I knew, I wasn't riding *toward* my dream, I was riding *away* from it." His voice grew husky, his eyes turned the gray, smoky-blue of the mountains behind him. "Those mountains hold no dreams for me now, Dr. Emma Allen. My dream—all I want—is standing right here in front of me. I've shown you my future. I want you to share it with me. I love you, now and forever. Will you marry me?"

She nodded and stepped into Zach's arms, joy flooding her heart. "Yes. Oh, yes, I will marry you. I love you, Zach—"

He caught her to him, drew her against his hard chest,

his lips covering hers. A kiss like she remembered, only so much more.

She opened her heart, parted her lips beneath his and gave all her love in return.

Epilogue

Emma rose from her chair, rested her hands on her swollen abdomen and walked out onto the porch. A smile touched her lips. Every time she came outside and looked over the budding orchards she was more thankful she had won the argument over where they should build their home. Zach had wanted to build in town, next door to the Hargroves', in the lot where her wagon had sat, so she could be near her patients. But she had wanted their home here on the plains, by the barn, so she would be near Zach while he tended the apple orchards and watched over their cattle and horses.

She turned and looked across the river at the sturdy iron rod with a bell on the top, and a side arm from which dangled a hand-carved sign that read Doctor Emma. She smiled and rubbed her hands over the bulge beneath her skirt. Zach had promised the bell was loud enough to be heard over the clamor of any and all future children. And the neighing and snorting of Comanche's get.

She sank down onto the porch swing Zach had hung so she could sit and look toward the fields and barns while she waited for him to come to the house at the end of the day. Things had worked out so well. And, looking back, she could see God's hand clearly guiding them and blessing them. The furniture Zach had purchased from the Widow Canfield was enough for all five rooms, with some left over for expansion. Those items, awaiting the births of future little Thatchers, were in the loft of the second barn they had built by the house for storage of apples.

Emma sighed, pushed her toes against the porch floor and set the swing in motion. This was her favorite spot. Would the baby she carried like to sit and swing here with her? She laughed and pushed harder. Probably not, if they were the energetic, adventurous sons she hoped for. As soon as they could walk they would be off exploring their land, learning to ride Comanche's colts and fillies. Of course, she could have a little filly of her own. The daughter Zach wanted…one, he said, who would look like her and be just as stubborn. Tenacious, she always corrected, because she loved to hear him laugh.

She heard the thunder of hoofs, looked up and saw Zach riding Comanche across the field, heading home. To her. Her heart filled. How blessed she was. She stopped the swing and closed her eyes. "Thank You, God, for leading me on the path to Your blessings. For fulfilling my dream of being a doctor, and giving me so much more than I even knew to ask for."

The hoofbeats pounded close, stopped. She smiled, rose from the swing as Zach swung from the saddle then hurried forward to step into her husband's strong, loving arms.

* * * * *

Dear Reader,

When I began writing *Prairie Courtship* I knew the story would be based on the scripture: *"Delight thyself also in the Lord; and he shall give thee the desires of thine heart. Commit thy way unto him; trust also in him; and he shall bring it to pass."* Psalms 37:4–5. But then I realized there is another scripture that is equally appropriate: *"For my thoughts are not your thoughts, neither are your ways my ways, saith the Lord."* Isaiah. 55:8

Emma's dream was to become a respected doctor, a goal all but impossible for a woman in the year 1841. She prayed that God might answer her prayers. But she was so certain how that should be accomplished she did not recognize that God was answering her prayer all along—just not *her* way.

I have learned that God's answers to our prayers are far better than any our minds or hearts can conceive, and that His will and plan for us is always one of love and blessings.

Thank you, dear reader, for choosing to purchase *Prairie Courtship*. If you would care to contact me, I can be reached at dorothyjclark@hotmail.com or www. dorothyjclark.com.

Until next time, dear reader... May God give you the desires of your heart. And may you recognize and rejoice in His answers to your prayers—however they may come.

Dorothy Clark

QUESTIONS FOR DISCUSSION

1. The characters in *Prairie Courtship* all have a dream they are following—their own or someone else's. Have you ever followed a dream?

2. In 1841, Emma's dream to be a doctor was all but impossible for a woman to attain. Do you believe it was God's intervention in her life that placed her in a position that overcame the era's overriding prejudice against female doctors to make Emma's dream come true?

3. What are the circumstances that led to Emma's being in that place where her dream could come true? Do you believe all that happened was a coincidence? Why or why not?

4. Emma looked on the circumstances that caused her to join the wagon train as God's refusal of her prayers. Do you think that was true?

5. Do you think God can turn the unhappy circumstances of life into good for His children? Did he do that for Emma and those who traveled with her? How?

6. Zach was a strict wagon master, insisting on traveling sometimes when they should have stayed

in one place. Was he right to be so strict with the emigrants? Why or why not?

7. We know very little about Zach's past, except that he was in the army. Do you think he had a family? A sweetheart? What type of past do you think he had that led him to this point in his life?

8. Emma had a double burden of caring for her sister, Anne, and plying medical knowledge for the emigrants. How did she handle the stress?

9. At first, it seems as though Zach didn't like Emma. When did this change? Can you cite the first instance where their relationship changed?

10. Did you ever think that the men on the wagon train would accept Emma as a real doctor? Why or why not?

11. Zach expresses the need to travel and not be tied down in one place. How does this change for him once he meets Emma?

12. Emma's sister, Anne, never overcomes her grief over her lost family. Do you think it was a good idea for Anne to go to the mission without Emma? Why or why not?

13. Did it surprise you that Zach decides to become an orchard farmer? Why or why not?

HISTORICAL

TITLES AVAILABLE NEXT MONTH

Available November 9, 2010

MAIL ORDER COWBOY
Brides of Simpson Creek
Laurie Kingery

SOARING HOME
Christine Johnson

REQUEST YOUR FREE BOOKS!

2 FREE INSPIRATIONAL NOVELS
PLUS 2
FREE
MYSTERY GIFTS

Love Inspired
HISTORICAL
INSPIRATIONAL HISTORICAL ROMANCE

YES! Please send me 2 FREE Love Inspired® Historical novels and my 2 FREE mystery gifts (gifts are worth about $10). After receiving them, if I don't wish to receive any more books, I can return the shipping statement marked "cancel". If I don't cancel, I will receive 4 brand-new novels every other month and be billed just $4.24 per book in the U.S. or $4.74 per book in Canada. That's a saving of over 20% off the cover price. It's quite a bargain! Shipping and handling is just 50¢ per book.* I understand that accepting the 2 free books and gifts places me under no obligation to buy anything. I can always return a shipment and cancel at any time. Even if I never buy another book, the two free books and gifts are mine to keep forever.

102/302 IDN E7QD

Name	(PLEASE PRINT)	
Address		Apt. #
City	State/Prov.	Zip/Postal Code

Signature (if under 18, a parent or guardian must sign)

Mail to Steeple Hill Reader Service:
IN U.S.A.: P.O. Box 1867, Buffalo, NY 14240-1867
IN CANADA: P.O. Box 609, Fort Erie, Ontario L2A 5X3
Not valid for current subscribers to Love Inspired Historical books.

Want to try two free books from another series?
Call 1-800-873-8635 or visit www.morefreebooks.com.

* Terms and prices subject to change without notice. Prices do not include applicable taxes. Sales tax applicable in N.Y. Canadian residents will be charged applicable provincial taxes and GST. Offer not valid in Quebec. This offer is limited to one order per household. All orders subject to approval. Credit or debit balances in a customer's account(s) may be offset by any other outstanding balance owed by or to the customer. Please allow 4 to 6 weeks for delivery. Offer available while quantities last.

Your Privacy: Steeple Hill Books is committed to protecting your privacy. Our Privacy Policy is available online at www.SteepleHill.com or upon request from the Reader Service. From time to time we make our lists of customers available to reputable third parties who may have a product or service of interest to you. If you would prefer we not share your name and address, please check here. ☐

Help us get it right—We strive for accurate, respectful and relevant communications. To clarify or modify your communication preferences, visit us at www.ReaderService.com/consumerchoice.

LIH10R

*See below for a sneak peek from
our inspirational line, Love Inspired® Suspense*

Enjoy this heart-stopping excerpt from
RUNNING BLIND
*by top author Shirlee McCoy,
available November 2010!*

**The mission trip to Mexico was supposed to be an
adventure. But the thrill turns sour when Jenna Dougherty
and her roommate Magdalena are kidnapped.**

"It's okay. I'm here to help." The voice was as deep as the
darkness, but Jenna Dougherty didn't believe the lie. She
could do nothing but lie still as hands slid down her arms,
felt the rope around her wrists.

"I'm going to use a knife to cut you free, Jenna. Hold
still."

The cold blade of a knife pressed close to her head before
her gag fell away.

"I—" she started, but her mouth was dry, and she could
do nothing but suck in air.

"Shhh. Whatever needs to be said can be said when
we're out of here." Nick spoke quietly, his hand gentle on
her cheek. There and gone as he sliced through the ropes on
her wrists and ankles.

He pulled her upright. "Come on. We may be on
borrowed time."

"I can't leave my friend," Jenna rasped out.

"There's no one here. Just us."

"She has to be here." Jenna took a step away.

"There's no one here. Let's go before that changes."

"It's dark. Maybe if we find a light…"

"What did you say?"

"We need to turn on the light. I can't leave until I know that—"

"What can you see, Jenna?"

"Nothing."

"No shadows? No light?"

"No."

"It's broad daylight. There's light spilling in from the window I climbed in through. You can't see it?"

She went cold at his words.

"I can't see anything."

"You've got a nasty bruise on your forehead. Maybe that has something to do with it." His fingers traced the tender flesh on her forehead.

"It doesn't matter *how* it happened. I'm blind!"

Can Nick help Jenna find her friend or will chasing this trail have Jenna running blindly again into danger?

Find out in RUNNING BLIND, available in November 2010 only from Love Inspired Suspense.